THE FIGHTER

DOCTOR #4

E. L. TODD

Hartwick Publishing

The Fighter

Copyright © 2019 by E. L. Todd

1

COLTON

IT WAS SATURDAY MORNING. ALL WEEK, CRAP PILED UP IN MY garbage can, and I kept stuffing more and more inside until everything started to overflow. Only when I couldn't fit even a napkin on top did I finally take out the garbage.

I stepped into the hallway with the overstuffed bag at my side, ready to throw it down the trash chute. But instead of entering an empty space, I spotted Pepper saying goodbye to some guy at her door.

I tried not to make it awkward, so I walked away and headed to the trash chute down the hall, but I could still hear their conversation.

"I had a good time last night." A man I'd never seen before wrapped his arms around her waist and kissed her on the threshold, gripping her tightly like he didn't want to return wherever he came from.

"Me too." She pressed against his chest then stepped back, ending the affection. "I'll see you around."

"You want to get dinner tomorrow night?" The man was in a leather jacket and dark jeans. He was tall, really tall.

"I already have plans tomorrow. Maybe some other time." It

was obvious she was brushing him off, kicking him to the curb like every other guy she met. She'd become a numb shell, picking up a different guy every weekend and tossing him aside when she was done with him. It'd been going on for a while.

"Alright, I'll call you." He finally walked away.

I dropped the bag in the trash chute then headed back to my apartment. I crossed paths with the guy, checking him out briefly before I arrived in front of her door. Then I checked out his ass until he took the stairs. "Wow, he's hot."

"Yeah, he was." She was dressed in a long shirt that almost touched her knees. She didn't seem to care if anyone saw her half naked in the hallway, and since I'd seen her naked hundreds of times in the past, she cared even less about showing skin to me. "You want to get brunch? I've been craving strawberry waffles all week."

"He was?" I asked. "I'm guessing you aren't going to see him again."

She shrugged. "He just wasn't my type."

"Tall and handsome isn't your type?"

She walked inside her apartment. "I'm going to change, and we'll get going. And I'm buying. I had a really good week at work."

"Well, I can't say no to that...since you never pay for anything."

She flipped me off before she shut the door in my face.

WE WENT to our favorite boutique restaurant, where the waffles were so fluffy, they served pecan butter, and their orange juice was freshly squeezed. One of the best things about being gay was enjoying brunch without judgment. It was definitely my favorite meal.

"So, what was his name?" I dunked my waffle into the cup of syrup before placing it in my mouth.

"Who?" Pepper was stuffing her mouth like she hadn't eaten in weeks.

"The guy you just slept with." Had she forgotten about him already?

"Oh." She dumped so much syrup on her waffle that it was drenched in the ultra-sweetness. "It was Adam...or Alan. Something like that."

Something like that? "You aren't going to see him again?"

She shook her head. "Nah."

Nah? "What was wrong with him?"

She shrugged. "Nothing. Just didn't like him."

"But you slept with him."

She turned to me, her eyebrow raised so high it looked like a mountain. "Enough with the condescension, alright? If I were Zach, I wouldn't be getting this third-degree judgment. It's sexist. Look, I slept with him because he was hot and I wanted to get laid. Jesus, leave it at that."

"No, it's not sexist. It's just not you." When Finn left, Pepper was a mess. It was just like our divorce all over again. But after three months of licking her wounds, she suddenly snapped out of it and put herself out there again. But instead of dating and getting to know different people, she'd turned into a heart-breaking playgirl. She was never with the same guy twice. All she did was sleep with them and never call them again.

"Not me? I'm living my life and enjoying it. That's the new me."

On the outside, she seemed perfectly happy. It seemed like she'd bounced back from Finn and forgot about him. Maybe she even believed that too. But this new behavior had been going on for so long, I worried she was in a worse spot than when Finn left six months ago. He destroyed her, ruined the optimistic romantic she used to be. Now she'd become just like everyone else, filling her loneliness with meaningless sex. "I just worry that—"

"Well, don't." She grabbed her orange juice and took a deep drink. "Damn, that's good. It's seven dollars, but so worth it." Her need to change the subject quickly told me that this wasn't up for debate, that she wasn't ready to talk about how she really felt, so it was pointless.

I guess I'd have to wait for it to run its course.

Both sets of fingers rested against the beer on the table. Loud music played overhead, along with the sounds from the TVs in the corners. People mingled at the bar and at the tables, talking about whatever.

Zach and Stella sat across from me, Stella close to him so the girls wouldn't look his way.

"I just worry about her." I continued to talk about Pepper, the woman I loved more than anything in this world. I was worried about her but had no idea what to do. "She slept with this other guy last night and couldn't even remember his name."

"So?" Stella asked. "If a guy did that, you wouldn't question it."

"I'm not questioning it because she's a woman," I argued. "I'm questioning it because that's not Pepper. She doesn't just sleep around."

"She picked up Jax in a bar," Stella countered. "All she wanted from him was sex, but she didn't get it. Look, the woman is finally single and in a good place. Let her enjoy it. Let her figure out what she wants. Just because she's sleeping around doesn't mean there's something wrong with her."

"I don't know about that..." Pepper wasn't just sleeping

around with guys on the weekend. She was meeting them on Tuesdays and Thursdays, finding guys in random places like the gym...even though she didn't work out. "She's going out of her way to pick up these guys. It's not like she's at the bar on a Friday night and sees someone she likes. She's hunting them down."

"I could say the same about dudes," Stella said. "All guys ever want to do is get laid. That's what their goal is all the time, whether they are at the grocery store or the gym. How is Pepper any different?"

"I get what he's saying." Zach finally entered the conversation. "There's nothing wrong with what she's doing...it's just not like her. She'd only slept with a few guys her whole life leading up to this, and now she's slept with more guys in the last few months than in her entire lifetime."

"Exactly," I said. "It's like she's using sex to make herself feel better."

Stella raised her glass. "More power to her."

"I will admit that it's better to see her like this than how she was before," Zach said. "She was so low, man. Like a zombie or something. She'd be looking right at you but not even know you're there. Maybe this is just another phase, but let her do what she needs to do to feel better."

"Maybe," I said. "I'm just worried that this isn't a phase. That she's given up on love or something..."

"Maybe she has," Stella said. "After everything she's been through, I don't blame her."

I'D JUST PULLED out the pizza box from the fridge when my phone started to ring.

Finn's name was on the screen.

I stared at it and debated whether I should answer. He'd tried calling me a few times after he left, but I kept dodging his calls. I was too pissed at him to have a normal conversation. But then he stopped calling me for a long time, probably getting the hint.

After the third ring, I finally answered. "Yeah?" That single word came out hostile because I had so much pent-up rage directed toward him. He'd hurt Pepper a million times more than I ever did—and I didn't think I could forgive him.

"Didn't expect you to answer."

"Almost didn't." Now that my brother was on the phone, I'd lost my appetite. I shoved the box of pizza back into the fridge. "What do you want?"

"I'm not sure," he said. "I was expecting to have a conversation with your voice mail."

I ignored his smartass comeback. "How's Africa?"

"Africa is a continent. That's like me asking you how the United States is."

"You're paying two bucks a minute just to be a smartass to me?" I asked incredulously.

"I think it's a fair price." His smile was audible through the phone. "How are things with you? Mom told me Tom is still in the picture... That's good. It seems like Mom and Dad really like him."

"What's not to like? What about you?"

"Well, Kenya and Uganda are both beautiful places. There's poverty and civil war, so sometimes tensions run high. We're also close to the Congo, so there're a lot of drug wars taking place. But other than that, no complaints."

He left Pepper for poverty and war? Fucking idiot. "I'm glad you're having a good time..."

He turned quiet, wasting a ton of money just to sit in silence with me.

I knew what he wanted to ask, but I didn't make it easy on

him. As far as I knew, he'd never tried to contact Pepper after he left. So if he wanted to know how her life was, he would have to ask me.

But I wouldn't give him what he wanted so easily.

When he spoke again, he was serious. "How is she?"

"Your ex-fiancée?" I asked, reminding him of the commitment he'd made and broken.

"Colton, look—"

"It would have been one thing if you'd just broken it off to travel across the world, but you asked her to marry you first. You asked her to spend her life with you—and then you left. I've never heard of an emptier proposal in my life."

"I meant every word…"

"Whatever, Finn. She's fine now. She's moved on. She's in a good place." Even if she wasn't, I wouldn't tell Finn the truth. I would make her seem indifferent to him. I would make her seem like the person who got the better deal out of the situation. "Her shop is doing well, she's dating, and we have brunch together every Saturday. Life is pretty good."

He was quiet for a long time. "Good…I'm glad to hear it."

"She's over it, Finn. But I'll never forgive you for what you did to her."

"Loyal as always."

"Through and through."

The door opened, and Pepper walked inside. She was dressed in skinny jeans, heels, and a flowery blouse.

I kept the phone to my ear as I looked at her, feeling awkward that I was talking to Finn while she was in the room.

She walked right up to me. "Do you have some wine? I have a guy over, and I realized I'm totally out."

I wondered if Finn heard that. "Yeah, check the cabinet."

Finn didn't say anything. He must have heard her. Otherwise, he would question the long-term silence of our conversation.

She looked through the cabinets as she made her selection. "Are you talking to Tom? Tell him thank you for those cookies he made me. My hips are fatter, but I don't even care." She grabbed the bottle she wanted and shut the door.

"Actually...I'm talking to Finn."

Her eyes should have dropped in sadness and she should have stiffened when she heard his name. But like my words meant nothing to her, she smiled and carried the wine with her as she left. "Tell him I said hi." She strutted her hips then walked out, like the awkward situation hadn't happened at all.

I spoke into the phone. "I'm not sure if you heard, but—"

"Yeah," he said quickly. "I heard her..."

2

PEPPER

I walked into the bar and found them all gathered around one of the high-top tables. I'd just picked up a new dress I'd ordered online, and I was happy it fit perfectly and matched a pair of heels I already had in the closet. Skintight and see-through along the outer part of my legs, it was scandalous and classy at the same time.

Stella dropped her jaw. "Girl, you look fucking amazing."

"Shit, I can see your abs through the material," Tatum said. "I would kill for a body like that."

"Well, she worked her ass off in my classes," Stella said proudly. "She lost ten pounds of fat and gained ten pounds of muscle. She is one fit chick." Stella gave me a thumbs-up.

I came to the table and set down my clutch. "You are the worst trainer ever."

"What?" Stella asked in offense. "Excuse me?"

"Because you're so damn hard," I said. "Every day, I feel like I'm going to die."

"Hey." Stella slammed her hand on the table. "That's how you know I'm the best."

Colton looked me up and down appreciatively. "You definitely aren't buying your own drinks tonight."

"She better not." Tatum lifted my clutch. "Not sure why you brought this."

"You can have any guy in this bar," Stella said. "Gay or straight, married or single."

"I'd rather be with a gay man than a married one." I'd been playing the field and sowing my oats, but I wasn't interested in married men. I didn't believe in love, but that didn't mean I didn't respect the institution. "I'm going to get a drink." I grabbed my clutch and walked away.

Colton caught up with me. We hadn't talked about his phone call with Finn and I had no interest talking about it now, but that was obviously what he wanted to discuss. "Pepper, I wanted to talk to you about something."

"Finn?" I reached the bar and waited for the bartender to notice me. "How is he?" When he left, I was a mess. I didn't go to work for weeks, the shop almost closed, and I cried so much that I became dehydrated enough that I had to go to the emergency room. To top it off, Layla was my doctor. That just made it worse.

As the months passed, I imagined all the women he'd been with. I wondered if he ever thought about me, if he missed me enough to come home. But by the time three months came and went, I became exhausted with being pathetic. I got back on my feet and brushed it off. The man destroyed me, and I was tired of being broken. I wanted to move on and forget about it.

Colton was a little taken aback by my question. "Uh, I guess he's fine. Didn't really say much."

I waved the bartender over and ordered a vodka cranberry. "Then what is there to talk about?"

"I just wanted you to know he called me. He's been trying to get a hold of me for months, but I kept ignoring his calls."

I didn't know why we were still talking about Finn. He was a man who was no longer in our lives. I wanted to forget he ever existed and just move on. "You don't need to ignore him, Colton. He's your brother. You should talk to him."

"But I'm still pissed after what he did to you—"

"Colt." I rested my hand on his shoulder. "I'm over it. It was a long time ago. I'm in a good place, and I'm sure he's living the dream doing whatever he's doing out there in the jungle. You need to let this go."

His eyes shifted back and forth as he studied me. "I'm not sure if you're really over it, Pepper. Sometimes I worry that you're sleeping around to make yourself feel better, that the pain is too much to bear, so you're masking it with an endless line of good-looking guys."

"I like sex, Colton. A lot of people like sex."

"But this isn't you—"

"I'm fine, okay? I'm just living my life and having a good time. You need to stop worrying about me."

"You know I'll never stop." He continued to hold my gaze like there was no one else in that bar. "I just don't want you to do something you regret. I don't want you to find comfort in other guys when you always have me. We can talk about it as much as you want until you're over it."

"I told you I am over it, Colton. I appreciate your concern, but I'm fine. So instead of wasting another moment on a guy who's not in our lives anymore, let's have a good time." I grabbed my drink from the counter and raised it to him for a toast.

Colton still wore that uneasy look, like he didn't believe a word I said but felt powerless to fight it. He lifted his glass and clinked it against mine. "Alright. To good times."

COLTON HAD LEFT the bar an hour before because he already

had someone special to go home to. Stella and Zach left, heading back to his place because they were a serious couple now. They'd been together for almost a year. Tatum went home with some guy.

So I stood at the bar and finished my last drink.

The bar was quiet because most people had already gone home for the night. I never thought I'd be one of those people who lingered at bars because I had no one to go home to. Now I stood with all the other lonely people, reexamining my life and wondering where I'd gone wrong. My first marriage ended because I fell in love with a gay man. My second engagement ended because he didn't love me enough.

I reflected on that relationship so many times because I wondered why I'd been so stupid. There were plenty of times when it seemed like what Finn and I had was real, something so strong and special that it would last a lifetime. But in reality, I was just a stepping stone until something better came along. If Finn preferred to devote his life to helping people away from Seattle instead of staying here with me, he clearly didn't love me enough.

If he ever loved me at all.

Maybe the breakup wouldn't have hurt so much if he hadn't proposed. Maybe it would have just been a breakup, something ordinary and predictable. But I knew I'd still be just as heartbroken.

I finished the rest of my drink then opened my clutch. It was time to pay the bill and go home, to pass out on my bed with my dress still on. The later I stayed up, the longer I slept in. I wasted as much of the day as possible because there was nothing to look forward to.

I pulled out a couple of twenties.

A man appeared at my side and slid a fifty to the bartender. "Her drinks are on me."

I stared at the crisp bills in my hand and fought the smile that stretched my mouth. This guy thought he was so suave, throwing down money like that, but I wasn't easily impressed. I'd been with a lot of men in the last few months, and they all seemed to be the same. "You really don't need to do that." I lifted my gaze and looked into his, encountering the unexpected. I'd been with handsome men with rock-hard bodies, but I hadn't come face-to-face with a guy like him.

His jawline was chiseled from granite, the line so pronounced and sharp, he possessed statue-like qualities. His neck had corded veins that protruded from his skin like he was constantly flexing. His hands were exactly the same, a web of veins that looked like rivers on a map. He had tanned skin as if he ran shirtless through the park on every sunny day that graced Seattle, or he owned a yacht in the Mediterranean that gave him that olive-gold glow.

With dark hair on his head and a matching shadow along his jaw, he had the masculinity that made him so manly, but he also had such full lips, they seemed fake. Green eyes that were vibrant in color looked into mine with all the confidence in the world.

This man wasn't just handsome. He was an entirely different breed. Part man and part divine, he was a mortal god. I wasn't even sure why someone like him would be standing in this bar, ten minutes before it was about to close. He could have grabbed a hot piece of ass the second he walked in the door.

How he managed to be alone until the end of the night was a mystery to me.

The bartender took his money as we continued to stare at each other.

The man helped himself to my cash and returned it to my wallet.

I noticed the Omega watch on his wrist and the beautiful

texture of his black jacket. He wore an olive-green t-shirt underneath, the fabric hugging his muscular physique. He looked like someone who belonged in Manhattan, getting free drinks handed to him because he was more beautiful than all the women in the building.

"Brutus." He extended his hand to shake mine.

I took it, my grip a little weak. "Pepper."

He didn't make a comment on my odd name, not like most people did. He lowered his hand then leaned against the counter. "The bar closes in ten minutes. You want to continue this conversation at my place? Or I can give you a ride home?" This guy went straight for the kill, not having any shame for seizing what he wanted.

A year ago, I probably wouldn't have been interested. I needed to have a connection with a man before I slept with him. But now, my prerequisites were at an all-time low. I wanted a beautiful man to entertain me for the night, to make me feel desirable. I wanted that closeness, that intimacy. But I didn't want the heartache, betrayal, and disappointment.

It was the best decision I'd ever made.

"Your place."

THIS GUY WAS LOADED.

For one, we drove to his place in a Bugatti. I didn't know anything about cars, but I knew that shit wasn't cheap.

And two, his apartment overlooked the bay, sitting on the top two floors of a tall building. With an enormous living room visible the second you stepped out of the elevator, the place had to be at least ten thousand square feet.

Did a single guy need this much space?

I tried not to react to his ridiculous wealth, but it was hard not to look around and admire the perfect lighting, the paintings on the wall, the rug that was probably selected in Morocco then shipped here on a private plane.

He stepped into his kitchen and poured two glasses of wine. Then he came back to me, standing nearly a foot taller than me. His eyes weren't kind the way Colton's were. They were so deep and masculine, he seemed like a predator more than a human.

I took the glass and suddenly felt afraid.

He studied me, watching the way I slouched and diverted my gaze. "What is it?"

I handed my glass back to him. "I'm sorry. I should go." The elevator was right behind me, so all I had to do was get to the sidewalk and call an Uber. Then I could forget this terrible night ever happened.

"Why?" He set the glasses down on the coffee table beside him. "What's wrong?" Without raising his voice, he conveyed his concern. It was obvious he didn't want me to leave, even though he knew nothing about me besides my name.

I stepped back, putting a little space in between us. "I don't sleep with married men." A man like this didn't live in a mansion all alone. There was no need for this much space, no matter how rich he was. His wife probably went out of town and took the kids with her. I refused to be the other woman in the bed she slept in, to enjoy a man she probably loved with all her heart. A man so beautiful, so fit, and so rich obviously had the heart of whatever woman he wanted. Maybe she would never find out about this, but if even she never did, I wanted no part in it.

His eyes narrowed in confusion before they softened in relief. "Why do you think I'm married?"

I took a look around. "You live in this big place all alone?" I asked incredulously. "Twenty people could live here and not be crammed. Why would a bachelor need all this space to himself?"

"Whatever the reason may be, it's none of your business. And no, I'm not married." He grabbed the glasses again and handed one to me.

I didn't know this man, so he could be lying, but I took the glass anyway.

"If you don't believe me, raid the closets and see if there is any women's clothing anywhere. Search for clues that hint my wife is out of town and I'm sneaking around behind her back." He drank his wine and pressed his lips tightly together, clearly offended I suggested such a horrible thing. "I know you don't know me, but I'm the kind of man that's honest to a fault. If I had a wife and you had a problem with it, I would just find someone else. But I don't." He took another drink of his wine, downing half of it in a single go.

Now I felt low for accusing him of such a thing. "I'm sorry... I just assumed."

"Assumptions are dangerous things." He set his empty glass on the coffee table, as if someone would magically appear out of nowhere and clean it for him. "But I admire your honor. Most people don't care about those sorts of things. They don't realize how their actions affect other people, how their deceit poisons their blood." He took off his jacket and let the material slide down his chiseled arms. When he stood in just a t-shirt, his toned biceps and triceps were visible. That warm, sun-kissed skin was beautiful, even under the dim lighting of his apartment. When he stared at me, he didn't seem unnerved by the intimacy between our gazes. We were strangers, two people who'd barely said more than a few words to each other, but he was so confident that it didn't affect him at all. Even when I insulted him, he didn't let it affect his solid presence.

I gripped the glass between my fingers, the warmth in my

belly having nothing to do with the smooth alcohol he'd given me. This man was mysterious, but I liked it that way. I didn't want to ask him what he did for a living, if he lived here full time, or his favorite restaurants in the city. I liked it like this, this mutual anonymity toward each other. That was what my life had become, a serious of meaningless one-night stands that chased away the loneliness. I'd had two perfect relationships in my life, and they both ended the same way—with the men leaving. I would never put myself in that vulnerable position again.

He took a step and moved into my space, his fingers sliding to my neck as his cologne surrounded me. With a light touch, he guided my chin up, then pressed his lips to mine, getting his toes in the water.

The glass of wine nearly slipped through my fingertips.

His full lips were so soft, so delicious. They slipped past mine in an erotic dance before he released a quiet breath against my trembling lips. He kissed me again, this time harder, like he felt the same electric pulse I did. There was an inferno between us, the kind of chemistry passionate lovers possessed. So we both ran with it, kissing each other harder and feeling the other.

He took the glass from my hand then wrapped his arm around my waist, squeezing me against him. He didn't end our kiss or stop to look at me. His movements were so slick.

With unburdened hands, I let my fingers explore his body, feeling the hardness underneath his t-shirt. It was like solid concrete, strength that was so profound, I moaned in his mouth. I imagined those chiseled abs underneath his shirt, the tanned skin that deserved to be licked.

My fingers found the hem of his shirt, and I pulled it toward his head, eager to get to the good part now that my blood was boiling with hormones.

He set the glass down then stripped it off.

My eyes swept over his frame, appreciating every single inch of that man. "Mmm..." I gave a gentle bite on my lower lip, my hunger insatiable. I'd been with a lot of men in the last few months, but I'd never been with someone like him.

He moaned quietly under his breath as his hand moved into my hair again, and he kissed me. He gripped the bottom of my dress and yanked it over my hips, revealing nothing underneath. The way the dress was made inhibited me from wearing anything underneath because the sides were extremely sheer. When he noticed, he gave another moan and finished pulling it over my head, revealing my naked body.

My dress landed on the floor, and he guided me backward until we hit the wall. One large hand gripped my tit as he kissed me while the other gripped my ass.

I got his jeans undone and pushed everything down, getting his beautiful body out of those clothes.

When his clothes were around his ankles, I looked down and saw a cock that made me bite my lower lip again. Long and fat, it was the perfect tool to make me come all night long. It was a man's dick, a package built for pleasing a woman. "Hurry up and fuck me." There was nothing stronger than getting lost in unbridled passion, physically enjoying someone to the exclusion of all else. It was easy to forget about the bullshit in life. It was easy to forget about all your problems. This man was beautiful and endowed. He was the exact prescription I needed for my disease.

He rolled a condom to his base then hiked my leg over his hips. Then he slid inside me, sinking in so smoothly because I was soaking wet. Inch by inch he moved, getting farther inside me until he was sheathed to the hilt.

"Yes..." My arms wrapped around his neck, and I breathed against his mouth.

He moaned against my mouth then started to fuck me, pounding my ass into the wall as he gave me one of many orgasms that night.

I woke up the next morning in his bed.

At some point during the night, we made our way down the hallway and into his Alaskan king bed. His room was surrounded by floor-to-ceiling windows with breathtaking views of the city as the morning sun poked through the clouds.

He was dead asleep beside me, his hand resting on his chest while the sheets were bunched around his waist. Tanned skin stretched over his strong muscles. He had the deep V in his hips, like he hit the weights religiously and swore off carbs forever.

It was a nice sight—but I had to leave.

I slowly slipped out of his bed and made it to my feet without waking him. Then I tiptoed out of the bedroom and down the hallway until I found my dress sitting on the floor. My heels were still on because I'd never taken them off during the night. Whether we were doing it up against the wall or on the couch, my four-inch heels stayed on my feet.

That was kind of hot.

I got inside the elevator then descended to the ground, my hair a mess and my makeup smeared around my eyes. In this kind of scandalous dress, it was obvious I was doing the walk of shame, but I was so satisfied, I couldn't care less.

I pulled my phone out of my clutch and looked at a screen covered with text messages from Colton.

Are you awake?

When will you be home?

Pepper, you okay?

It was hard to believe this man used to be my husband because he acted like my father. I made it to the street and waved down a cab. Then I took the short ride to my neighborhood. I was excited to get these heels off and catch up on some sleep before work tomorrow. I texted him back. *I'll be home in five minutes. Chill.*

We're having game day at my apartment. You want to join?

Depends. Food?

He sent me an emoji of someone rolling their eyes. *Yes.*

What kind of food?

Does it matter? You'll eat anything.

Just tell me!

Alright. Waffles, bagels, bacon (crispy the way you like it)...

Sold!

He rolled his eyes again.

I went to my apartment to change first then headed across the hall.

The dining table was covered with the breakfast buffet. Everyone sat on the couch and ate while the TV was on. Board games were piled on the coffee table because they obviously hadn't decided which to play first. "Wow, this looks bomb." I grabbed a plate and piled the food on top, pouring the syrup over everything because I was a weirdo and couldn't get enough of it.

"So where did you end up last night?" Stella sat on Zach's lap, her legs draped over his thighs as they shared the armchair. Since it was Sunday, she was in her leggings and a sweater, but that woman could make a trash bag look sexy.

I took a seat beside Colton and Tom. "You know, up against a wall...on a couch...a bed at some point."

Stella chuckled. "Damn, you're living the single life and nailing it."

"Yes, *nailing* is the right word." I ate a strip of bacon covered in syrup and felt Colton's disappointed stare. He wasn't happy about my newfound sexual appetite. He treated me like a person who'd gotten hooked on drugs and was slowly fading away. But sex was better than drugs—and I was definitely hooked.

"Who was the guy?" Zach asked. "Anyone special?"

"What was his name?" Colton asked. "Or can you even remember?"

I was about to bite off the final piece of bacon but decided to throw it at his face instead. "Brutus."

"Ooh...he sounds hot," Stella said. "Super manly."

"He was super manly," I said, returning my attention to the food on my plate.

"Are you going to see him again?" Tom asked.

"No." I blurted out my answer fast, because the idea of spending any more time with that man didn't seem appealing. He was from a different world, a world I would never be part of.

"What's wrong with him?" Colton asked. "He's hot enough to sleep with but not good enough for a cup of coffee?"

"Colton." Stella stared at him. "This sexist bullshit needs to stop. I can't count the number of times Zach has come home after a promiscuous night, and he doesn't get the third degree."

"Thank you," I said to her.

"I'm not sexist," Colton countered. "I just know this isn't you."

"This is the new me," I said. "People change all the time."

"But how can you not like any of them?" he asked incredulously. "You refuse to give anyone a chance, so what if this guy is good for you?"

"Trust me, he's not." I smeared cream cheese across my toasted bagel then took a bite. "The guy drove me to his apartment in a *Bugatti*." I chewed the bread and watched all my friends do a double take.

Zach's jaw was practically on the floor. "You serious?"

"That's like a million-dollar car," Colton said. "Are you sure?"

"I don't know much about cars, but I know what it was." I took another bite and kept chewing. "Then he took me to his apartment, which was a fucking mansion. It was two stories with a grand spiral staircase. It had to be at least ten thousand square feet. At first, I assumed he was married so I tried to bolt, but he convinced me he wasn't."

"Why did you think he was married?" Stella asked.

"Why would a single person need that much space?" I countered. "That doesn't make any sense to me."

"Brutus..." Colton rubbed his jaw.

"So this guy is super rich?" Zach asked incredulously. "And you *don't* want to see him again?"

"Girl, that's the kind of man you chase after," Stella said. "You could be Mrs. Bugatti."

Colton pulled out his phone and started typing.

"I don't want to be Mrs. Bugatti," I countered. "His wealth doesn't interest me. He's a typical arrogant playboy who just wants pussy. Why would I want to get involved in that? Besides, I never gave him my contact info."

"Did he say anything when you left?" Stella asked.

"No. I snuck out." I finished everything until my plate was empty, with the exception of a few streaks of syrup.

"Girl, you're crazy," Stella said. "You should have stuck around and made that man fall madly in love with you."

I'd loved two men in my life, and I could get neither one of them to fall in love with me. This guy wouldn't be any different. "He's not my type. He's the kind of guy you have fun with, not the kind of guy you have anything serious with. And if he's that rich, he's probably the biggest jerk on the planet."

"Was he a jerk to you?" Stella asked.

"No...but we didn't do much talking." He was the strong and silent type—just the way Finn used to be. That's how I knew to steer clear of him. I could recognize a heartbreaker from a mile away now.

Colton held up his phone to me. "Is this him?"

I glanced at the screen and saw a handsome man stepping

out of a large building in a designer suit. He had the same dark hair, same shadow across his jaw, and the same webbed veins on his hands. A different watch was on his wrist. "Yeah...it is."

"Brutus Hemmingway?" Colton asked incredulously. "You slept with Brutus Hemmingway?"

"Is that name supposed to mean something to me?" I asked, still not caring if this guy was a billionaire.

"Holy shit," Zach said. "He's like one of the richest guys in the country. He opened up a shipping business like a decade ago. They get packages and deliveries done in a few hours. It's crazy."

Stella snatched the phone to look at the screen. "And damn...he's fiiiiiiine."

Zach glared at her.

"What?" Stella held up the phone to him. "I'm sorry, but this guy is gorgeous. Don't act like he's not."

Zach finally gave a shrug.

Colton took the phone back. "This guy is worth like a hundred and fifty billion dollars."

Millions, billions, what difference did it make? "Money is just money, Colton. It can't buy you happiness." I could have all that money this very moment and still be just as miserable.

"That's not what I'm trying to say," Colton said. "But you slept with a celebrity."

I shrugged. "I guess that's kind of cool."

"Kind of?" Zach asked. "It's badass. It's crazy that you aren't going to see him again, though."

His money didn't impress me. The only thing I was interested in was his rock-hard body and kissable lips. What I craved in a man was someone who was happy with nothing at all, who cared more about helping people than making money. I wanted a man who was selfless and made sacrifices. I wanted a man who didn't need much in life. But that man was gone, on the other side of the world, fucking every beautiful woman he saw. He wasn't thinking about me. So I shouldn't think about him. "There are plenty of other fish in the sea."

ONCE A WEEK HAD PASSED, I forgot about Brutus altogether. He was just another notch on my bedpost, a former lover who wouldn't live long in my memory. The weekend had arrived once more, and I would go out and hit the town as always.

I was working in the shop on Friday when Colton walked inside.

In a suit and tie, he was clearly taking a long lunch break from work. He reached the counter and rested his elbows on the surface, looking handsome with his new haircut. Even though he had different features from Finn, it was hard for me not to see the resemblance. "How's it going?"

"It's going. Pretty slow day."

"A lingerie shop should never be slow." He pulled out his phone and checked his messages. "You wanna get lunch? Mega Shake?"

I rubbed my stomach behind the counter. "Nothing heavy. I've been eating too much lately."

"Too much? You've never been in better shape."

"But when I work out with Stella in the morning, I feel my dinner bouncing around in my stomach. So nothing greasy or heavy."

He stuck out his tongue in disappointment. "Lame."

"What if we go to the deli?"

He shrugged. "I guess that's okay."

The bell over the door rang when a new customer walked inside.

"Just let me take care of this person, then we'll go." The

person might not buy anything, but most of the time, women walked in here with a purpose. They didn't browse then walk out empty-handed.

"I'll take a seat." Colton moved to the side and sat in the leather armchair, scrolling through his phone to check his newsfeed.

I lifted my gaze to meet my customer, but my eyes locked on a man I already knew. His appearance caught me by such surprise that I forgot to speak. My hands rested on the counter and stayed still, but I had the urge to flinch in fear.

Brutus approached me with perfectly straight shoulders, a strong back, and a slight smile on his lips. His green eyes were beautiful in such a handsome face. He wore dark jeans and a t-shirt again, a navy blue jacket on top. With his eyes set on me, he reached the counter then rested his arms on the surface, his fingers almost touching mine.

I kept up my confidence even though my tits were starting to sweat. Brutus and I ended our night the way most couples did, but I still felt like I'd done something wrong—when he looked at me like that.

Colton peeked over his phone when the silence stretched on, and his eyebrows jumped up his face when he spotted Brutus.

I pulled my eyes away from Colton and faced the man who hadn't blinked once. "What are you interested in? Panties? Stockings? Bodysuits?" Being a sarcastic smartass was the right way to go.

"All of the above."

Okay...maybe it wasn't the right way to go.

"As long as you're the one wearing them." He occupied the space like he owned the store instead of me. His presence was like a heavy cloud, about to drop pounds of rain on my head.

I kept a straight face even though bumps danced over my arms. The sex we had was good, some of the best I'd ever had.

He fucked me against the wall, doggy style on the couch, and then made me come over and over in his bed, missionary style. But he probably had incredible sex like that all the time—because he was the reason the sex was so good.

I glanced at Colton, who had his eyebrows raised all the way to his forehead.

I wished we were having this conversation in private, but Brutus obviously he didn't care who eavesdropped. "How did you find me? Or is this just a coincidence?"

"Not a coincidence. I don't usually shop for lingerie in the middle of the day on a Monday."

"So Tuesdays, then?"

His eyes dropped in their intensity as a soft smile entered his lips. "Let's have dinner tonight." He spoke with such confidence, like he assumed there was no possibility I would say no.

Arrogant, just like I thought. "I can't." I was tempted to say yes, but I'd already been down this road before. Beautiful men didn't settle down. Sometimes their hearts softened enough to let someone in—but only so far. This guy was no different. All I wanted in life was to be single forever, to have a few kids on my own when I had more financial stability. Men were useless to me —except for sex.

"Alright. Tomorrow, then."

I didn't do back-to-backs because I didn't want any type of intimacy. I didn't want to have deep conversations about our pasts. I didn't want to talk about anything besides sex and booze. I didn't want to open my heart to anyone ever again. I was done with that shit. "You're a good-looking guy, but I'm just not interested."

The room turned deadly quiet. Brutus stared at me with an expression identical to stone. Heartbeats passed, but he didn't blink and stir. Like he couldn't process the rejection that just came out of my mouth, he continued to stare at me.

Colton lowered his phone and stared at me like I was crazy. "Are you nuts?" he mouthed.

This guy clearly wasn't used to hearing the word no from anyone. I held my ground as I continued to be his target, the focus of that steely gaze. "Not interested in what, exactly?" His clipped voice came out deep.

"Dating."

"Alright. You want to fuck instead?"

That was the most attractive option of the two, but I wasn't interested in that either. "I don't sleep with the same guy twice. Nothing personal."

Again, he stared at me like he couldn't believe what I'd just said.

Colton looked like his head was about to explode.

Wordlessly, Brutus turned away and walked out of the store. He continued to hold himself straight, walking like a man who still had all the pride in the world after being rejected twice.

"What the hell is wrong with you?" Colton stood up when the door shut behind Brutus. "He's fucking gorgeous, and you just turn him down?" He gripped his skull like he was going to have a meltdown. "One of the richest dudes in the world just hunted you down to ask you out, and you rejected him?"

"I already said I don't care about his money."

"What about that ass? And those arms? Seriously, what's wrong with you?"

"I don't want anything serious."

"He just asked for a date—not a weekend getaway."

"Whatever." I came around the corner as I grabbed my purse. "I know guys like him. They're confident and quiet. They want something just because they can't have it. And once they have everything, they throw it away. Been there, done that."

When Colton knew I was referring to Finn, he sighed under his breath. "I knew you weren't over it..."

"How can I be over it, Colt? The guy asked me to marry him, but then something better came along. He preferred to live in a hut somewhere than be with me. I'm not in love with him, and I've moved on with my life. But...I'm just jaded by everything. I don't want to be in a relationship ever again because they don't work."

"That's not true—"

"The two men I fell in love with broke my heart."

His eyes filled with guilt.

"I'm just tired of it. I don't want to do it anymore."

"It won't always be like that. You'll find the right guy—"

"He doesn't exist, Colton. I just want to enjoy life, and maybe someday I'll be making enough money to start my family."

"On your own?" he asked incredulously.

"Why not? There are single parents everywhere."

"I think you're jumping the gun, Pepper. Brutus could be exactly what you're looking for, but you aren't giving him a chance."

He definitely wasn't what I was looking for. A man that rich and pretty would never commit to one woman. "I'm done talking about this. You want to get lunch or not?"

When Colton knew my mood should go unchallenged, he dropped the subject. "Yeah...let's go."

3

FINN

Nightmares flashed across my mind as I lay in the darkness of my apartment. A grenade blast shattered my eardrum like it was exploding right beside me. Blood sprayed into the air, sprinkling my skin like a series of freckles. My friend died in my arms, his eyes filled with terror as he prepared to face the unknown. It was a cosmic explosion of random events. But the worst part of my nightmare was the brunette with green eyes.

With her hair pulled over one shoulder, she sat on the couch in my living room, wearing a comfortable dress as she watched TV with Soldier by her side. More beautiful than I'd ever seen her, she glowed as if she were a radiant diamond. She turned to glance at me, that special look in her eyes just for me. Love collided with affection, admiration, and trust. She rose to her feet, her dress fitting tightly against her stomach because it was distended by several inches.

She was pregnant.

I looked at her with so much love in my heart, but something nagged at my insides. Without reason, I turned my back to her and headed to the door, ignoring the sound of my name from her lips.

Then I woke up with a jerk.

I sat up in bed, surrounded by the darkness of my apartment. My bag sat on the chair, and the TV was off. The only thing I could hear was the sound of my own breathing, along with the distant sirens that seemed to parade through the streets every few hours. It was a hot night, the kind of heat that made you sweat in your sleep—even with AC.

Jane lay beside me, her blond hair across the pillow and mattress. Buck naked, she was on my side of the bed, reaching for me like she wanted to snuggle despite the humidity.

I couldn't look at her, not when Pepper was still so fresh in my mind.

I pulled on my pants and walked to the balcony outside. I was a few hours from Uganda, staying in my apartment while I had a couple days to rejuvenate from the care center. Tall skyscrapers extended to the heavens, a small metropolitan city surrounded by the African landscape. Like most big cities, it was overpopulated and dirty.

I stood at the edge of the balcony and rested my arms on the wall, feeling the nighttime breeze but getting no reprieve from it. I'd been given the title of Chief Physician for the operation, an honor that would glow on my resume. The adventure was exactly what I'd expected it would be, thrilling and rewarding.

But as I stood in the evening air, I felt the tightness of my throat, the hot, sickening feeling deep inside my chest. My lips pressed tightly together to fight the tremble of my bottom lip. My eyes squinted as moisture flooded the surface from nowhere. Drowning in my own sorrow, I'd never been so overcome with grief, been filled with so much regret.

This was exactly what I'd wanted—but it came at a price.

A price I never should have paid.

I closed my eyes and focused on my breathing.

Deep breath in. Deep breath out.

I lowered my heart rate and subdued my emotions. I brought myself back to pragmatism and opened my eyes once more. The moment had ended, and I was back to my stoic self.

But the regret was still there.

The pain of my mistake.

This opportunity was supposed to fulfill me, to make me feel so alive. After watching friends die left and right, I'd promised myself to live each day to the fullest, not to get trapped in mediocre relationships that gave me a bland existence.

But now I couldn't enjoy any of it.

Every time I wanted to turn back, I forced myself to stay.

But now, so much time had passed, I couldn't go back even if I wanted to.

She was over me.

I heard her tone over the line, the indifferent way she said hello. She'd spoken just moments before, asking about wine because she had a date over. When she realized I was on the phone, her tone didn't change at all.

She didn't care.

It shouldn't hurt me, but it did. I should be happy that she was in a good place, that she moved on after what I did to her.

But I couldn't help but hate myself.

I hated myself for so many things. But I hated myself most of all for making the wrong choice. Every day was a halfhearted existence. I was privileged to help people, but I wasn't as invested as I used to be. Something was missing.

And I knew exactly what it was.

I threw away the woman I loved.

And now I couldn't take it back.

4

COLTON

We went out to our favorite bar that night, and Pepper stole the show like she always did. Drinks were constantly sent to her throughout the night, but instead of flirting with her admirers, she stayed with us.

"You aren't going to pick up anyone?" Tatum asked.

Pepper shrugged. "Maybe later. I'm hanging out with you guys right now."

"She can get that D later," Stella said. "Because she can get it whenever she wants."

I enjoyed the moments when Pepper was just Pepper, being herself and making sarcastic jokes at my expense. I hated watching her walk off with some random guy. Her personal life was none of my business, but I was afraid she was making mistakes she would regret later.

"I don't know about that," Pepper said with a chuckle. "But thanks."

Like a shark that swam out of the shadows, Brutus Hemmingway appeared from out of nowhere and approached our table. With a short glass in his hand, he seemed to be drinking a Jack and Coke. He came to the spot beside Pepper and joined our group like he'd been invited.

We were all stunned, like fans who were immediately starstruck by a celebrity. Zach was about to drink from his glass, but he chose to stare at Brutus instead, his mouth gaping open with a stupid look on his face. Stella's eyes were wide open, and she licked her lips instinctively. Tom was even drooling all over him, which forced me to nudge him in the side...even though I thought Brutus was beautiful too.

He turned to Pepper. "I'd offer to buy you a drink, but it seems like every guy in the bar already has."

Pepper was clearly unnerved, but she kept her composure. "You could buy one of my girlfriends a drink, then."

"How about a round for the whole table?" he asked. "On me."

"Ooh...I could get on board with that," Zach blurted.

He turned to me first, probably recognizing me from the store last week. "I'm Brutus. You must be a good friend of Pepper's. I see you two together a lot." He shook my hand with masculine strength, his tight arms flexing with mounds of muscle.

"Yeah, we're best friends." I stepped out of the way so my date could be seen. "This is my boyfriend, Tom."

Brutus shook his hand then introduced himself to the rest of the table.

Pepper gave me a furious look. "This guy can't take no for an answer, can he?"

"Maybe that's a good thing."

"No. It's just an annoying thing." She turned back to him. "So what's your next plan? To impress my friends?"

He stared at Pepper like she was the only woman in the room. He'd probably paid a guy to sit at the bar and alert him if she walked inside. Then he showed up and tried to sweep her off her feet. "Is it working?"

"Yes," Zach blurted.

Pepper glared at him.

Brutus smiled slightly then turned to me. "How long have you guys known each other?"

"About..." I tried to think of the total time since the night we met. "About six years now—"

"We used to be married." Pepper used her best ammunition to get herself off this guy's radar. Telling men she used to be married to a gay man was her best method to shake their attention. "We got divorced almost two years ago. And I'm sure it's obvious why." She drank from her glass, victorious in her scheme.

Why did she want to shake this guy so much? This one actually had potential.

His eyes narrowed, and he continued to stand there as if he were intrigued. "It's great to see that you guys are still friends. That's quite a testament to your relationship."

She did a double take because she couldn't believe what he'd just said.

I liked this guy.

Brutus remained as cool and suave as ever, drinking from his glass while admiring the earrings that hung from her lobes. He stared at her like she was land he had already claimed for himself. She thought she was on the market, but he obviously thought she was already his.

I wondered when Pepper would figure out that this guy wouldn't let her go without a fight.

He turned to Stella. "What's your story?"

"I'm her best friend," Stella said proudly. "And I've been dating Zach for almost a year now."

"You're a lucky man." Brutus raised his glass to Zach.

Zach clinked his glass against mine. "And you'll be a lucky man if you can ever tame a woman like Pepper."

Pepper's cheeks immediately reddened.

Brutus took a long drink before he set his glass down. "I've always been a lucky guy…"

I'd never seen a man so smitten with Pepper. The guy was crazy rich and so sexy it was stupid, so he could have whoever he wanted. So if he really had his sights on Pepper, it must be for a good reason. "Tom, let's head out. I'm a little under the weather."

Pepper snapped her neck in my direction. "You aren't going anywhere." She knew exactly what I was doing and wasn't buying my excuse.

I rubbed my stomach. "Must have been those hot wings I had earlier."

"You didn't eat any hot wings today," Pepper said coldly.

"No, I'm pretty sure I did." I grabbed Tom's hand and motioned to Stella and Zach.

Zach caught on. "Yeah…we've got to go too."

"You are all traitors." Pepper rolled her eyes then drank from her glass.

Brutus wore a slight smile, knowing he must have gained our approval if we were giving them some privacy. "It was nice to meet you all."

"You too." I waved to Pepper then walked out with everyone else. When I turned back to look at her from the door, she was flipping me off.

I gave her a thumbs-up and darted out.

———

WE WERE RELAXING on the couch of my apartment when Finn called.

Tom eyed my phone on the coffee table. "It's almost eleven. Why is he calling so late?"

"It's probably eight in the morning his time." I was taking his calls now, but I still resented him for what he did to Pepper. She was fucking every guy she saw because she was still so devastated by his betrayal. She talked about having a family on her own because the idea of ever trusting someone again was just too hard. I knew I was to blame for her feelings as well, but Finn did the biggest amount of damage. I took his call. "Hey." I spoke with a somewhat positive tone, but I was still annoyed that I had to have a conversation at all. Maybe when Pepper was married to a good guy, I would finally stop hating Finn.

"Hey." His tone was the complete opposite of mine, full of melancholy, like he didn't have the energy to even have this conversation. "How's Seattle?" He sighed into the phone, like I was the one who'd called him and interrupted his day.

"Cold, wet, rainy. The usual. How's Uganda...or Kenya? Wherever you are."

"Hot and humid."

"Wow, polar opposites."

"Yeah."

I watched the TV while my feet rested on the coffee table. I expected him to tell me about saving someone's life or his adventures with the villagers he was treating, but he was quiet on his end of the line. He'd never been much of a talker, but conversation was essential for a phone call. "Everything alright?"

"Yeah...I've just been going through a rough time. I don't have anyone to talk to about it."

When I realized my brother was actually hurting, I dropped all my resentment and opened myself up to him. I left the living room and headed into the kitchen so I could escape the sound of the TV. "What's going on, man?"

"I've been thinking about Pepper a lot…"

If he called me to tell me he'd made a mistake, I didn't want to hear it. If he said he wanted her back, I wouldn't help him. He'd made his decision six months ago, and he had to stick with it for the rest of his life.

"She's seeing someone?"

I wanted to slam the phone down when I heard the question. "You're joking, right?"

"No."

"You heard her on the phone the other day. Yes, she's seeing someone." She was seeing tons of people. I would never let him have the satisfaction of the destruction he caused. I wouldn't let him know that Pepper was still suffering, still processing this break up in a self-destructive way.

He was quiet for a long time. "Is it serious?"

"You've got to be kidding me, Finn. Look, you dumped her and took off. You don't get to call and snoop on her—"

"I'm not snooping, okay? I just—"

"It's over. When Pepper said you would never have another chance with her, she meant it. Stop asking about her because I won't give you answers. And don't you dare call her either. She wouldn't answer anyway." I couldn't believe Finn was pulling this shit. I also couldn't believe it took him six months to figure out what he'd lost.

"You really think I have no chance of getting her back?"

She had a billionaire pining for her affection. She talked about being alone for the rest of her life. She would never take back Finn in a million years, even if she did have feelings for him. "None."

He sighed into the phone. "Are you going to tell her what I said?"

"No. I'm sure time is standing still over there because you're alone, but we've all moved on. Tom and I really like her boyfriend. He's hot, rich, and treats her like a goddamn queen. No one is thinking about you, Finn. No one is thinking you two should be together. We've all moved on, and we're in better places. You're just going to have to live with the consequences of your stupidity—because you deserve to." I hung up and shoved the phone into my pocket.

Tom stared at me from his seat on the couch. "That was pretty cold."

"He deserves cold."

"You lied and said she has a boyfriend. I don't think that's fair."

"I'm not letting Finn think she's still heartbroken over their breakup...even if she is. I'm not letting her look weak. He ripped her apart into so many pieces, they may not fit together again. I'm not giving him any hope whatsoever. I don't want him anywhere near her, and neither does she."

"But are you sure about that? Maybe she would take him back."

"Trust me, she wouldn't."

Tom kept staring at me.

"What?"

"I just think if Finn really feels that way, maybe Pepper has the right to know."

I came back to the couch and avoided his gaze. "If he really felt that way, he could leave his post and come home and try to win her back. I'm not stopping him. She's just a phone call or text message away if he wants to do it the coward's way."

"But maybe he never will because he thinks she has a boyfriend."

"Whatever. They never should have gotten together in the first place. I'm not letting that shitshow happen again."

5

PEPPER

Now it was just the two of us at the table in the bar.

Because those bastards abandoned me.

He stayed beside me with his hand around his glass, keeping a respectable distance between us even though he'd already licked the valley between my tits and eaten my pussy. Our night together had gone on for hours. We didn't get to sleep until six, which was why it was so easy for me to slip out when he was dead to the world.

Dressed in a t-shirt and jeans, he didn't look like the rich man with a fat wallet. He seemed like a regular guy, which was why I went home with him in the first place. His jeans fit him so nicely, and the fabric of his shirt stretched across his chest because he had such a solid build. His masculine physique was softened by that pretty face. If being a billionaire didn't last, he could always do modeling—or porn.

"Your friends are nice." He pivoted his body toward mine.

"They're backstabbing assholes, and we both know it."

A soft grin stretched his face. "I think they liked me."

"They just think you're hot."

"And you don't think that?"

"Well…I do. But they also think you're rich."

"I am rich."

"And that's exactly why I'm not interested…" I took a drink.

"Because I'm rich?"

"Because you're arrogant about it."

He studied me while his fingers tapped against his glass. "It's impossible for a self-made man not to be that way."

"I'm sure it is." I didn't mean to be rude to this guy, but I'd already rejected him, even though he refused to accept my disinterest. He popped up in random places, cornering me so he could have my attention. If he weren't such a good-looking guy, people would find it creepy.

After a long bout of silence, he spoke again. "I'd really like to take you out sometime."

"I told you I wasn't interested."

"Why?"

I turned back to him, doing my best not to turn vulnerable when I looked at his sexy features. "I'm not looking for anything serious. If I were a man, that answer would have been sufficient."

"But I asked you to fuck, and you turned that down too."

"Because I don't like to be with the same man twice. Again, if I were a man, you wouldn't be blinking an eye over this. So you continue to ask me because you don't like my answer…like it's going to change."

"I have to try, right?"

"Or you could move on to someone else. A man like you could probably get any woman he wants." He could pick them up in his expensive car and drive them to the airport where his private jet was waiting. He didn't need to spend time hunting me down if he wanted a hot piece of ass for the night.

"I can get any woman I want. But I want you." Full of arrogance but also with a hint of sweetness, he threw out a line that softened me.

I looked into my glass.

"You want me too. So tell me why you won't let yourself have me."

"I already said—"

"I want the truth. Don't waste my time with that bullshit answer." A new watch was on his wrist, another Omega that was solid black. It seemed like every watch he wore was the price of a nice car.

"I didn't realize I owed you an explanation..."

He finished the rest of his drink and left the empty glass on the table. "How about I go first, then?"

"Go first for what?"

"Why I'm bending over backward to get ten minutes of your time." One arm rested on the table, and he stared at me with the same heated expression he gave me the night we slept together.

"I guess I would be curious to know. You've seen a lot of beautiful women in your lifetime, so I can't be that impressive to you. We've hardly had a real conversation, so it's not like we have a lot of in common. Your interest in me is a mystery, honestly."

"Have you ever Googled me?"

The only information I knew about him was what I learned from Zach and Colton. "No."

"I figured. Then you don't know that I'm divorced."

This guy couldn't be more than a few years older than me. He seemed too young to have already settled down and then called it quits. "Oh...I didn't know that." I assumed that a man like him would be a terminal bachelor until old age humbled him.

"It's the same story that's been told a million times. I fell stupidly in love with her, married her, and then she had an affair. She took half of everything, all of my hard work. I'm not sure which stung more, signing those divorce papers or writing her a fat check. She publicly humiliated me...and I was crushed."

Just minutes ago, he was a handsome stranger who meant nothing to me. But now, my heart beat a little harder, my eyes softened a little more, and I actually felt something for this man. It was pity mixed with respect, the way he told me about the most humiliating thing that ever happened to him with such vulnerability.

"So when you got upset because you thought I was married...I respected that. If only more people were like that, perhaps that affair never would have happened. Perhaps I would still be married right now, not that I wish that were the case."

"When did this happen?"

"The divorce was finalized three years ago, when I turned thirty."

"I'm sorry..." I pitied him because I understood his pain all too well. Losing someone you thought would be yours for the rest of your life was one of the hardest pains to ever endure. Divorce was ugly.

"Sometimes I wonder if she just wanted my money. If that guy hadn't slept with her, then she would have found someone else. Either way, she got half of my wealth, so it didn't matter. The fact that you didn't stick around the next morning and kept blowing me off told me you couldn't care less about my money."

I gave a slight nod. "Money is the root of all evil. You can trace back every problem in the world to greed. Every time."

He studied me for a full minute. "I think you might be right about that."

I turned back to my glass and took another drink.

"Now that I know you're divorced, I realize we have something else in common. Ever since things ended with my ex-wife, I haven't been interested in a real relationship. The idea of getting married again sounds like a headache. It's all fucking and partying for me now. But with you...I guess I wanted a little more. I'm attracted to your honor. I'm attracted to your indifference to my wealth. Now I'm attracted to you because that divorce must have been hard, but you overcame it." He moved a little closer to me, as if we were alone in his apartment and no one was around. "Tell me your story."

I gripped my glass a little harder. "It doesn't have a happy ending."

"Maybe the story hasn't ended yet."

"Alright." I released my glass and let it sit beside me. "I was married to Colton for three years. I was very happy. Being married to him was like being married to your best friend. I thought we would be together forever...until one day he told me he was gay."

His features softened with pity.

"It was really hard, letting him go and starting a new relationship. It took a long time, but we finally came to a place where we're best friends again."

"That's real love. It survives the harshest conditions."

"But then something worse happened..."

He kept listening.

"I fell in love with his brother, Finn. He's a veteran and a doctor. It kinda just happened, and we couldn't stay away from each other. We started a relationship, and we were very happy... he even proposed to me."

"Don't tell me he's gay too."

I chuckled, because Finn was the straightest guy on the planet. "No. He got offered a position in Africa with Doctors Without Borders for a year before he'll get a position at the Mayo Clinic in Minnesota. And he took it..."

He shook his head slightly. "Makes his promise sound a little empty."

"It was completely empty...and it hurt more than when

Colton left. Truth be told, I'm still not really over it. I'm over him, but that kind of abandonment really screwed me up. My mother got pregnant when she was really young, so she gave me up for adoption. I stayed in the system for eighteen years. I thought I'd overcome my abandonment issues when I was a young adult, but watching him leave brought everything back…"

"When did this happen?"

"Six months ago."

"So it's still a bit fresh."

"Yeah. I'm tired of getting hurt. I'm tired of watching the men I love walk away. So I'd rather be alone. It's just easier that way." I drank the rest of my glass then set it on the table. I was surprised I'd confided that information in him when I hadn't even told Colton the truth.

"It looks like you and I have a lot in common."

"Yeah…maybe we do."

"Well, I have an idea… How about we be alone together?"

I turned back to him, finding comfort deep in the beauty of his eyes. Now he didn't seem like an arrogant douchebag like all the rest. He seemed like a broken soul the way I was, someone who understood the same kind of suffering. "Okay."

He smiled. "I've never had to work so hard for a date…but it was worth it."

WE LAY in my bed together, the morning piercing through the slits in my blinds to fill my bedroom with a minute amount of light. Last night, we came to my place because it was so close. Clothes fell on the floor, and then we were fucking like we hadn't gotten laid in weeks. It was still just sex, but this time, I actually felt a connection to him.

He wasn't just some guy I would forget about the next morning. His face was permanently engraved in my mind. Our conversations were committed to memory. He was someone I would see again… and again. It wasn't a relationship. But it was definitely something.

When I opened my eyes, he was already awake. He was on his side facing me, his hard body making the old mattress dip in his direction. His hard chest rose and fell with his relaxed breathing, and his large biceps were a beautiful thing to see in the morning. "You're still here."

"You thought I would sneak out the way you did?" A slight smile was on his lips, full of amusement.

I shrugged. "I would have deserved it."

"No. This bed is too comfy."

"It's a ten-year-old mattress," I said with a laugh.

"It's not comfy because of the mattress. It's comfy because of the sexy naked woman beside me." He scooted closer to me and wrapped his arm around my waist, enveloping me in his masculine warmth.

I chuckled. "Good answer."

He pressed a kiss to my shoulder then continued to look at me, the shadow along his jawline a little thicker than it was last night.

"I'm surprised you agreed to come here. My apartment isn't fancy like yours."

"I would have slept behind a dumpster if it meant I got to fuck you."

I laughed, picturing the two of us sleeping on a pile of newspapers. "That would be so gross."

He shrugged. "Still would be worth it."

I lifted myself from the bed and pulled my hair out of my face. "I'm glad you don't think my eight-hundred-square-foot apartment is a dump." I got out of bed and picked up his t-shirt from the floor. I pulled it over my head and let the cotton settle around me. "I'm going to make breakfast. You hungry?"

"Always."

We walked into the kitchen and worked together to make pancakes and bacon. He didn't have any spare clothes so he stood in his boxers, his muscular thighs stretching out his shorts. His butt was tight, and his back was chiseled.

I'd have to steal his clothes more often.

I stood at the stove and flipped the pancakes in the pan. "I'm not a good cook, but I'm a lot better than I used to be."

"You can't be worse than me." He leaned against the counter with a mug full of Folgers coffee. He was probably used to freshly ground roast every morning because his assistant had the best beans flown from out of the country every single day. But he didn't complain about the cheap stuff I had. "I never cook."

"Then what do you eat?"

"I have a personal chef. He leaves things in my fridge throughout the week."

"That sounds nice." I scooped the pancakes onto a plate and poured more batter into the pan.

"This is better, though." He ripped off a piece of a fresh pancake and popped it into his mouth.

"Liar."

"I'm serious. Having a sexy woman cook me breakfast in my shirt...that's pretty hot."

I rolled my eyes. "You're probably used to that too."

"No. I don't invite them over for breakfast, and I don't let them wear my clothes."

He and I were both wounded, so we cut off all emotion from other people. But now we both seemed to open up to each other. "And I don't cook breakfast for anyone."

"I assumed so. You ducked out of my apartment right after we were finished."

I shrugged. "I got what I wanted."

"Too bad for you I wanted more."

I turned off the stove and slid the remaining pancakes onto a plate.

The door to my apartment opened, and Colton walked inside uninvited. "Hey, do you have any..." He halted on the doorstep when he saw Brutus beside me, and slowly, a mischievous grin stretched across his face. "Sorry, didn't know you had company." His eyes looked over Brutus's perfect physique, not even bothering to be discreet about it. Then he turned back to me and waggled his eyebrows.

Brutus didn't seem uncomfortable with the unexpected company or the fact that Colton was my ex-husband. He raised his mug in greeting. "Good morning. Pepper just made breakfast. You want to join us?"

Jax was put off by Colton the second he knew about our previous relationship. Instead of feeling the same way, Brutus seemed to see Colton as a friend, the least threatening person on the planet.

"I don't know..." Colton joined us then looked down into the pan of bacon grease. "Sometimes Pepper cooks food...and sometimes poison."

"Oh, shut up." I left the spatula in the pan and pulled out a few plates from the cabinet. "I'm such a better cook now, and you know it."

Colton leaned toward Brutus and whispered something.

"Hey." I flicked him on the arm. "Knock it off, or no food for you."

"I guess I'll take my chances," Colton said. "You probably wouldn't poison Brutus, so I should be safe."

We sat down at the dining table, and Colton couldn't stop

sneaking glances at Brutus's phenomenal physique. He'd direct his fork to his mouth to take a bite but would miss because his eyes devoured Brutus's arms and chest.

I knew Brutus could feel Colton's attraction, and I was glad he was nice enough not to say anything. I wouldn't like it if someone were gawking at me like that, man or woman. "What's Tom doing?"

"He went home," Colton said. "He had laundry to do and had to get ready for the workweek."

"You ever think about moving in with him? You've been together for a while now."

Once Tom was mentioned, Colton stopped gawking at Brutus. "It's crossed my mind, but since our relationship is going so well, I don't want to mess it up by asking."

"If you do move in together, you should shack up at his place," I said. "That way I don't have to live across the hall from you anymore."

Brutus sipped his coffee. "I was wondering where you came from."

"If I didn't live across the hall, you'd starve," Colton countered. "So you need me."

"I'd prefer Tom's company over yours." Now we talked like two bratty friends rather than former spouses. Our previous relationship seemed like a lifetime ago, and neither one of us viewed each other that way anymore.

Colton took a dramatic bite of his bacon, the crunch audible. "You know what? I'm taking this back to my apartment and eating it on the couch." He left the table and headed to the door.

"Wash that plate before you bring it back."

"Ha." He stepped out and shut the door behind him. "We know that's not going to happen…"

When he was gone, Brutus drank his coffee and continued to look at me. "You guys are closer than I realized."

Brutus and I weren't in a relationship, but I didn't want to head in the same direction I had with Jax. I didn't want to waste my time with this guy if he was going to be weird about my relationship with Colton. Colton was the closest thing I had to a family, and I wasn't throwing that away. "I don't know what's going to happen between us. Maybe nothing will ever happen. But I can't be with someone who has a problem with my relationship with Colton. I know it's a little weird because we used to be married and we live across the hall from each other, but that's nonnegotiable."

He took a bite of his bacon and seemed relaxed, like my speech meant nothing to him. "Why would that bother me? He's clearly gay."

I stared at him blankly for a moment, surprised that was so easy. "I dated this guy a while ago who had a problem with it. Said I had to choose between him and Colton...I chose Colton."

"Insecure and controlling...you made the right decision." He finished his food so his plate was completely clean. Even if he had a gourmet chef to prepare all of his meals, he didn't seem to care about the pancake batter I got from Walmart.

Just like that, he overcame the biggest hurdle in my relationships.

"I don't know where this is going either...but I hope it's going somewhere." He rested his hand on top of his mug as he turned his head and looked at me. "By the way, I have this dinner thing tomorrow night. It's a birthday party for a friend at the Four Seasons. You want to tag along?"

"Are you serious?"

"You can come as a friend if that makes it easier for you."

"Why are you asking me?"

He shrugged. "I like you. Do I need to have a better reason than that?"

"I just figured you'd want to go alone..."

"So dozens of women can hit on me because they know I'm a billionaire?" He shook his head. "That gets old after a while. It would be nice just to go and not have to worry about that. But if you aren't interested—"

"No, I'll go." I'd decided I wouldn't date anymore, but I enjoyed spending time with Brutus. He seemed harmless because of his past heartbreak, and it was refreshing that he knew about all of my suffering. I felt like I could be myself completely, to not be judged for my pain. "It'll be fun."

"Great." He smiled. "We'll have a good time. There will be more food and booze than we can consume."

"Ooh...then we really will have a good time."

6

FINN

I RETURNED TO MY APARTMENT AFTER A ONE-WEEK ROTATION IN Uganda.

Every time I drove into the village, I was filled with dreadful isolation, like I was driving off the face of the earth.

But every time I drove into Kenya, it was worse.

There was nothing waiting for me there.

Suffocated by my own thoughts, the loneliness made me drown. If only Pepper had come with me, I would have had everything I wanted. But now I had nothing...because I was too depressed to enjoy what I was doing.

Jane was usually in my bed—but she meant nothing to me.

She tried to talk to me, but I tuned her out. All we did was fuck, a poor attempt to chase away the feelings in my heart. Sometimes I pretended she was Pepper just to finish...but that usually made me feel worse.

When I walked inside my apartment, I sat at my desk and opened my laptop.

The conversation I had with Colton weeks ago kept replaying in my mind.

She'll never take you back.

She's seeing someone else.

She's over you.

Every sentence hurt more than the previous one. I'd made my choice when I decided to come here—and now I couldn't take it back. I couldn't make it right. I couldn't get on my knees and beg for another chance.

I made my bed. It was time to lie in it.

How could I have been so stupid? Maybe this decision would have made sense years ago, but meeting Pepper changed my life drastically. My priorities were different now. I was trying to live my old life, when my soul was only happy in the company of its other half.

I didn't want to be here anymore.

I didn't care about it anymore.

I looked at my laptop and scanned the news from the United States. I stayed updated on both places, wanting to know what I was dealing with at home and abroad. It seemed like my mind was playing tricks on me, torturing me even more, because a woman in a photograph looked identical to Pepper.

Billionaire and business tycoon Brutus Hemmingway was spotted at the Four Seasons Seattle with a new woman on his arm. It's the first time he's been photographed with someone since his high-profile divorce from supermodel Cassandra Newton. The identity of the woman is unknown at this time.

I stared at the picture, seeing a good-looking guy with his arm around a gorgeous brunette with green eyes. He escorted her into the hotel, a foot taller than her, with confidence in his gaze. He was lean and muscular, and he had a jawline most men would be envious of. Maybe the reporter couldn't figure out who the woman was, but I could.

It was Pepper.

She'd won the affection of a handsome billionaire. A man every woman wanted.

But he only wanted her.

She wasn't just over me...she'd forgotten about me.

7

COLTON

I STOOD AT THE TABLE IN THE LIVING ROOM AND PICKED UP MY watch. It was a gift given to me by Tom, and the back of the watch was engraved with the date of the night we'd met. I slipped it onto my wrist and clicked it into place.

Pepper entered my apartment in a short dress with a deep vee down the front. A silver necklace was around her throat with a diamond in the center. It was a necklace I'd never seen, and judging from the quality of the diamonds, it was expensive.

Which meant it was a gift from Brutus.

A month had passed since she'd accompanied him to that birthday party at the Four Seasons, and they'd been inseparable ever since.

Which made me very happy.

Thankfully, Finn had backed off and didn't call me about Pepper again. Hopefully, he'd given up on her and moved on with his life. It shouldn't have taken six months for him to figure out the mistake he'd made, so I didn't pity him at all.

I just wanted Pepper to be with a good guy. And Brutus checked all the boxes.

"Ready for our double date?" She walked inside, her four-inch heels echoing against the hardwood floor. With her hair in soft curls and a brilliant shade of lipstick on her lips, she looked stunning.

"Yes. But not as ready as you are. The dress is perfect on you."

She spun around and struck a pose. "Thank you. You look nice too." She was a ray of sunshine now, bursting with happiness every time I saw her. The melancholy Pepper I knew was long gone, and so was her past of sleeping around. In fact, I'd never seen her happier...with the exception of her time with Finn.

But at least the hard days were behind her.

"Is Brutus coming here?" I wrapped my arm around her waist and kissed her on the cheek.

She rolled her eyes. "You really need to stop gawking at my boyfriend."

"Come on, he's gorgeous. What am I supposed to do?"

"You shouldn't be checking him out in front of your boyfriend."

"Are you kidding me?" I asked with a laugh. "Tom gawks at him harder than I do."

"Well, hands off." She poked me in the chest. "He's mine."

"You can have him...but we like to look at him."

She walked into the kitchen and poured herself a glass of wine. "I'm excited to try this new steakhouse. The waiting list is weeks-long, but Brutus managed to get us in with the snap of his fingers."

"Because he's a billionaire. He can make anything happen. He might own it for all we know."

"True..." She sipped her wine and smeared her lipstick against the glass.

"How's it going with him anyway?"

"Good."

I grabbed a glass and filled it with the white wine I'd picked up at the grocery store. "Come on, you guys have been inseparable ever since that party at the Four Seasons. It seems like you really like him."

"I do like him." She smiled before she took another drink.

I didn't feel guilt for not telling her about Finn's regret. She was finally in a good place, and I wouldn't let his feelings confuse her. I never thought I would say this, but Finn was the kind of man who talked about doing things...but never actually did them. Maybe he really did regret going to Uganda. That didn't mean he would ever come home and commit to her. Even if he did, Pepper was too smart to take him back.

"I like him a lot." She swallowed her wine then set the glass on the counter. "At first, I just wanted to get rid of him, but he really wore me down. He told me he's divorced."

"Yeah...I read that somewhere." But I couldn't figure out what happened. His representatives just said they were uncoupling without explanation.

"I'm not one to gossip, but he told me his wife cheated on him. She took half of his assets and broke his heart. He said it really hurt and took a long time to get over it. That was music to my ears...because he really understood how I felt. And he couldn't care less about my relationship with you. It just felt so easy..."

I was so glad they'd met in that bar. Pepper kept going through guys like water, and thankfully someone stuck. He was handsome, easygoing, and got along with all of us so well. But more importantly, he gave Pepper exactly what she needed. "So, it's pretty serious, then?" I picked up the bottle and refilled our glasses.

"I wouldn't say it's serious. But we aren't sleeping with other people. I'm not ready to fall in love again. I'm still so broken over everything that's happened over the last few years. But with

Brutus, we're friends and lovers. We can be honest with each other, and that's really refreshing. Neither one of us is in a rush to be anything serious because we've both been hurt, so it just makes the arrangement easy."

They were healing together, and in the process, falling in love. Brutus hadn't been around that long, but I could tell he would be the right one. He would be the one she married and started a family with. I didn't say that, obviously. I kept it to myself. "I really like him, Pepper. He's a really good guy. The second he came around, he just fit with our group. And he's so fucking hot."

She laughed into her glass and smacked my arm. "Oh my god, Colton."

"What?" I asked innocently. "How often do you meet a guy in real life with those kind of abs?"

"You're ridiculous."

"If only he were gay..."

"Oh...he's definitely not gay."

Someone knocked on the door.

"Come in," she announced.

"Do you still live here?" I asked sarcastically.

Brutus walked inside, wearing dark jeans, a deep blue V-neck, and a black leather jacket. He had the looks of a bad boy but the smile of a saint. When his eyes settled on Pepper and her dress, it was like I wasn't even in the room. "Damn, you look good in that dress."

Pepper couldn't hide her smile as she set down her glass and moved into his chest. Her arms wrapped around his neck as he gripped her around the waist. Together, they pulled themselves together and kissed. He bent his neck down to kiss her hard on the mouth, his hands gripping the material of her dress and pushing it up slightly in the process.

I looked into my wineglass so I wouldn't be creepy.

When Pepper pulled away, she dragged her hands down his chest. "You look good too."

"Not as good as you." He kissed the corner of her mouth. "But thanks anyway." He squeezed her ass with both hands before he pulled away. He turned his attention to me and stuck out his hand. "Hey, Colt. Nice to see you."

I ignored his gesture because this man deserved more than a boring handshake. He came in here and put a smile on Pepper's face. That made him my hero. "Yeah, it's great to see you too."

When he pulled away from my hug, he smiled. "Looks like I have the approval of the best friend."

A knock sounded on the door, and Tom walked inside. "Hey, guys."

Pepper walked to the other side of the apartment to greet him.

And left the two of us alone for a second. "Yes, you have my approval—a million times over. You make Pepper really happy, so you're my favorite person in the world. Thanks for being so good to her. I really appreciate it." I clapped him on the back.

"Are you just saying that because you think I'm hot?" he asked, grinning playfully.

"I mean...it helps." I chuckled.

"It's ironic. I was actually worried you would never like me since Finn is your brother."

"What does that have to do with anything?" I glanced at Pepper, who was absorbed in a conversation with Tom by that time. They hugged then kissed each other on the cheek.

"Well, if they'd ended up together, she'd be your sister-in-law. I don't know, I just thought you might be loyal to him since you're related."

I wasn't loyal to him at all. He went behind my back and slept with my ex-wife. Then he proposed to her and dumped her. Good riddance. "I'll always love my brother, but he never deserved her. I'm relieved he's on the other side of the world and out of her life. She deserves to be happy."

"Do you think he really loved her?"

The answer immediately popped up in my mind. The instinct was so clear. I had so many memories where Finn wore his heart on his sleeve, the way he spoke of her so highly, the way he stayed faithful to her when he could have fooled around. "I do. But I don't think he loved her enough either. If he did, he wouldn't have left."

"Well, I hate that she got her heart broken, but I'm glad it happened. At some point, he's going to realize he made a huge mistake. It'll hit him when he least expects it. Hopefully, it'll be too late for him to do anything about it."

It was incredible that Brutus predicted that outcome so easily.

"About eighteen months after I got divorced, Cassandra came back to me. Every man she was with only wanted her for her money. They would use her then spit her out again. No one actually cared whether she lived or died. That's when she appreciated me, realized what she threw away."

"What did you do?"

"She gave me the revenge I'd been hoping for. So I smiled and slammed the door in her face. Never saw her again."

WE DEVOURED OUR GOURMET STEAKS, our red wine, and Pepper ate all the bread in the bread basket. We were given a private table in the corner near the window, but women still gawked at Brutus.

"That was so good," Tom said. "But I'm not taking my shirt off tonight. We'll do it clothed."

"That's fine with me," I said. "My belly is bigger than yours.

Brutus is the only one who looks thinner now than when he walked in."

Brutus chuckled. "You guys are my biggest admirers. Pepper doesn't even compliment me like that."

"Fucking you is my compliment." She moved her hand to his thigh and leaned in to kiss him on the cheek.

He melted right before my eyes, like he'd never been more infatuated with a woman in his life. His hand went to the back of her neck, and his fingers got lost in her blanket of hair. He leaned into her and kissed the corner of his mouth, his affection implying that he wanted to do more than just kiss her.

It used to gross me out when Pepper and Finn were like that. But with Brutus, it was a welcome sight. Brutus adored her.

When the waitress brought the check, Brutus pulled away. "I got it, guys." He grabbed the black pad then reached for his wallet in his back pocket.

"No. We split it." I grabbed my wallet and threw down my card.

"Yes." Pepper grabbed her wallet. "We split it three ways."

"Not gonna happen." Brutus grabbed her wallet and placed it on his other side so she couldn't reach it. "I'd consider splitting the bill with the guys, but no way in hell am I letting you pay."

Pepper didn't fight since her wallet was out of her reach. "You've got to let me pay sometime."

"No, I don't." Brutus took my card and slipped them both into the folder. "Good, the check dance is done. I hate that shit."

I liked the fact that Brutus wasn't an arrogant asshole who refused to let anyone chip in. He didn't make us feel poor, like there was no way we could afford a place like this. He wasn't stuck-up like I imagined a billionaire would be. He was chill.

The waitress took it, and the argument died.

"You know," Pepper said. "We live in the twenty-first century. Women pay for stuff."

"I agree. But you pay for your meals in a different currency." His arm moved around her waist, and he gave her that smoldering gaze again, like he couldn't wait to get her back to his place so he could fuck her into the sheets.

She blushed slightly. "I'm going to check my makeup before we go. Mind letting me out?"

"You could just slide over my lap," Brutus said, half teasing.

"I have a feeling there would be a huge log in the way." She smacked her hip against his in the booth.

He rose from the booth, let her out, and then gave her a playful smack on the ass as she headed to the bathroom. Then he sat down again, facing us like he hadn't just groped Pepper right in front of us.

I liked him.

He started a new conversation. "I'm thinking of taking Pepper to Fiji next week. The weather is beautiful right now, and we could use a vacation."

Man, I wished this guy would take me to Fiji to fuck for a week. "Wow, that sounds really nice."

"What about her shop?" Tom asked. "She's her only employee, right? She can't close that long."

"I've been helping Pepper with her business," Brutus explained. "I gave her a few pointers, helped her with marketing, and got her to hire a few girls to help her run the store. It's only been a few weeks, but her income has risen by three hundred percent, even with the cost of employees."

"I didn't know that..." Pepper hadn't mentioned it to me.

"She fought me at first, but I didn't like the fact that she had to work all the time. The nice thing about owning a business is not working all the time. My self-interest was my primary concern."

"That's great," I said. "She's also been making it check to

check, but she's never given up her business because she enjoys it too much."

"It's a great business," he said. "Women want something small like that. You go to Victoria's Secret and see models in a size double zero, and it's intimidating. At Pepper's shop, it's more intimate and more realistic. Makes women feel sexy. I knew she had a lot of potential the second I walked in there."

"Good. I've always wanted her to have more success." I had feared for her financial stability without me. I made a lot more money than she did, and when we first divorced, I kept putting money into her account until she threatened to rip my eyes out. "But I don't know about going to Fiji. Pepper is kind of a home-body, and she hates planes."

"She's afraid of flying?"

"No. The seats are just uncomfortable for her."

"Oh...that shouldn't be a problem," Brutus said. "We'll take one of my planes."

One of his planes? I'd forgotten this guy was worth a hundred and fifty billion dollars. He probably had planes all over the world. "Then she'll say yes in a heartbeat."

"I was hoping so," he said. "I have to be in New York on business in a few weeks, so I want to spend some time with her before I leave. It's just part of my job sometimes."

"Are you in Seattle most of the time?" Tom asked.

"Yeah, it's where my corporate office is," Brutus explained. "But I have headquarters everywhere." He didn't talk about work much, probably because it was an awkward topic.

And I never asked him anything because Pepper forbade me saying a word about it.

Pepper returned to the table a moment later. "Ready to go?"

Brutus rose to his feet and wrapped his arm around her waist. "Want to stay at my place tonight?"

"Sure. You have any dessert in the kitchen?"

He smiled at her. "I made sure my chef made a few things for you."

"So you knew I was coming this weekend?" she asked, being playful.

He rubbed his nose against hers. "I was hoping you were."

ON SUNDAY NIGHT, Pepper walked into my apartment. "Guess where I'm going tomorrow."

I didn't turn my gaze away from the TV. "Fiji."

"Wait...how did you know that?" She came over to the couch holding a bag with her store logo on it.

"He told me at dinner on Friday."

"And you didn't mention it?"

"Why would I ruin the surprise? He said he was going to take you on his private jet... That's gonna be cool."

"I know, right? It's so crazy. I've never taken a vacation my entire life, and now I'm going to Fiji on a private jet to a private island. Like...is this really happening? And Brutus is just so..." Her hand made a fist as she tried to describe her thoughts. "Sweet and sexy...and kind and funny. On top of that, he's rich? What the hell was his ex-wife thinking?" She shook her head. "There is no better guy out there than Brutus Hemmingway—even if he weren't rich."

"He told me she tried to get him back about a year and a half after they divorced."

"What did he do?"

"Slammed the door in her face."

"Good. She didn't deserve him...not after what she did." She pulled a few items out of her bag. "Look what I got myself for the trip. I found the sluttiest lingerie in my inventory...at his request." She smiled as she showed me the pieces, excited about running off to an exotic location with her sexy boyfriend.

"He'll like all of those—especially that black one."

She put everything back in the bag. "He's great, isn't he? You guys like him?"

"We love him." He was perfect, a blessing after Pepper had been cursed. "And I can tell you love him too. Well, not literally love him. You know what I mean."

"Yeah, I do. Our relationship is just so easy. It's really nice..." Her eyes wondered why, and a smile slowly faltered off her lips.

I studied her, wondering what she was thinking. "Where did your mind go?"

She shifted her gaze back to me and cleared her throat. "I was just thinking about Fiji...pretty long flight."

"But you'll be on a private plane, so it'll be nice. There will probably be a full bed, so you could even sleep and screw the entire way."

"True...I can't believe this is really happening. I'll take lots of pictures to show you."

"You better. And have a good time."

"I will. Keep an eye on my apartment, okay?" She hugged me then kissed me on the cheek.

"I will."

She rose to her feet and let her bag hang on the crook of her arm. "And thanks for forcing me to go out with him... None of this would be happening without you."

"Dr. Burke, I don't understand." William, the man who oversaw the various programs around the world, sat across from me in the tent just outside the village. The zipper was pulled up so we had our privacy, but anyone could hear through the thin material. "You've been doing exceptional work here on the ground. The team loves you, and the patients are grateful to have you here treating them. You still have five months to go before your commitment is finished. Why are you trying to leave now?"

The heat permeated the material of the tent and my clothes, constantly making me hot and sweaty. My hands were always slippery because the humidity kept my skin moist at all times. The bugs and spiders that crawled into unlikely places were the stuff of nightmares. But my discomfort had nothing to do with my decision. "I wish I could give you a better justification. I wish I could tell you that I'm sick or have other obligations. The truth is, I belong somewhere else. I thought this was what I wanted to do...but I realize this isn't my home. I should be in Seattle. This was a wonderful opportunity, and I'm so grateful you gave me a chance to be part of this wonderful program. But...my heart isn't in it." My heart was on the other side of the world, sleeping in another man's bed. Colton told me I had no chance at getting her back, that I'd fucked up too badly. But I still wanted to be home. I still wanted to see her. I didn't want to spend another day in this jungle when I could be looking into her face. Even if she never wanted me again, I still wanted her friendship. I just wanted to talk to her, to see those beautiful green eyes stare back at me.

Willian didn't hide his annoyance. "You realize this means you'll forfeit your position with the Mayo Clinic."

It was my dream job, to work for an organization that provided the best health care in the country. But I realized I had a different dream now. That dream could be a reality this very moment if I hadn't made the wrong decision. "Yes."

William sighed in disappointment. "Alright. If I can't change your mind..."

"You can't." I'd never imagined myself making a decision like this. A few years ago, this never would have happened. I never would have cashed in my dreams to spend my life with one woman...in one place. But she changed me in ways I couldn't explain. Now I wanted to come home to her every night, to live a quiet and mediocre existence that gave me so much joy. I was officially trading in my bachelor life because it gave me no further happiness. "Thank you for everything, William." I shook his hand and left the tent.

My bag was outside, so I grabbed it and headed to the Jeep parked at the dirt road. I would get on the next plane to the United States and leave this part of my life behind forever. I would return home to my house and my dog.

And hopefully...eventually...Pepper.

If I could get her back.

"Finn?" Jane's voice came from behind me.

I'd forgotten about her, hadn't given her a second thought at all. My mind had been wrestling with memories of Pepper, thinking about the regret I carried like TNT strapped to my chest. I turned to look at her.

The unease was written across her pretty face, the gleam of sweat on her forehead as her blond hair was pulled back into a ponytail. She was a doctor from the UK, so she had an English accent. But her eyes filled with dread, like she already knew what was happening without my needing to explain it.

"I'm going home, Jane."

Her feelings for me started the day we met, but she knew I didn't reciprocate her affection. I was just a lonely man trying to forget my pain by using someone else. She let me use her. Maybe she hoped I would change. Or maybe she knew I never would but didn't care. "I hope you get her back, Finn..."

9

COLTON

I SAT ON THE COUCH AND LOOKED AT ALL THE PICTURES SHE SENT me. There were some of the private pool attached to their room, the beach that was just steps away from the villa, along with other beautiful scenery.

Including a picture of Brutus in a Speedo.

My god...so beautiful.

She sent a smiley face emoji. *Just for you.*

Actually, I think it's just for you. But thanks for sharing. It was nine o'clock my time, so it must be late afternoon wherever she was at. Every picture had a stunning blue sky and so much sun that she would be so dark by the time she came back.

A knock sounded on the door.

Tom had just left an hour ago, so maybe he was coming back because he forgot something. I left my phone on the coffee table then opened the front door. I expected to come face-to-face with Tom. Then I would show him the sexy picture of Brutus that Pepper was so nice to share with me.

Instead, it was Finn.

As in, my brother Finn.

On the other side of the door in jeans and a t-shirt, he looked exactly the same way I remembered. His skin was a little darker from sun exposure, and he seemed leaner than before, like he couldn't keep up his strict diet while living in a third world country.

I stared at him blankly, thinking this was a dream...or a nightmare. "What are you doing here?" It wasn't the best first sentence to come to mind, but the words tumbled out on their own. I expected Finn to be a distant part of my life from now on, a guy I saw for the holidays every few years. I never expected to see him standing on my doorstep, especially when he looked dead inside.

"I've been gone for six months, and that's the first thing you want to say to me?" His tone was clipped like he was seriously offended by the way I addressed him.

My attitude fired back. "You've been gone for six months because you *wanted* to leave. And you caught me by surprise. I had no idea you were coming home for a visit. How long are you in town?"

His stature was the same, strong and straight. His chiseled arms were covered with veins, and his tanned skin looked tighter because of his activity in Africa. His muscle size had decreased, but he was as lean as ever. "You want to invite me inside before the interrogation begins?"

"Sure." I opened the door wider and let him enter my apartment. When I shut the door, I was suddenly overwhelmed with relief. Pepper was on the other side of the world and would never know he was here. By the time she returned, he would be gone again. The timing couldn't be more perfect. "You want something to drink? I think I've got—"

Finn grabbed me and pulled me into his chest. His hands gripped me hard as he brought me into a hug, squeezing me like it was the last time he would ever see me. His hand cupped the back of my head, then he patted me on the back before he released me. "It's good to see you. I missed you, man." He looked me in the eye as he said it, showing the kind of emotion Finn wasn't known for.

"I missed you too...everything alright?"

He shrugged. "You said you have some scotch?"

"Uh...I might." I stepped into the kitchen and looked through the cabinets until I found an old bottle he'd left behind. "You're in luck." I found a short glass then filled it completely, still processing the fact that my brother was standing in my apartment.

He looked around the apartment, like he expected to see something new. "I thought you and Tom would be living together by now."

"In good time." I carried the glass to him and handed it over.

He took a long drink then set it on the dining table beside him.

"So...are you in town for a week?" Hopefully, it wasn't longer than that. It would be impossible for me to hide Finn from Pepper if he was at my apartment all the time. "It's a pretty long flight, so hopefully you have more time than that."

"I do." He wiped his mouth with the back of his forearm.

"Oh?"

"I left the program."

My eyebrows shot to the top of my forehead. "Wait...what? What do you mean, you left?"

"I left," he said simply. "I gave up my position then got on the first plane home."

"But why...?" That was his dream job. He wouldn't give it up without reason.

"My heart wasn't in it anymore." He crossed his arms over his chest, his blue eyes filled with unquestionable pain. His gaze focused on the living room for several seconds before he turned back to me. "I wanted to come home."

This still wasn't adding up. "What about the position at the Mayo Clinic?"

"I forfeited that."

"Seriously? So you just abandoned everything?"

He gave a single nod. "Yeah."

"Again...why?"

"I told you my heart wasn't in it anymore."

"Then why did you leave in the first place?" Why did he break Pepper's heart for something he didn't want?

"Because I was stupid, Colt." His eyes were full of self-loathing. "I was a fucking idiot."

Our last conversation came back to me, when Finn told me he regretted leaving Pepper. He finally came to his senses, but he took way too long to figure out what he lost. His chances of fixing things were long gone. "You're an even bigger idiot for coming back here. Pepper is not in the same place you are."

"I knocked on her door, but she didn't answer..." The pain intensified even more, like he knew exactly where she was—in bed with someone else.

"Because she's in Fiji."

Finn nearly did a double take when he heard what I said. "Fiji?"

"Her boyfriend took her on vacation in his private jet."

Finn clenched his jaw and sighed. "What about the store?"

"He helped her adjust her business model and made it much more profitable. Now she has employees so she can take time off."

He didn't ask any more questions. Instead, he grabbed his scotch and took a long drink, nearly finishing the contents in one go. Then he set it aside and started to pace in my living room. His hands dragged down his face, and he sighed loudly, his shoulders slumping under an invisible weight.

I almost felt bad for him. "Finn, the guy she's dating is—"

"Brutus Hemmingway. Yes, I know."

"And how did you know that?"

He gave a simple answer. "The news." He turned back to me, his arms still crossed over his chest.

He came back to Seattle even though he knew Pepper was dating the most eligible bachelor in the world. He either had a crazy amount of confidence, or he was just stupid. "Finn, I have a pretty low opinion of you because of what you did to Pepper, but my opinion will be even lower if you try to sabotage her relationship with Brutus. She's really happy, Finn. Like, *really* happy. They are perfect together."

He lowered his chin toward the floor. "Thanks for being so sensitive about it…"

I threw my arms down. "You left. You broke her heart. You left her to cry in my arms for months. Why should I feel bad for you? You're the one who fucked up. You're the one who thought a better guy wouldn't pick her up. If you really want to waste your time trying to get her back, then fine. But I promise you, you aren't going to get the happy ending you want. Pepper will never take you back—not ever."

He kept his chin tilted toward the floor. "Be that as it may… this is my home."

"What?"

"My house is here. My dog is here. My family is here. This is where I belong."

"It wasn't where you belonged six months ago," I jabbed. "You had a fiancée, and you still left her."

"And that was the biggest mistake of my life." He lifted his gaze to meet mine, the emotion deep inside his look. "I'd give anything to go back in time and make the right decision. I spent months in Africa thinking I could go back to my old life and be who I used to be...but I can't. I keep having dreams about Pepper...with a ring on her hand and a baby in her belly. I have to try to get her back...or at least get some closure."

"All you're going to do is give her revenge—the satisfaction of slamming the door in your face."

He winced. "You really think she'd do that?"

I put my hands on my hips. "I really think you can't compare to this guy, Finn."

"Pepper doesn't care about money."

"That's not all he has." I started listing off his qualities. "He's been divorced. He understands what it's like to be left, so they have heartbreak in common. He knows she doesn't care about money—that's why he adores her. He couldn't care less about her relationship with me. He couldn't care less that the guy was she was married to is gay. And most importantly, this guy is smokin' hot."

Finn didn't roll his eyes or make a joke about the last thing I said. He continued to stand there, staring at a different spot in my living room while his chest rose and fell with labored pain.

"They have a lot in common, Finn. She trusts him."

He turned back to the table and grabbed the scotch. He took a long drink as his throat shifted and moved to get the booze in his stomach. When the glass was empty, he set it down with a distinguishable thud.

"You should see if you can get your position back in Africa. If it's only been a few days, they might cut you some slack."

"I'm not going back, Colt."

"Then what are you going to do here? You don't have a job or a place to live."

"The renters left my house a few weeks ago. That's where I'll stay."

"Oh...I thought you sold it."

He shook his head. "The equity hadn't risen high enough yet."

"And what about work?"

"The ER took me back in a heartbeat. They are short on doctors, so they were happy to welcome me back."

He left so easily, and now he returned so easily. So this was really happening. Just when Pepper finally found the right guy, Finn returned to Seattle to fuck it up. I rubbed my hand across my jaw and sighed, unsure how to handle this. I should give Pepper a heads-up so Finn didn't appear on her doorstep and catch her off guard.

Finn studied me. "You hate that I'm here." The tone of heart-break was in his voice, and his pain was audible.

"I just want you to leave Pepper alone. I don't think what you're doing is right. I think it's selfish. But you've always been selfish, so I guess it doesn't surprise me…"

His eyes fell further. "Colt."

My hands moved to my hips.

"I love her."

I couldn't stop myself from rolling my eyes. "Whatever you say."

"I do. I know I fucked up, but I love her. I have to try to make this right."

"Look, this is the guy she's gonna marry. You missed your chance. Get over it." I'd never been so cold to someone, but I wanted to protect Pepper. The last thing I wanted her to do was throw away the perfect guy for a man who didn't deserve her.

"She loves him?" His voice turned quiet, like he could barely get the words out.

I wanted to lie if that's what it took to get him to back off, but I didn't want to cross a line. "I don't know. But I've seen them together…and it just feels right. I'm sorry that you're in pain because you realized your mistake, but you have to live with the consequences. All you're going to do is upset her, and you'll never get what you want anyway."

"Colt—"

"Do whatever you want, Finn. I obviously can't change your mind."

He stepped back and looked at the floor for a second before he raised his gaze and met my look. "I'm ready to be whatever she wants. If she wants to marry me, I'll go down to the court-house today. She wants babies, we'll make them. I'm prepared to be whatever she wants...because I want those things too. I shouldn't have left, but it took that experience to make me realize this is the only place I ever want to be."

"And that would be fine if you were only gone for a few weeks or a month. But it took you six months to figure out your shit. I can only imagine how many women you slept with in the meantime..."

"One."

"I didn't ask, Finn," I said bitterly. "And your answer should be zero."

"So you aren't going to help me with this at all?"

"No." Finn was my flesh and blood, but Pepper was some-thing more. "I like Brutus. If she even thinks about taking you back, I'll remind her how much of an asshole you are. I'll tell her that Brutus is the safer bet. I will always be rooting against you because I don't think you deserve her. When you left, you didn't just hurt Pepper. You hurt me too. You slept with my ex-wife behind my back, and just when I finally accepted you, you dump her. You took off to save the world, and I had to pick up the pieces of her broken heart—again."

"You act like you're a saint, when you're the one who broke her heart the first time."

"Wow...that's low."

"No, it's true."

"Finn, they aren't comparable, and you know it. Say whatever you want to make yourself look better, but we both know you're the lesser man."

"Colt, I'm your brother."

"Yeah...which is pretty sad."

10

PEPPER

Brutus carried my bags to my door. "I had a great time."

"I had the *best* time." I unlocked the door and stepped inside. "My skin is so tanned, I'm still a little drunk, and the sex...wow. I've never done it in a hot tub before."

He set my bags on the couch and chuckled. "I'm glad I was your first."

"Thanks for taking me. That was my first-ever vacation."

"I'm glad I got to experience it with you." He wrapped his arms around my waist and kissed me on the mouth.

"You know, you don't have to do nice things like that for me. I'm happy just getting shakes at Mega Shake."

"I know, babe. But I like spoiling you." He kissed me again then pulled away. "I'd like to stay, but I've got piles of work waiting for me at my office. Maybe we can have dinner tomorrow."

"Yeah, sure."

The door flew open, and Colton appeared. "I thought I heard voices."

Brutus chuckled. "Wow, that didn't take long." He hugged Colton.

"I can't wait to hear about your trip," Colton said. "And see all your pictures." He came to me next and hugged me tightly.

"Brutus was just about to leave, so I'll tell you about it." I opened the front door and gave Brutus another kiss goodbye.

He squeezed my ass before he walked out. "I'll see you soon."

"Bye." I waved while I watched him go, admiring his tight ass as he walked away. When he was gone, I shut the door. "So, what do you want to hear about first? The food or the sex?"

"I want to see more pictures of Brutus in a Speedo."

I laughed then sat beside him, ignoring my bags on the floor so I could deal with them later. I pulled out my phone and told him all the details of the trip, flipping through the pictures and telling him about all the booze I had and the food that made my thighs expand.

He listened to everything, but as the minutes passed, he turned quiet, as if there was something on his mind. His eyes glossed over like he wasn't listening to anything I said. He gave the occasional nod, inserting it in places in the conversation that didn't really make any sense.

"I'm boring you." I locked my phone and realized I was bragging too much. The last trip Colton ever took was our honeymoon. Maybe talking about a five-star trip on a private jet made him feel sad about his own life.

"No, you aren't," he said quickly. "I've just got something on my mind."

"What?" I detected the sudden somberness in the room, like his sadness stemmed from a serious issue, not a spat with Zach about the last basketball game they played. "Come on, you can tell me. You know you can tell me anything." Maybe he felt bad for ruining the high from my trip, but when I went to bed that night, I would just dread work in the morning, so it didn't matter.

"Well..." He sighed. "I don't even know how to say this. But I know I should because I don't want you to be caught off guard and bombarded."

"Okay..." What the hell was he talking about?

He turned quiet again, as if he were searching for the right words before he spoke them into the air between us. He looked at the blank TV for a while, the weight of the situation obvious in the look in his eyes. He took a deep breath before he spoke. "Finn is here..."

I hardly ever heard his name anymore, so it was always a small shock when it was mentioned. But it also didn't make me pause. It didn't make my heart rate spike. That man was part of my past, a mistake that caused me endless grief. But I was over him, accepting the fact that he was screwing other women in a different country without thinking about me at all. So it didn't make me feel anything. "What's the big deal? He had to visit sometime, right?" If we crossed paths, I wouldn't make it awkward by pretending he didn't exist. I'd known this day would come eventually, and I wouldn't make it a big deal. I'd take the classy route. "We're going to have to deal with each other eventually. It's nothing to worry about."

That didn't console Colton whatsoever. "Well, he's not here to visit. He's here to stay..."

Since that was a curve ball, I didn't know how to react. I assumed Finn would always be away from Seattle, whether it was in a different country or different state. So I didn't know what to say. I stared at him for nearly a minute before my brain and mouth began to work together. "What do you mean, he's here to stay?"

"He moved back to Seattle. He's living in his old house. I guess he never sold it...just rented it out."

He'd only been gone seven months, so why was he returning to his old life already? "But why?"

Colton didn't answer me right away. "He said he never

should have left...he never should have left you. Now he's here because he hopes you'll take him back." He stared at the floor for a minute before he looked at me again.

Now, I was stunned. Completely stunned.

I'd stopped thinking about Finn and assumed he'd stopped thinking about me a long time ago. Now he was in Seattle, and he wanted to get me back. He left me for seven months like it was so easy for him. But now he returned...

"I'll let him tell you everything else. I just wanted you to have a warning. The last thing I wanted was for him to show up on your doorstep and catch you off guard."

I was still speechless, unable to believe this was happening. I used to fantasize about this moment months ago, of him returning home when he realized he couldn't live without me. But when three months came and went, I knew it would never happen. I moved on with my life.

"But I will say this." Colton's voice came out as a whisper. "Don't take him back. He doesn't deserve you, not after what he did. Brutus is the real deal. Brutus is the guy you should be focusing on. I know you loved Finn...but he didn't love you in the same way."

EVER SINCE COLTON told me about Finn, I'd been a walking zombie.

My thoughts were on Finn all the time, imagining the moment when he would make his move. Would he come to my apartment? Or would he stop by the shop in the middle of the day? Would he have new tattoos on his body that were inspired by his travels? Would he look different? Would he look the same?

I hadn't anticipated this would ever happen. I didn't know how I felt about it.

I wouldn't really believe it until he said those words to my face.

Why did it take him seven months to figure out how he felt?

It should have only taken him a month, even less.

The high I felt from my vacation quickly evaporated in light of the explosion that was about to happen. Finn was in Seattle, living in the house where we fell in love. He was sleeping in the bed we used to share. My presence surrounded him, so he must be thinking about me every moment I thought about him.

I'd been so happy with Brutus just a week ago.

Now, I was a wreck all over again.

I stopped by the grocery store on my way home and picked up a few frozen pizzas, some milk, and three bottles of wine. I unlocked the door and stepped inside, my heart racing because I expected Finn to appear at any moment. He'd been here for a week but still hadn't contacted me.

Maybe he was working up the nerve.

I put everything in the fridge then uncorked a bottle of wine.

A knock sounded on the door.

I recognized it right away. It was loud and short, a quick tap from strong knuckles. I stared at the red wine I'd just opened and tossed the cork on the counter. My heart pounded so hard, I could feel it in my ears. My entire body tightened, like it was prepared for war. My breathing quickened as the moment covered me like a heavy shadow.

It was him.

I just knew it.

He'd probably watched me walk into the building from his parked truck, making sure Brutus wasn't with me so he could get me alone. Colton didn't mention it, but he must have told Finn I was seeing someone.

I crossed the living room and stopped in front of the door. I'd been so shocked Finn was in Seattle that I hadn't decided how I felt about it. He was there to tell me he shouldn't have left, that he'd made a mistake. But what would I say?

My hand rested on the door, and I let the seconds trickle by. He probably heard my heels clap against the hardwood floor as I made my way over there. He knew I was standing on the other side of that flimsy door.

I took a deep breath and finally opened it.

I came face-to-face with the love of my life, the man I thought I would spend the rest of my life with. He was the man I wanted as the father of my children. He was the man who broke my heart worse than my own husband.

I studied his face, seeing his clean jaw and the sharp contours of his face. He was leaner than the last time I saw him, his muscle mass slightly less than it used to be. But he was still in remarkable shape, the tattoos on his arms still striking against his slightly tanned skin. He was tall like I remembered. He was just as beautiful.

His blue eyes were trained on me, and the second I met his look, his pupils dilated. He took a deep breath as his gaze took me in, like he'd been looking forward to this moment for years. As his chest rose with his breathing, his shoulders rose and his hands tightened into fists.

I was frozen to the spot, still surprised by his visit, even though I'd known it was coming. My hand continued to rest on the door because I needed something to hold on to. I kept my breathing under control, but I couldn't control the adrenaline that spiked in my blood.

The temporary high I felt when I looked at him slowly faded away. My heart beat a little less frantically, and I didn't ache for air. When I looked at his beautiful face, I remembered our passionate nights together, when his hand was fisted in my hair and he told me he loved me. I remembered the way he told Layla he was committed to me. I remembered turning around and seeing him on one knee, asking me to be his wife.

But I also remembered the day he left. I remembered his decision to leave me behind forever. I remembered leaving the diamond ring on the nightstand. I remembered the months that passed, when I would sleep on my living floor after drinking too much. I remembered when everyone worked together to keep my store open because I was too depressed to work. I remembered sleeping with any handsome guy who bought me a drink because that was my only way of coping.

I remembered how much he'd hurt me.

And that was when I knew how I felt. "No."

He took another deep breath, his eyes falling with disappointment.

"I told you I wouldn't wait for you. I told you I wouldn't take you back." It didn't matter how much I'd loved him in the past. His actions were unforgivable, and I would never trust him again. The beautiful relationship we'd had was poisoned by his departure. He couldn't take that back. "Goodbye, Finn." I closed the door in his face.

Then I locked it.

A WEEK CAME AND WENT, and he didn't bother me again.

Maybe that was the end of it.

Maybe I wouldn't have to deal with it anymore. Maybe we would only bump into each other once in a while. Colton didn't seem to like him, so it was unlikely they would be hanging out much.

When I got off work, I went to Brutus's apartment. He gave me the code to his elevator and encouraged me to visit him whenever I felt like it. I texted him before I made my way over then stepped out of the elevator into the living room. "I'm here."

Brutus exited the hallway, his sweatpants low on his hips while he was shirtless. He didn't have ink everywhere, but he was as hard as steel—and even sexier. "Hey, babe." He kissed me in the living room. "What a nice surprise."

"I missed you."

"Did you now?"

"And I was horny."

He chuckled. "You mean you were just horny."

I shrugged. "You caught me."

"That's fine with me. I'm glad you stopped by anyway. I'm leaving tomorrow, and I want to enjoy you as much as I can."

"Leaving?" I asked. "To go where?"

"New York," he said with a sigh. "I have work to do up there. I'll be gone for a few weeks."

He was telling me this now? "Oh...I had no idea."

"Yeah, I've been dreading it. I was actually going to ask if you want to come with me."

I'd never been to New York before. "How long is the trip?"

"About three weeks."

It was the perfect time for me to get out of town with Finn lurking around. "I can't be away from work that long."

"Yeah, I figured. Sometimes I think about buying your shop so you won't have to work anymore."

"But I like working."

He smiled. "I know. That's why I like you." He kissed me again before he took me by the hand and guided me into his bedroom. "I'm sorry I'll be gone for so long. But I'll make it up to you when I get back."

"You better." Without Brutus being in town, I would be stuck at my apartment all the time. That meant Finn could stop by whenever he wanted. If Brutus were still in town, I could just stay at his place for weeks on end and avoid it altogether.

"You alright?" He sat on the edge of the bed and studied me.

"Yeah…" I slipped off my heels and took a seat beside him.

"I didn't realize you were going to miss me so much."

Brutus and I weren't in a serious relationship. We were just comfortable with each other, finding comfort in each other's past pain. But we'd become so close that I didn't want to lie about Finn. It seemed deceitful, especially when he'd been hurt in the past. "There's something I need to tell you…"

"Alright."

"Finn came by my apartment last week."

His eyebrows furrowed. "I thought he was in Africa and was never coming back."

"I thought the same thing. But Colton told me Finn said he regretted leaving…and returned to Seattle to get me back."

When Brutus understood the gravity of the situation, he just stared at me. "What happened?"

"He came to my door, and I just stared at him. Memories came flooding back, all our nights together. I remembered the way he said he loved me, the way he made me feel…but then I remembered how much he hurt me. I remembered the moment when he threw us away. I told him I would never take him back…then shut the door in his face."

Brutus didn't have a reaction to the news.

"I just wanted you to know. Felt weird keeping it from you."

"Thanks for telling me." His hand moved to my thigh. "How do you feel about it?"

"I don't know… I guess I'm still processing it. Colton said Finn moved back to Seattle permanently. I just don't understand how he could leave me then change his mind. And I don't understand why it took so long to change his mind."

"Maybe he isn't that bright."

"I guess..."

He moved his hand to my back then migrated his fingers to the back of my hair. "I feel weird giving you advice because I'm biased, but I think you made the right decision. Maybe if he'd come back sooner, it would have been different. But seven months is a long time."

"Yeah..."

"When my ex came back to me, I didn't hesitate before I shut the door in her face. Her actions were obviously worse than Finn's, but it felt good shutting the door on her for good. It gave me closure. It really allowed me to move on with my life. Maybe this will give you closure too."

Maybe.

Maybe not.

"Wow..." Stella sat across from me, her drink untouched because she'd been too absorbed in our conversation to take a drink. "That's all you said?"

"Then you shut the door?" Tatum asked.

I nodded. "I remembered how much I loved him...but I also remembered how much he hurt me. I didn't think twice before I told him we would never get back together. Then I shut the door."

"I wonder what changed his mind," Stella said. "It's been seven months. What took so long?"

I shrugged.

"Do you think he'll ask you again?" Tatum asked.

I shrugged again. "We'll have to talk at some point. He's Colton's brother, so there's no way around it."

"I can't believe you've been with so many hot guys," Stella

said. "First, Jax and then Finn...and now Brutus. And Brutus is so fucking rich. That guy probably wipes his ass with cash."

Tatum laughed. "And he'd still look hot doing it."

"He's in New York right now," I said. "Wiping his ass with hundred-dollar bills, apparently."

"He's gorgeous," Stella said. "Imagine if you had a threesome with him and Finn."

I didn't want to think about sex with Finn ever again.

Tatum's eyes shifted to the bar behind me. A second later, they widened. "Speaking of the devil..."

Stella followed her stare. "He's sitting at the bar watching the game."

It was already happening. I was bumping into him at my favorite bar, infecting the same space just like I used to. I could be cold and ignore him, but I didn't want to be friends like we used to be...because we'd never really been friends. "Is he with anyone?"

"No," Stella reported. "He's sitting alone."

"Is he looking over here?" Had he already noticed us?

"Now he is," Tatum said. "He's heading over here."

Of course, he was. "Great..."

A minute later, he reached the table, holding a glass of dark beer. He was in a black t-shirt and black jeans, filling out his clothes with his masculine physicality.

I stared at my glass.

"Ladies, how are you?" He set his beer down on the table and addressed Stella and Tatum.

"Good," Stella said. "We were just talking about Pepper's super sexy and rich boyfriend."

I cringed at her description. I didn't want to be with Finn, but I didn't want to make him feel like shit either.

Finn didn't have a reaction to the comment. "Can I buy you guys another drink?"

"We're good," Tatum said.

Instead of walking away, Finn continued to stand there.

The silence stretched for a long time, until I was unable to ignore it. I finally lifted my gaze and addressed him. "Hi..." I looked into his blue eyes and saw the old intensity he used to flash me all the time, like I was the only thing on his mind.

He didn't say anything back. His focused stare was more than enough. "Ladies, could you give us a moment?"

"Hell no," Stella answered. "She could be all yours right now, but you left."

"Or did you forget?" Tatum asked. "Did you forget when you were screwing some whore in Uganda?"

Whoa...they were taking this too far. "Guys, could you give us a minute?"

Stella stuck her tongue out at him as she slid out of the booth, her drink in hand. Tatum rolled her eyes as she walked off. They settled on an empty booth on the other side of the room, far out of earshot.

Finn sank into the booth, sitting directly across from me so there was nowhere else for me to look other than his beautiful blue eyes. His beer rested between his hands, and he stared at me like I was a photograph, not a real person breathing. His eyes studied my features, taking in the appearance of my eyes and lips. Then he glanced at my neck, as if he hoped to see the necklace he'd given me.

It was in my nightstand drawer. I'd stopped wearing it a long time ago.

The silence seemed to stretch on forever, so I took several drinks of my wine, hoping the booze would keep me loose for this very rigid conversation. I'd made myself clear on my doorstep, so hopefully, he wanted to talk about something else —like moving forward with our friendship.

He finally spoke. "I'd like to tell you a few things."

So, this wasn't over. "It's not going to make a difference, Finn." I kept my voice low and suppressed my rage. I was less angry at him when he left me and forgot about me. But listening to him admit it was a mistake just made me furious. He broke my heart for no reason. All of this could have been avoided if he'd just stayed. His remorse somehow made the situation worse.

"Then there's no harm in listening." He moved his beer to the side, as if it might be a distraction from this conversation.

"Other than wasting your time…" I never knew I could be so cold, but right now, I was freezing.

His eyes closed for an instant, as if he were wounded by what I said.

"I really hope you didn't think you'd show up at my doorstep and I'd run into your arms like nothing happened. I may have loved you, but I have a lot more self-respect than that."

"No, I didn't think that. But I didn't think you'd hate me either."

I felt a lot of negativity toward Finn, but I certainly didn't hate him. "Hate is a strong word, and I don't use it unwisely. And I certainly won't use it now…" He might have broken my heart, but he was a good man who was selfless and caring. He would make a woman very happy someday…when he was truly ready to settle down.

"I made a mistake. I shouldn't have left. And I'll regret that mistake for as long as I live."

My eyes shifted to my glass, unable to tolerate the emotional sincerity in his gaze.

"I thought that life was what I wanted, but then I realized I wasn't that man anymore. I knew I belonged here—with you."

"If that's true, why did it take you seven months to figure that out?"

"It didn't take seven months." His arms rested on the wood

between us, his powerful shoulders making an outline in his t-shirt. He glanced down at his hands then looked up to meet my gaze again. "It took a lot less. In the beginning, I pushed through my work and tried to stay busy so I wouldn't think about you. But eventually, my sorrow caught up to me. When I kept my mind focused on other things, you would visit me in my dreams. They were always the same, the three of us at the house."

"Three of us?"

"Soldier."

I hadn't seen him much since Finn and I broke up, and I missed him so much.

"And you're always pregnant..." He sighed as he looked at me. "The dream woke me up, and I went to the balcony of my apartment. I looked into the dark night and cried... I cried."

I pictured this beautiful man weeping tears for me, a man so strong and stoic that he never showed his emotions to anyone.

"When my buddies passed away, I didn't shed a tear. When other terrible things happened, I never got choked up. But that dream killed my soul...because that's the future I was supposed to have." He lowered his gaze and stared at the table between us, unable to hold my look any longer.

It was a moving story, but the number of tears he shed wouldn't compare to mine.

"I told Colton how I felt, but he told me I'd missed my chance. He told me to forget about you."

Colton never told me that.

"Months passed, and I couldn't take it anymore. Uganda isn't my home. Seattle is my home...you are my home. So regardless of what happens between us, I want to be near you. I want you in my life. I'm prepared to show you that I'm not going to run off again...not ever. I'd marry you tomorrow if you said yes."

My defenses slowly softened at his confession. I used to fantasize about our wedding day until the dream was cruelly taken from me. It was a nice picture, but it wasn't nice enough. "As lovely as that sounds, it's meaningless now. You didn't offer those things when it mattered. You didn't stay when it mattered. I've never told you this, but I've struggled with abandonment issues my entire life. My mother put me in a home because she didn't want me, and I've been on my own ever since. When Colton left, I felt like I was losing my family again. That's why that divorce was so hard for me. Then we got together...and I realized you were the person I was supposed to be with. I felt complete. You would be my family...and we would make a family together. But then you left..." I swallowed the lump in my throat so I wouldn't cry. "If you broke up with me because it just wasn't working, that would have been different. But you asked me to be your wife, to be your family...and then you took off. It opened up my old wounds, made me feel abandoned once more. That hurt most of all...and that's why I can't forgive you."

He bowed his head slightly, his eyes closing as he suffered through the pain.

"I'm sure Colton didn't tell you this, but those months after you left were the hardest of my life. I was so depressed, I couldn't work and I almost lost my store. I cried so much and became dangerously dehydrated, so I had to go to the ER...and be treated by Layla. Finn, it was really hard for me. After three months passed, I finally accepted the horrible truth—you weren't coming back. I forced myself to move on with my life. I started sleeping around, picking up guys at bars every weekend because it was better to sleep with a stranger than be alone. And now I'm still broken because I never want to fall in love again. I just want someone who wants the same things I do, a friend who wants a family. That's how I found Brutus. It's a weak thing to say, but your departure killed me. Now I'll never be the same..."

Finn kept his head bowed for a while, his hands resting against his lips. He was still for a long time before he lifted his head and looked at me, moisture in his gaze that reflected the light hanging from the ceiling between us. The water didn't thicken into tears, but it was enough to show how hurt he was. "Baby, I'm so sorry..." His voice cracked slightly, so heavy with remorse that his apology was derived from the heart.

Despite how much he'd hurt me, I didn't want to hurt him. I didn't want him to feel the pain I'd felt a million times over. I didn't want him to suffer. In a moment of pity, my hand reached for his across the table. "If you stay in Seattle, we can be friends. I'd never come between you and Colton. But I don't want you to waste your time hoping there's ever a chance we can get back together...because we can't. You should sell your house and start over somewhere else. I've moved on with my life, Finn. You should too." I pulled my hand away and slid out of the booth.

He continued to stare straight ahead, his eyes watering until a tear broke free and slid down each cheek. He didn't seem to care that he was in a public place. He didn't care about wearing his heart on his sleeve. He was so broken that he didn't care about anything anymore.

Staying was only making it worse, so I turned away and walked off.

I got no satisfaction out of what I'd just witnessed. If I had it my way, I would take away all his pain...so he would never have to feel as terrible as I did.

"You alright?" Colton stood at the kitchen counter and watched me enter his apartment. "You look shaken up..." He sprinkled parsley over the pan of lasagna and placed it in the oven. He shut the door then ripped off his oven mitts.

"I just had a long talk with Finn..." The image of him succumbing to tears would haunt me for a long time.

"Please don't tell me you took him back…"

"No."

He released a satisfied smile. "Good."

"But he seems genuine, Colton. I know you're angry with him, but you need to be there for him right now. He needs you."

He cocked an eyebrow and wore an incredulous look. "He's the one who chose to leave—"

"Doesn't matter. You're his brother—be there for him. He's going through a really hard time, and he doesn't need to be reminded of his shortcomings. He's in a dark place, and he needs support. You need to be that support."

"What did he say to you?"

"It wasn't what he said…" I believed Finn was genuine, that it was a mistake he wished he could take back, but no amount of remorse could erase the damage inflicted. He broke me into so many pieces that I would never be whole—thanks to him. We could never have a relationship after everything that had happened. I would never trust him again, no matter how sincere he was.

Colton continued to watch me. "Is he going to stay?"

"I'm not sure. But I encouraged him to leave and start over somewhere else."

Now that Colton knew we weren't getting back together, he dropped his venom. "Are you alright?"

"Yeah…I'm okay. I don't want him to feel like this. I want him to be happy."

He crossed his arms over his chest. "I always knew you were the most compassionate person I've ever met, but you still surprise me. After what he did to you, he doesn't deserve your kindness."

"I'll always love him…so he'll always have my kindness."

I TALKED to Brutus on the phone and told him everything that happened with Finn.

After a long pause, he spoke. "That's heavy..."

"It wasn't a fun conversation."

"I almost feel bad for the guy...almost."

I hated how much Finn was hurting.

"But he was an idiot to let you go. Now he's paying for his stupidity."

I didn't know what to say to that, so I changed the subject. "How's New York?"

"Eh, it's fine."

"I thought New York was exciting?"

"I've been here a lot. I get tired of the crowds and the weather. It's either a million degrees, or it's covered in snow— one or the other. And I'm in meetings most of the time, so I'm working most of the time."

"That's too bad."

"It is what it is. It's actually pretty late here, so I'll let you go."

We started off as two people casually seeing each other, but now we talked every day like we were a couple. We didn't have deep conversations about the future, and we didn't say the L-word to each other either. "Alright. I'm getting tired. Good night."

"Good night." He hung up.

I looked at my phone and noticed the battery was about to die. I carried it into the kitchen and plugged it into the charger. I always kept the wire in one place because if I ever moved it, I lost it.

A knock sounded on the door.

It was nine in the evening and it wasn't Colton, who would just let himself inside.

That meant it was Finn.

I used to pray for a moment like this, to hear his knock in my most desperate hour. But his presence never came. He never carried the light into the darkest time in my life. But now he was here...and he wasn't going away easily.

I opened the door and came face-to-face with him. I'd seen him a few hours ago at the bar, and since then, his tears had stopped. There was still a tint of redness to his gaze, a puffiness around his eyes. Our conversation happened hours ago, but it was obviously still heavy on his mind.

He entered my apartment without being invited and shut the door behind him.

I backed up, feeling him take charge of the moment without saying a single word. "I'm staying in Seattle. I'm not moving somewhere else to start over. My family is here. My house is here. My dog is here."

"Alright..." He would just make it more difficult for himself —for both of us.

"And you're here."

I released the air from my lungs, not surprised he hadn't been deterred.

"I gave up on us when I shouldn't have. I left you when I should have stayed. I'm not making that mistake again. Baby, I'm here until you're ready to have me again. I will wait until you trust me again. I will wait as long as it takes. If all I can be is your friend, that's fine. I'll gladly take it."

"Finn, I'm seeing someone."

"I don't care."

"But I like him—"

"You don't love him."

"You don't know how I feel."

He stepped nearer to me, our bodies coming closer together than they had been in months. "Yes, I do. I know what it's like to be loved by you...and I don't see that when you talk about him. And you told me you wanted someone for convenience, someone who's safe. You're with him because he won't hurt you...and that's not love."

"Well, I've done the love thing a couple of times, and it didn't work..."

"It didn't work *once*," he corrected. "Because our story isn't over yet."

"Finn, you're wasting your time—"

"Then let me waste it." He stepped back, the vein in his forehead pounding as I imagined the adrenaline spike in his blood. "You may not be mine anymore, but I'm still yours. Whether it takes months or years, I'll wait for you. I'll wait until this guy screws up or the next one does. The story ends with us together. I just have to wait for the pages to turn." He placed his hand over his heart. "I'm your family, Pepper. You already have my last name. Our kids will have that last name. I won't leave you again, not ever. I know you don't trust me...but someday you will."

11

COLTON

I RANG THE DOORBELL.

The weather was surprisingly nice, clear and sunny, so I thought I'd ask Finn if he wanted to shoot some hoops.

He opened the door, just wearing his sweatpants without a shirt. He regarded me with a cold look, immediately suspicious of my presence since I'd been a dick to him ever since he returned to Seattle. "Why are you here?"

I couldn't stop a small smile when my own words echoed back at me. "Wanted to see if you wanted to shoot some hoops."

"Again...why?"

"Because it's fun."

"Last time we spoke, it seemed like you wanted nothing to do with me."

"Well...Pepper talked some sense into me. She said you were going through a hard time so I should be there for you... That's what brothers are for."

He sighed as he opened the door wider. "Of course she did." He walked into the house and left the door open. "I'll grab the ball from the garage."

When he stepped out of the way, Soldier bolted toward me,

his tongue hanging out of his mouth. He jumped on me and dragged his paws down my legs, his tail wagging a million miles an hour.

"Hey, boy. I missed you too." I kneeled down and gave him a good rubdown. "You liked staying at Grandma's?"

He barked then licked my face.

Finn returned with his Nikes and a ball under his arm. "He gained a lot of weight staying with Grandma and Grandpa."

"Shut up, he looks fine." We headed to the driveway, and Soldier took a seat in the grass.

Finn dribbled the ball then made a shot, sinking it through the net on his first attempt.

"Nice." I got the ball and dribbled to the road. I tried to sink the shot, but I missed by a foot. "I'm a little rusty."

Finn got the ball again, and we took turns shooting.

"So...are you staying in Seattle, then?"

"Don't look so happy," he said sarcastically. He dribbled the ball then passed it to me. "I'm not leaving. This is where I've settled down for good."

"Finn, I'm happy to have you back, but I really think you're wasting your time." I didn't say these things to hurt him. I said them to protect him. If he kept putting his heart on the line, it would keep getting smashed.

"I don't."

"Brutus is pretty—"

"She doesn't love him."

"Not yet." I lined up the shot and made it.

He grabbed the ball from under the hoop. "Say whatever you want, Colton. I won't change my mind. I wasn't there for her when I should have been, but I'm here now. I'll wait as long as it takes, be whatever she needs...even if that's only a friend."

"You're just gonna get your heart ripped out, man."

"Even so, it hurts far less to be near her than far away from her."

"And what about when you see them together?" I asked.

He dribbled the ball and stared at the hoop, either thinking about his shot or the question I'd just asked. "I'll deal with it."

"I don't think it's just something you can deal with."

"I'll do whatever I have to do to get her back. So if I have to suffer for a while, so be it. This guy may be rich and good-looking, but he'll never have what I have. He'll never give her what we had. She'll have to choose between what's safe and what's real...and I know exactly what she'll choose."

PEPPER ENTERED my apartment with chips and salsa. "I have extra wine at my place. You want me to grab it?"

"No, I think we have plenty of stuff." I set the bean dip on the table. "I should tell you that I invited Finn...is that okay?"

She patted me on the arm. "Don't be ridiculous. He's always welcome."

"Are you sure? Because when I saw him a few days ago, he seemed pretty determined to get you back."

She shrugged. "I tried discouraging him, but it didn't make a difference."

"Does that change anything...?"

"No." She said it without hesitation. "He hurt me in a way we can never recover from. I made that perfectly clear. He might hang out for a couple of months, but he'll lose interest. We both know how he is...he'll never stay in one place too long." She rolled her eyes and walked away.

Finn had developed a bad reputation, but I didn't defend it. It was dead on.

Pepper greeted Tom while Stella walked up to me. "You invited him?"

"He's my brother, Stella. What was I supposed to do?"

"How about, not invite him?" she asked. "You can see him at Thanksgiving and shit. But not on our turf."

"Look, Pepper told me to be nice to him since he's going through a hard time..."

"Boo-hoo. Pepper cried her eyes out every day for three months. You think I give a shit that he's going through a hard time?" She flipped her hair over her shoulder. "Bitch, please." She strutted back to the couches in the living room where Zach was watching the game.

I felt bad for my brother... He had a tough crowd.

He knocked on the door a moment later.

I answered it then spoke at a low level so only he would hear. "Just a warning...everyone hates you."

He held a case of beer in his hand, and a slow smile crept onto his lips. "Trust me, I already know." He clapped me on the back. "But thanks for the heads-up." He carried his case of beer to the fridge. "Hey, guys."

All he heard were crickets.

Pepper was the only one who acknowledged his existence. "Hey, Finn. I'll take one."

He grabbed her a bottle, twisted off the cap, and then handed it to her. In the small interaction, he looked at her like she belonged to him, like she lit up the room and he was a moth attracted to her flame.

She turned away and pretended not to notice. She was in the mood for wine but drank his beer to be polite, to make him feel less ostracized from the group.

Stella's eyes smoldered with fire. "So how rich is Brutus, again? Isn't he worth like two hundred billion dollars?" She spoke loudly and obnoxiously, doing her best to make Finn feel like shit.

Pepper looked mortified. "Stella."

"And how big is his dick again?" Stella asked. "Anaconda, right?"

Pepper narrowed her eyes. "*Stella*."

Stella didn't look the least bit remorseful as she drank from her wineglass. "Let's just say I wish he were sitting here playing games with us instead of *you*." She gave Finn a dark look before she turned to ignoring him.

I was pissed at Finn too, but even I thought that was a little cold.

Pepper clearly didn't appreciate it either. "Stella, don't—"

"It's fine." Finn took a seat on the couch with his beer in hand. "She's right."

"Damn right, I'm right," Stella snapped. "You can't just dump her, take back her ring, and then chill with us like we're all friends. Bitch, we'll never be friends. That charming smile and those tattoos won't work on anyone anymore. We know what you really are—a piece of shit."

"Jesus, knock it off." Pepper slammed down her beer. "Enough is enough. Take the high road and be classy. I know you just want to have my back, but I don't need it. Finn is Colton's brother, and we need to include him. I don't care if he's here or if he's not here. If I can deal with him, so can you. That goes for all of you." She pointed to everyone in the circle. "Now let's have some fun."

WHEN GAME NIGHT was over and everyone left, Finn helped me clean up and do the dishes.

Pepper stuck around too, preserving all of the leftovers and rolling up the bags of chips.

Finn looked up every few minutes to stare at her.

She was oblivious to it, concentrating on her hands. When her phone rang, she looked at the screen. "It's Brutus. I'll see you guys later." She walked to the door as she answered. "Hey, how was your day?" She walked out and shut the door behind her.

Like a dog that was devastated when its owner left, Finn stood at the sink and stared at the spot where she'd been a moment before. The water continued to run as he abandoned the dishes at the bottom of the sink.

I couldn't unsee the devastation in his eyes. I actually felt bad for him.

He finally lowered his gaze and kept washing the dishes. "What do you think of him?"

"I told you I liked him."

"But what do you think of him? Why do you like him?"

"Do you really want to have this conversation?" I asked in surprise.

"Yes."

"He adores Pepper. I guess that's my biggest reason. The second he saw her, he was smitten. She kept trying to brush him off, but he wouldn't give up."

"She didn't want him at first?" He stacked the washed dishes on the counter so I could put them in the dishwasher.

"No. She blew him off twice, actually."

"How did he change her mind?"

"He told her he was divorced. He'd been hurt just the way she had."

He kept scrubbing, listening to our conversation while he focused on his work. "What's their relationship like?"

"I feel weird giving you this information..."

"But I'm your brother, and you're going to tell me."

"Finn, I haven't changed my mind about anything. You may be my brother, but I still prefer him for Pepper."

He stopped his actions, looking at me like that wounded his soul. "I know I fucked up, but don't be cruel."

"I'm just being honest. Before you got here, I told Pepper you were coming. She didn't care. But she did say you would be gone in a few months...because you're never in one spot too long. You'll lose interest and move on. And I agree with her."

He turned his gaze to the sink, visibly crushed by his reputation. "I don't blame her for thinking that...but it's not true. At least, not anymore." He started to do the dishes again. "Now, answer my question."

"I don't know...it started off casual, but now they're a couple. They're together a lot. She usually sleeps at his place. They have a really open relationship. They aren't afraid to tell each other the truth... They're really honest with each other."

"Did she tell him about me?"

I nodded.

"Why hasn't he shown his face? Why isn't he coming to game night with her friends?"

"He's in New York."

He set the dishes on the counter and turned off the faucet. "Why?"

"For work."

"How long will he be gone?"

I shrugged. "A few weeks."

He stared at me as he considered the information. Then he looked at the sink again. "The timing couldn't be more perfect."

"You aren't going to get her to change her mind in a few weeks."

"No. But I'm definitely going to try."

12

PEPPER

SINCE I HAD EMPLOYEES AT THE STORE, I DIDN'T WORK AS MUCH. I took long lunches, worked on paperwork, and went home early. On top of that, my store was open longer hours, and I was doing bridal parties every weekend. I was working a few hours a week but making twenty times what I made before.

Brutus had the Midas touch.

Since there was nothing to do at the shop, I changed at my apartment and headed to the gym. I'd been working out with Stella in the mornings, but now that I actually enjoyed exercising, I hit the gym on my own in the afternoons. Plus, I had a lot of extra time now.

I walked inside the gym and spotted a familiar face.

Finn.

He was lying on one of the benches and pumping enormous weight. Weights were on either side of the bar, making the total weight over two hundred pounds. He did his presses, his chest thick and tight, and sweat accumulated all over his body. He was shirtless just like he was at home—and he was attracting a lot of attention.

Almost every woman in there was staring at him.

When he finished his set, he sat up and patted his forehead with his towel. He didn't notice me because he wasn't looking into the mirror in front of him. His eyes were on the ground, his features forlorn.

A perfect ten walked over to him, her blond hair slick in a ponytail. She wore only a sports bra and leggings, showing off her incredible definition and killer ass. She was the kind of woman that didn't get rejected often...if ever. Even without makeup, she was still flawless.

Music was loud overhead so I couldn't hear their conversation, but it seemed like Finn wasn't interested in anything she had to say. He hardly looked at her as she talked his ear off for nearly five minutes. When he finally spoke, he must have said something offensive because she immediately looked pissed.

Finn placed his earbuds in his ears and tuned her out completely.

She stomped off, all the guys checking out her ass as she went.

Finn looked just as miserable as he had before she approached him, like he'd lost everything.

I shouldn't feel anything for him, but I somehow felt terrible for him. I knew exactly how he felt...because I'd cried for three months straight.

I went to the free weights and grabbed a few ten-pounders. There was a mirror on the opposite side of the room, so I did my workout. I worked on my arms and shoulders, sculpting them even though Stella had kicked my ass in her early morning classes.

A few minutes later, I noticed him approach me from behind, his expression visible in the mirror. I kept working out even though his stare was focused with laser-like intensity. I glanced at him from time to time, but I eventually stopped what

I was doing when he was directly behind me, his smell registering in my nose.

I pulled out my earbuds and turned to look at him. Instead of wearing a sexy outfit like most of the girls, I just wore an old t-shirt and leggings. I was making more now, but the last thing I was going to spend it on was workout clothes.

He continued to stare at me like he could hardly believe I was there. Then he pulled his buds out of his ears. "Pepper?"

"Yes...it's really me."

"I noticed your arms looked tighter, but I didn't think it was from hitting weights."

"Stella got me working out. I've been addicted ever since. It's a great way to release all that bad energy..."

He gave a curt nod in acknowledgment. "Colton told me your store is doing well. I guess that's why you're here in the middle of the day."

"Yeah, I work fewer hours now. It's been nice." Even when we discussed friendly topics, it never felt like we were really friends. There was always this tension between us. "What happened with that girl?"

"What girl?" he asked, seeming sincere about his confusion.

"The blonde. I saw you two talking."

"Oh..." He shrugged. "Just chitchat."

"Because it looked like you said something that pissed her off."

He shrugged again. "She asked me out, and I said no. Nothing more to it."

"Well, you shouldn't have said that. She's beautiful."

His eyes narrowed like my comment offended him. "I'm taken."

His devotion was sweet, but also pointless. "Finn—"

"My mom told me you didn't see Soldier much while he was living with her. I know he'd really like to see you. He's at my house if you want to stop by. I'm free now if you aren't doing anything."

Was this just a scheme to get me to come over? "I don't think that's a good idea..."

"I don't have a trick up my sleeve. I just think he'd like to see you. That's all." He faced me, ignoring all the people grunting as they did their reps and set their weights on the floor. Upbeat pop music played overhead, obnoxiously loud and pointless since everyone wore headphones. Shirtless and sweaty, he kept staring at me.

"I would like to see him..." That dog felt like my own at one point in time. Losing him was almost as hard as losing Finn. It was like losing our child, the person we spent all our evenings with. He kept me company while Finn was away for a month, sticking by my side because he knew how heartbroken I was.

"Good. I'll give you a lift."

BEING in his truck made me feel like we were back in time.

I sat in the passenger seat near the window and did everything I could to avoid his stare. I watched the cars go by, watched the businesses fade in the background as we headed to his home in the suburbs. The music wasn't on, so we only had silence for comfort.

The tension was suffocating because the silence was filled with memories. I remembered when we had sex in the back seat of his truck because we couldn't wait until we got home. I remembered the nights he would give me a lift to my apartment and the air would be charged between us. It was impossible not to think about it. "So, how was it over there?" He hadn't given me any details of his trip.

He drove with one hand on the wheel. "Exactly what you'd expect. Hot. Dusty. Dirty."

"I've never been to Uganda, so I don't have expectations."

"There's a lot of beauty to it. The people are interesting, the culture is fascinating. But it's an entirely different world from the one we're used to. Crime is rampant, and the government is corrupt. Unfortunately, that is the only way of life those people know. They don't have access to healthcare and die prematurely from illnesses that are easily treatable." He kept his eyes on the road as the passion escaped his voice. Even though he'd left his position, it was obvious he still cared about the region. "Personally, I think healthcare should be a right, not a privilege, and that should apply to every being in the world, humans and animals."

It was one of the reasons I'd fallen for him so hard. He was selfless, caring about others more than himself. He was a cold man showing little emotion, but he had a big heart in that hard chest. "Do you regret leaving?" We were never getting back together, so his actions seemed in vain.

"No. Remember what I told you about the military?"

"That it was time for you to leave."

He nodded. "Same thing. It was time for me to leave. I've entered a new phase in my life...and that's where I belong." He didn't look at me as he confessed his deep commitment to me, that he wanted to be there with me rather than anywhere else.

It was a kind gesture, but it fell on deaf ears.

We arrived at the house moments later, and he parked his truck in the garage.

I was taken back in time, back to the old lives we used to have. The garage was cleaner than it'd been before he left, probably because he'd organized everything before he'd let the renters move in.

We entered the house, and instantly, a huge dog charged right at me.

Soldier jumped on me, knocked me to the ground in the kitchen, and licked my face until saliva dripped down my cheeks. His tail wagged so hard, it seemed like it would fling off his butt and across the kitchen.

I laughed as I felt him smother me with love. "Aww, I missed you too."

Finn kneeled down beside me. "You okay?"

I kept laughing, feeling Soldier cover me with his heavy body as he continued to kiss me. "Yes...but I might die from his kisses."

Soldier whined as his entire body shook, so happy I was in the house again.

"Aww, you're so sweet." I rubbed his fur then wrapped my arms around him for a hug. I missed this dog so much, it brought tears to my eyes. I finally got some air and sat up, looking into those coffee-colored eyes that were full of innocence. "I missed you too, honey." I cupped his cheeks and rubbed the backs of his ears. "You know I love you."

He pressed his head to my chest and tried to sit in my lap, like he was a puppy rather than a full-grown dog.

"Oh wow..." I felt his heavy weight on my legs, like he was a fat kid and I was Santa Claus. "Grandma really has been fattening you up, huh?"

Finn continued to kneel down and watch us, a slight smile on his lips with affection in his eyes. He moved down to the tile and leaned against the doors of the pantry as he watched the two of us together. "He was happy to see me too...but not that happy."

"Because I bought him toys," I teased. "Unlike you."

"Yeah..." He watched me play with Soldier, his large chest rising and falling slowly as he breathed.

I hugged Soldier and petted him as he got comfortable on top of me.

Finn watched him for a long time before his eyes lifted to meet mine. Even when he didn't say a word, his eyes were full of remorse. He carried the weight of his regret, the pain of his mistake. He used to be difficult to read, but now his expression was like a book. "When I was in Kenya, there was a British doctor there. We kinda had a fling. But it didn't mean anything. I told her I loved you, and when I left, she said she hoped I would get you back."

I stopped petting Soldier because his words took me by surprise. I knew he'd slept with other people because six months was too long to be celibate. Just when I thought I didn't care, I realized I did. It did bother me. Picturing him with someone else still made me sick to my stomach. But I refused to show that pain. "Your personal life is none of my business."

"I just wanted you to know. She was the only woman I was with during that time."

I should have been the only woman he was with. But he'd chosen to leave me. "Again, it doesn't matter."

"I didn't want you to think I was chasing tail the way I used to. I was with Jane because I was depressed. And anytime I was with her, I thought about you. Sex used to feel good, but then it turned painful." He rested his head back against the wood. "When it didn't get better, I realized it never would. The weight of my mistake started to hit me, started to suffocate me. Then it became intolerable..."

I knew these kinds of conversations would happen any time we were alone together. They seemed inevitable. "Finn, our relationship is in the past. I'd appreciate it if we could just be friends, talk about Soldier or the weather."

"Friends don't tell friends about their suffering?" he asked.

"Not when it's about our old relationship."

He tilted his head to the ground and sighed.

"I really don't want you to waste your time, Finn. You should leave."

"No." He held my gaze. "Never." The determination was so bright, his eyes were vibrant like the sun.

"I still care about you, and I don't—"

"You still love me."

I didn't break eye contact because that would make me seem weak, make his statement true. There was no doubt I would always love this man, even if I never wanted to be with him again. But that also meant nothing. "Love isn't enough this time, Finn. There's too much heartbreak, distrust, and pain. Even if I were still madly in love with you, it wouldn't change anything. Everything else overrides it." I looked down at Soldier, who had his eyes closed. He wasn't asleep, but he seemed so comfortable in my lap. "I like Brutus, and I would appreciate it if you didn't try to come between us."

"I'm not trying to come between you. You're the only person I care about."

I lifted my gaze to meet his.

"I know you're a loyal person, so I would never try to get you to cheat on him. That's not how I'd want our relationship to start anyway. My goal is to make you realize you can trust me again, to make you realize you should be with me. You can stay with Brutus because he's safe, because he won't hurt you. But when you finally trust me again, you'll want love. You'll want that fiery, passionate, deep love we used to have. You're still hurt by my betrayal...and I can wait until whenever you're ready to feel that way again. You gave yourself to me completely, and I threw you away when I shouldn't have. I understand why you're broken. I understand why Brutus is appealing to you. But you'll change your mind eventually...and I'll be here when you do." Finn had never been passionate about anything besides his work, but he seemed focused now. He cared about me more than anything else, even his job.

But the damage had been done. I petted Soldier on my lap and tried to ignore the tension between us. He'd just given a speech that would make any other woman fall to her knees. But that wasn't going to happen with me. "Were your parents happy to see you?"

He didn't answer for a long time, as if he were disappointed that I changed the subject. "Yes. But my mom is still disappointed in me."

"Because you left her again?"

He shook his head slightly. "Because I left you."

And just like that...we were back to where we started. "Well, I'm sure she's happy you're home..." When we were together, I always kept my feelings in check because I didn't want to scare him off. I wasn't used to getting this kind of attention from him.

"Yeah..."

I leaned down and pressed a kiss to Soldier's forehead, so happy this wonderful dog was in my life again. If only I could keep him. "Saying goodbye to Soldier was so hard...I lost it."

He studied me for a while, watching me interact with his dog.

"When you were gone that one month, he was always there for me. He knew when I was sad and tried to cheer me up. He was always there to lick my tears away...like he could feel what I was feeling." I'd never had a pet before in my life, and now it made me want to have a dog of my own...but nobody would compare to Soldier.

"How about you borrow him for a few days?"

I looked up, shocked by the offer. "What?"

"Take him. He's housebroken, so he'll let you know when he needs to go outside. And he would love to crash at your place for a bit."

"You're going to let me borrow your dog?" I asked incredulously.

He shrugged. "Why not? He'd love it."

"I don't know...I feel weird taking him from you."

"You're just borrowing him. Think of it as babysitting."

Like Soldier understood what we were saying, he lifted his head and looked at me, showing me those literal puppy-dog eyes.

"Dammit...I can't say no to that face." I patted his head.

"I need to learn to make that face, then," Finn said, teasing me.

I heard his words but refused to react. "Does he still snore?"

"Like a freight train," he said with a chuckle. "But it's got a nice ring to it." He rose to his feet and grabbed the dog food. "I'll pack up a couple of things for you."

"Are you sure about this? I feel bad taking your baby."

He dumped the food into a plastic bag and grabbed one of the toys I'd bought for Soldier. "He's our baby. We can share."

WE ENTERED MY APARTMENT, and Soldier immediately felt comfortable, as if he could smell my scent on every piece of furniture. He took a look around and smelled the couches then ventured into my bedroom, helping himself like he already lived there.

Finn put the bowls on the ground and filled them with food and water. "I'll pick him up in a few days. Let me know if you want to keep him longer." He rose to his feet and moved to the door as if he was going to stay goodbye and not look for an excuse to linger.

"Thanks."

"I just hope he'll agree to come home with me." The door

was still open so he stepped into the hallway. When he turned his back on me, his broad shoulders stretched out his t-shirt. He started off wider then became narrower around the hips, making the perfect triangle that every woman fantasized about.

"He'll get sick of me eventually."

"I doubt it." He turned around and gave me a soft smile.

"You did."

He dropped his smile immediately.

It was a low blow, but it sprung to my mind instantly. I didn't want to hurt him even though no one would blame me, but that popped out on its own. "I'm sorry…"

"No, I deserved it." He started to close the door. "Good night, baby."

Baby. He used to call me that every day. Used to whisper it when he made love to me. "Finn, you can't call me that anymore."

He halted on the doorstep, staring at me like my request was ridiculous. "I can call you whatever I want."

"I'm not your baby."

"Doesn't matter. I called you that even when you weren't my baby…and I'll keep calling you that until you are again." He closed the door, and his loud footsteps echoed as he disappeared. When it turned silent, I knew he was really gone.

I sat on the couch and thought about my afternoon. I'd spent most of it with Finn, running into him at the gym when I least expected him.

My phone started to ring.

It was Brutus, so I answered. "Hey, having a New York minute?"

"Clever," he said sarcastically. "More like a New York eternity."

"If you hate it so much, why don't you come home?"

"Because I love money."

The sentence was a bit of a turn-off, but I knew he had to run a company, and that took sacrifice. He would only do that if he were being compensated for it...and jetting off to Fiji.

Soldier jumped on the couch and barked.

"What was that?" Brutus asked.

"Oh...Soldier."

"Am I supposed to know who that is?"

"It's Finn's dog."

He was quiet for a while. "Are you at Finn's house?"

"No. He let me borrow him for a few days."

He turned quiet again, his unhappiness obvious. "Why would you want to borrow his dog?"

"We used to be really close. He feels like my dog. I don't know...Finn offered and I accepted." I petted Soldier beside me and felt the tension grow over the line.

"So, are you hanging out with Finn a lot now?"

I could sense his jealousy, which was surprising because he didn't seem like the kind of guy to get jealous. "No. I ran into him at the gym."

"Then went to his house?"

"Yeah...that's where the dog was."

He didn't seem to appreciate my sarcasm. "You said you didn't want to get back together with him, but you seem to be spending a lot of time with him."

"But I'm not. Colton had game night a few days ago and he was there, but we didn't hang out one-on-one. There's no way I can avoid him. It's just not possible. And then I happened to run into him at the gym. You're overthinking it."

"Maybe...I just think it's weird you have an attachment to his dog."

"I was living with Finn at one time, so I was with his dog all the time... I developed an attachment."

Brutus finally backed off when he realized this conversation was going nowhere. "How was work?"

"Weird."

"Why was it weird?"

"Because I was gone by noon."

He chuckled. "It's nice, right?"

"I'm used to working long hours without pay. But now I get paid when I don't work...it's crazy."

"You're just being more efficient. Running a business is difficult, so it's nice to have someone with experience to give you advice. I'm glad I could help."

"And I'm still repaying you for that help..."

When sex was mentioned, he lightened up even more. "Just another week and I'll be home. Better stock up on that lingerie."

"Now that I have some extra money, I can actually afford to buy a few things from my shop."

"Good. Then I'm really glad I helped you."

I chuckled. "That's all you care about...sex."

"I distinctly remember when that was all you cared about."

I had rejected him constantly, doing my best to stay away from him after I got my fix. But he eventually wore me down... because he didn't give up. "I know it's late there, so I'll let you go."

"Alright." He sighed into the phone. "I miss you."

Brutus and I weren't serious, but we'd started to speak to each other like we were. He was the perfect guy, and I'd finally found someone who really understood all of my fears. But Finn popped into my mind, the deep pain in his eyes as he looked at me. I shook off the thought. "I miss you too..."

13

COLTON

I WALKED ACROSS THE HALL AND LET MYSELF INSIDE HER apartment. Now I never knew when she was home since she was working fewer hours. Taking her toilet paper and salt became a lot more difficult.

Soldier hopped off the couch and ran toward me, his tongue hanging out as he pawed at my legs.

"Soldier? What are you doing here?"

Pepper stepped out of her bedroom. "He lives here. What's your excuse?"

After I gave him a good rubdown, I rose to my full height. "Finn gave him to you."

"He let me borrow him. We kinda share custody now."

"Divorce is always the hardest on the kids." I patted him on the head. "At least I can run into my buddy once in a while."

"So, what brings you here?" Her hair was slightly damp, so she'd probably come home after the gym and showered. She worked out hard—and now her body was even hotter than it used to be.

"Do I need a reason?"

She gave me a look full of attitude. "What are you here to take now?"

"What?" I asked innocently. "I'm not here to take anything."

With that glare, she clearly didn't believe me. "There's extra toilet paper under the sink."

"Actually..." I tiptoed into the kitchen and approached the cabinet. "Tom is coming over, and I need a bottle of wine."

She rolled her eyes. "Knew it. I just went to the store, so you're in luck."

I opened the door and grabbed a bottle of white wine, seeing all the bottles she'd stocked up on. "You know what? Think about all the free food and toilet paper you've gotten from me throughout the years. This is payback."

"If it is, I'll make sure to get you back double." She grabbed Soldier's toy off the ground and tossed it to him. "Have fun with Tom. You really should grow a pair and ask him to move in. You've been together for a year now."

"I don't know... He's the only guy I've ever been with."

"So?" she asked. "If you love him, you love him."

I'd thought about marriage a couple of times, the two of us getting a house together where we could have our two kids. "We wouldn't be neighbors anymore."

"Good. You won't steal my stuff."

I chuckled then headed to the door. "You got plans tonight?"

"Just with Soldier."

"You wanna join us?"

"No, it's okay." She moved to the couch and took a seat. "You guys enjoy your time together."

I felt bad leaving her alone when Brutus was away and Finn was sniffing around. "Brutus will be home next week."

"Yep. Hopefully, he doesn't leave for another trip soon. I'm not a fan of long-distance relationships."

"I'm sure it'll be a while before that happens. Has Finn bothered you?"

She shrugged. "He keeps saying the same stuff over and over...that he's not giving up on me." Her gaze faded away like her thoughts drifted somewhere else. Instead of being indifferent like she used to be, she was blanketed in melancholy. "It's weird to think he was gone for so long and now he's here...on my doorstep. I still can't believe he's in Seattle. I wonder how long he'll stay."

I used to think he would take off because he hadn't changed, but being around Finn now made me question my assumption. That man had never been more determined in his life. It was the first time he was completely devoted to a person rather than a job. It was a big change for someone like him. "I don't know..."

I said goodbye then returned to my apartment so I could chill the bottle of wine. Just when I shut the door to the freezer, my phone rang.

It was Brutus.

In the limited time he'd been dating Pepper, we hadn't spoken on the phone once. We texted occasionally, mainly if we were doing something as a group. I liked the guy and considered him to be a friend, but we weren't that close. Whatever he wanted must be important. "Hey, man." I stood at the kitchen counter and stared into the living room of my apartment.

"Hey, Colt. Is Pepper around?"

"She's in her apartment. Are you having a hard time getting a hold of her?"

"No. I just wanted to make sure she wasn't around..."

Ooh...this just got interesting. "You should know, when it comes to Pepper, I'm not good at keeping secrets."

"That's fine. I just want some answers, and I know you'll be straight with me."

Answers about what? "Alright..."

"You told me you think I'm good for Pepper."

"I did…"

"I know this may be awkward for you, but I want to know the details about your brother. Pepper told me his dog is staying at her place… She's seeing him a lot. She told me he wanted her back, but she said no. What I want to know is…should I be worried about him?"

"If Pepper turned him down, that's a pretty clear answer—"

"I mean, is he chasing her? Is he trying to get her back while I'm not around?"

He was right. This was an awkward conversation.

"Colton."

I always seemed to be in the middle of Pepper's relationships. Somehow, someway, it always happened.

"You there?"

"Yeah…I'm here."

"Your silence doesn't bode well."

"I guess I don't want to get in the middle of it."

"I just want to know if he's trying to take my girl away. He has access to you, and if we're friends, then I should have access to you too. Unless I'm wrong?"

"No, of course not."

"Then what's your answer?"

I didn't want to betray my brother, but I didn't want to lie to Brutus either. He was a great guy and a perfect match for Pepper. If they stayed together, she would be happy for a long time. If she went back to Finn…I wasn't sure what would happen. "The whole reason he's in Seattle is because he loves her and wants to be with her…"

He was so quiet, it seemed like he hung up.

"There's your answer…"

PEPPER WALKED INSIDE MY APARTMENT. "What do you think I should wear tonight?" She was carrying two dresses, both black. "This one or this one?" She held up each to her body.

"Depends. Where are you going?"

"Dinner at a steakhouse."

"Are you going with Finn?"

"Uh, no." She weighed the two dresses from side to side. "Brutus."

"Brutus? I thought he was gone for a few more days."

She shrugged. "He came home early. So, which one?"

I wondered if he'd come home early because of our conversation. "The second one."

"Excellent. Thank you." She headed to the door. "Finn is coming by to pick up Soldier, so just let him in."

"Alright."

She blew me a kiss and walked out.

A few hours later, a knock sounded on my door.

"It's open."

Finn stepped inside, in black jeans and a gray V-neck. In the short time he'd been here, he'd managed to increase his muscle size dramatically. He was obviously hitting the weights pretty hard and eating more calories. My brother used to enter a room with distinguished purpose. Now he just looked like a shattered piece of glass. "I'm here to get Soldier. Pepper isn't answering."

"She's out with Brutus."

"I thought he was in New York?"

"He came home early."

Finn closed his eyes for a second, like this was a major blow to his plan. "I guess he's not as stupid as I thought."

"You weren't going to make something happen in a week. Even if Brutus didn't exist, you would still struggle to get her back."

"But it would be easier because she'd be home right now. I'm not worried about Brutus. I'm worried about getting enough time with her. I can't just knock on her door whenever I feel like it."

"Never stopped you before..."

"But this is different."

I walked across the hall and unlocked the door so Finn could put Soldier on a leash. Finn gave him a good pat on the back then left his food and water behind.

"What about his bowls?"

"I'm gonna take a gamble and assume Pepper will want him again." As Finn walked him out of the apartment, Soldier whined.

I shut the door and locked it. "That dog loves her..."

"She's easy to love." He patted Soldier on the head and sighed. It was only seven in the evening, but he looked tired. Extremely tired.

"I'm sorry, Finn." I knew this was entirely his fault, but I felt bad for him anyway. I could tell he truly regretted what he did, and he would do anything to erase the past.

"I know, man." He stared down at his dog, his eyes lifeless. "You think I have a chance?"

"Uh...I don't know."

He lifted his chin to look me in the eye. "Has she said anything about me to you?"

Again, stuck in the middle. "Nothing different, at least."

He released a loud sigh, his frustration spilling out.

"You have slim odds of getting her back. Very slim. Maybe you should just—"

"I'm not giving up. I was just hoping to make some progress with her."

"Finn, even if you were successful...it's gonna take months."

"It could take a lifetime, and I still wouldn't give up." He rolled up the leash in his hand then headed down the hallway. "I'll see you later..."

I watched my brother go, feeling terrible for him. This new Finn was much better than the old one, but Brutus was still the better man. At the end of the day, I wanted Pepper to be happy. I just wasn't entirely sure who she would be the happiest with.

14

FINN

I WAS NOT AN IDIOT.

I didn't expect to return to Seattle and get her back overnight. I didn't expect to make her forget about her billionaire boyfriend just by confessing my profound feelings. After what I did, I deserved to work my ass off to prove myself to her.

But fuck, I missed her.

I wanted a reprieve, just a moment to treasure her. I wanted to hold her in my arms, rest my head against hers so I could smell her hair. My hands ached to feel that deep curve of her lower back, the way it arched before leading to that beautiful ass. I used to love her figure because of the curves, but now I loved those curves more because they would get more pronounced when she was pregnant.

In this fantasy, I was the father of her baby.

Never thought I would have a fantasy like that.

When I looked back on my life, I realized I'd been going a million miles an hour constantly. Always eager to get to the next destination, I didn't stop and appreciate what I had. I came to Seattle because I didn't know what my next move would be. I met Pepper, but my old instincts didn't die. I took off again.

But that should have been my last stop.

I could apologize forever, but it wouldn't change anything.

I hurt her...so fucking much.

When she told me she felt abandoned...I wanted to die. I left her just the way her parents did. I left her the way Colton did. I was supposed to be her family, her happily ever after at the end of the road.

But I hurt her more than everyone else combined.

She shouldn't forgive me.

But fuck...I wanted her anyway.

I wanted to prove to her I could give her the life she wanted, that I would be by her side every single day for the rest of my life. Another woman couldn't tempt me. A job couldn't entice me. I'd become a married man without a wife, a father without a family. She rooted me so hard into the ground that I was ready to sprout branches.

But she couldn't see that.

I sat on the couch while my beer rested on the coaster. It was easy to get hooked on liquor after not having it for so long, but I needed to stay sober. Light beer was the only alternative I would allow myself. One mishap and I'd be using booze the way I used to use women. Now I had to suffer my way through this.

Soldier sat on the couch beside me, and as if he could hear my thoughts in his head, he watched me with those compassionate eyes. He was a smart dog, a loyal companion, but he could read minds...I swear. He always knew when I was done, always knew when something was wrong.

He moved his paw on my thigh, giving a quiet whine.

"I'm sorry, boy." I stared into those brown eyes and felt like a disappointment. "I'm trying to get her back... I know you miss her."

He whined again.

"But I think I miss her more." I grabbed my beer and took a drink, cringing because the light stuff tasted like shit.

Now I sat alone in my house and reflected on the last six months. I had to question my sanity because all of my decisions seemed so stupid. "What the fuck were you thinking...?" How could I walk away from that woman? How could I not listen to my brother's advice? I was so afraid to be the man I didn't want to become, I'd failed to realize I was already that man. I was already settled down. I was already committed. I was already in love. There was no going back.

But I'd tried to run anyway.

"You think I'll get her back?" I whispered.

Soldier didn't respond, but he kept his paw on my leg.

"I've got to, right? We're supposed to be together... I know it."

He pulled his paw back and laid down again.

"God, I'm so fucked up. I'm talking to a dog." I dragged my palms down my face and wished Pepper could see all the women I was rejecting. When I returned to the hospital, the offers came in. Other doctors asked me out. Patients asked me out. When the blonde had approached me at the gym, she'd bluntly invited me over to fuck. I didn't just turn her down to show my commitment to Pepper. There was only one woman I wanted to be with.

The doorbell rang.

Soldier was on his feet, his eyes narrowed and his rigid body prepared for battle. He was usually excited when someone came to the door, but something about tonight made him act strangely.

"Please be Pepper..." Shirtless and in my sweatpants, I walked to the front door.

Soldier stopped in the entryway and started to growl.

"Boy, it's alright." I looked through the peephole first.

It was Brutus.

Brutus was on the other side of my door.

Like Soldier could see right through the wall, he continued to growl, taking a stance that showed he was ready to attack.

I didn't need to wonder what Brutus wanted. We were both after the same thing—which made us competitors. "Boy, stand down." It was the first time Brutus would see my face, so I was glad I was shirtless and I'd pumped up at the gym. He would see my pretty face and sculpted body and know he'd met his match. Maybe he had a bigger wallet than I did—but he didn't know how to fuck like I did.

I opened the door and looked him in the eye. He was just a smidge shorter than me. With green eyes and a shadow along his jaw, he looked exactly the way he did in photos. He wore an expensive jacket, a shiny watch, and his Bugatti was parked at the curb in front of my house. He clearly wanted to show off.

If I wanted to show off, all I had to do was drop my pants. "Brutus Hemmingway, can I get an autograph?" Sarcasm dripped from my mouth, like venom from fangs. I smiled just to make it worse. Our relationship became hostile the second he rang my doorbell late at night. If I'd met him at the bar and Colton introduced me, I would have shown him respect because he'd done nothing wrong. How could I hate a guy for wanting Pepper? All men wanted Pepper. But he'd crossed a line when he tried to catch me off guard. If he thought he was going to intimidate me, he was wrong. I'd been in battle many times. I'd seen things far scarier than this little rich boy.

Soldier came closer to the door and growled again.

"Back, Soldier." I used my leg to keep him back without taking my eyes off Brutus.

He hadn't blinked once since I opened the door. "I have an offer for you."

"You're going to threaten me to leave Pepper alone?" I asked incredulously. "I'm going to cut you some slack because you've obviously never fought your own battles before, but you don't show up on a veteran's doorstep and make demands."

Like Soldier was backing me up, he growled louder.

Brutus didn't flinch as he pulled out a check from his pocket. "Cashier's check." He held it up so it could be visible under my porch light. "A billion dollars—and you leave Seattle tonight." He held it out to me as he waited for me to take it.

A billion dollars dangled in front of me, a check that wouldn't bounce. It would entice anyone. I pictured myself sailing the Mediterranean on my yacht surrounded by pretty girls. I could do all the volunteer work I wanted and never have to worry about money again. Anyone would take it. Pepper probably wasn't going to take me back, so I should take it.

But then I realized how depressed I would be. An endless line of beautiful women would never satisfy me. That yacht wouldn't be a vacation unless Pepper were there to share it with me. My life would be empty without her...because it was empty now.

I took the check from his hand.

"I want you gone tonight," Brutus said. "If you aren't gone by tomorrow—"

I ripped the check in half.

His jaw snapped shut as he watched the pieces drift to the concrete of the porch. He watched as a billion dollars floated away. He'd been so arrogant to assume I would take the money that he got a cashier's check...which meant he could never get it back. His eyes moved back to my face, this time full of fury. He was pissed that I'd wasted the money—but he was also pissed that I didn't take it.

"She's worth a lot more. If you think otherwise, you don't deserve her."

15

***

PEPPER

We stood at the table in the center of the bar, Brutus with his arm around my waist and Zach with his arm around Stella.

"I've never been to New York," Stella said. "I've always wanted to go, but I never have time to travel. Did you love it?"

Brutus shrugged. "I've been there a lot, so to me it's just a big city with lots of traffic and grumpy people."

"But what about the food?" she asked. "The pizza? The bagels?"

"The pizza is alright," he said with a shrug. "But the bagels are really worth their reputation."

"Well, there's no such thing as carbs tasting bad, so I believe it." Stella held on to her drink like a crutch. She'd already had too much tonight and needed to be cut off soon. But since Zach liked it when she was drunk, he never cut her off.

"I'm going to use the restroom." Brutus turned his face toward mine, his lips just a kiss away. "You want another drink?"

"Yes," I said. "Always assume my answer is yes."

He chuckled. "Alright." He kissed my cheek before he walked away and headed to the bathroom.

"Girl, he is so delicious," Stella blurted. "That ass...that wallet in that back pocket."

Zach knew she was drunk, so he just went along with it. "Yeah, he is pretty hot."

"He is the perfect way to make Finn pay. I bet when Finn realized who he was, he felt like shit." She slammed her hand down on the table. "As he should."

Stella was a lot more vicious with Finn than anyone else, including Colton. Everyone else kept their distaste bottled inside, but Stella was too loyal to be polite. She had taken shifts at the lingerie shop to keep the place afloat, so she knew better than anyone how much Finn had hurt me. Maybe one day Finn would earn forgiveness from everyone...but probably not her.

A man appeared at my side, and he placed a drink in front of me. It was a vodka cranberry. "I made it a double." Finn stood in a black t-shirt and dark jeans, his tattoos matching his somber attire. He stepped out of the shadows like he was born from the darkness. He'd clearly waited until Brutus stepped away before he made his move—which meant he knew he would return.

Stella immediately narrowed her eyes. "Oh, look who it is. That mother—"

Zach placed his hand over her mouth. "Stella, chill."

She mumbled against his palm.

I was on alert once I realized Finn was beside me. My entire body went rigid anytime he was near. I was nervous that Brutus and Finn were about to meet, but I was also tense around Finn for other reasons. My heart still soared when he was near. My lungs still ached like I couldn't get enough air. When he'd first come back to Seattle, I was too angry to give him a second thought. But slowly, my hard walls were softening. He didn't care if Brutus was here because he wasn't afraid of anything.

Finn stared at me like I was his. "I think Soldier wants to stay with you again."

"I don't know. I don't have a beautiful backyard for him to play in."

"But he likes your walks. And he likes going to the store with you."

Sometimes I took Soldier to the lingerie shop and let him sit in the corner. Customers loved seeing a dog, and Soldier loved to people-watch.

"You can borrow him whenever you want."

"The change in ownership might confuse him."

"He deserves more credit than that." He had a light beer in front of him instead of his usual scotch.

I glanced at the bottle. "Change in taste?"

He shrugged. "I'm trying to cut back. When I came back to Seattle, I was drinking way too much scotch. The liver can regenerate, but not at a fast-enough pace to keep up with my drinking."

"I'm glad you're taking your health seriously."

"Well, I need to live a long time. I'll have a wife and kids someday who will rely on me."

I hoped he didn't think I would be his wife, that I would be the one waddling around his house with a pregnant belly. I continued to grip my glass without taking a sip, unsure what to say. That used to be my dream.

Brutus returned, another vodka cranberry in hand. He didn't react to Finn overtly, but he stood on the other side of me, his arm immediately wrapping around my waist and keeping me close to his side.

Finn drank his beer and stared at Brutus. He clearly knew who he was because there was hostility in his gaze, like he wanted to slam his head into the table. He took a long drink before he set his bottle down.

Brutus stared at him too, like he'd deduced his identity.

"Brutus, right?" Finn asked, standing at his full height.

Stella glanced back and forth between them. "Oh shit..." she whispered.

Brutus stared at him for several seconds before he responded, as if he didn't know what to say.

"It's ironic," Finn said. "Some guy came to my door a couple of nights ago, and he looked just like you."

Brutus was still quiet.

"Yeah." Finn snapped his fingers. "He was asking for donations for a penis enhancement. I remember now."

Brutus naturally looked a little cold, and right now, he looked absolutely frozen. He stared at Finn with a silent stature, like a monster about to come to life.

I had no idea why Finn said that. He was purposely antagonizing Brutus—and doing a great job.

Brutus didn't respond.

What the hell was going on?

Finn took another drink of his beer, a smile in his eyes.

Brutus took the vodka cranberry Finn had gotten for me and dumped it on the floor. Then he slid the glass across the table toward Finn before he set his own drink in front of me.

Normally, I would cause a scene for him making a mess like that, but right now, it was so tense, I didn't dare say a word.

Finn didn't take his eyes off Brutus, standing his ground with a calm posture.

Brutus was a strong man, but he was no match for Finn. I'd have to warn him not to throw a punch—because he would get his ass beat. "I buy her drinks. Not you." With a deep voice and terror in his eyes, he held his ground like he wasn't the least bit afraid of Finn.

This was one hell of a pissing contest.

Finn drank his beer, relaxed like this encounter wasn't as unnerving for him as it was for everyone else. "You aren't a man because you can buy her a drink. A fat wallet can't solve all your problems. It can't fight your battles. But I'm sure you figured that out recently..."

BRUTUS WAS quiet the entire ride home.

Even when we arrived at his penthouse, he didn't say a word. He made himself a drink in the kitchen then downed it like water. As if I didn't exist and he didn't want me there, he ignored me.

I didn't know how to broach this conversation. It would only end negatively. Finn was a major thorn in our side, and I didn't know what to do about it. Finn was at the bar because it was a public place and he could do whatever he wanted. I had no control over it. It would be ridiculous for Brutus to be upset with me. "Are you sure you want me to stay?"

Brutus wiped his mouth with the back of his forearm then came back to me. He stripped off his jacket and tossed it on the couch like he didn't care in the least. "Yes."

I crossed my arms over my chest. "You seem grumpy."

"What gave me away?" He leaned against the edge of the couch, his arms crossed over his large chest. The window behind him gave a breathtaking view of the city, the lights, and the harbor in the distance.

"What was that about?"

"What?"

"The things Finn was saying...have you met him before?" It seemed unlikely because Brutus just got back to town and didn't even know Finn's last name. He would have had to hunt Finn down, or vice versa. I didn't think either of them would be so childish. "I knew it would be awkward once the two of you met, but I didn't expect it to be a battle."

He stared at the floor, ignoring me.

I told Finn I didn't want him to come between Brutus and me, but he already was.

Brutus turned back to me. "If you want us to be together, you need to get rid of Finn."

I raised an eyebrow at the order. "Sorry?"

"You heard me." He rose to his feet. "If he's really just part of your past, then he needs to disappear."

I didn't appreciate being told what to do, especially when it came to something I had no control over. "And what do you expect me to do? Tell him to leave the bar?"

"Yes."

I raised an eyebrow. "It's a public place. I can't tell him what to do...and he would never listen to me anyway."

"Then you need to stop borrowing his dog."

"His dog?" I asked incredulously. "Brutus, it's a dog. It's harmless."

"He's using it to manipulate you."

"You're being ridiculous. I had a really close connection to that dog, and I'm not going to stop loving him because of Finn. And Colton is my best friend, so there's no way I could avoid Finn even if I wanted to. You're just going to have to trust me... which I understand is difficult for you to do. But I'm not a cheater or a liar. I already told Finn not to come between us and he better not try to seduce me."

"And what did he say?"

"That he would never put me in that position anyway...and I believe him."

"So, let me get this straight." He stood up and came toward me. "He wants to get you back, but he doesn't want to sleep with you?"

"He doesn't want to get me back by making me into someone I don't want to be. He doesn't want me to undermine my honesty and integrity. He wouldn't want to start a relationship with me if

I were in a relationship with someone else. I understand why you don't like him, but he's an honorable man."

His eyebrows furrowed in annoyance. "So he'll just try to get you to leave me?"

I shrugged. "I guess."

"And that's not going to happen, right?" He looked at me so hard, it seemed like his eyes had frozen in place. We hadn't been together long, but he'd already become possessive of me, no longer being laid-back and easygoing. Now he was a bit controlling.

"Brutus, I don't know what's going to happen with us. We agreed this was supposed to be casual. But Finn hurt me too much, and I don't trust him anymore. Even if I wanted to be with him again, I couldn't allow myself to be in that position again. He really hurt me...more than I can explain."

My speech made his eyes soften. His body relaxed too, like I'd just said the magic words.

"I understand why you don't like Finn, but I wouldn't worry about him. He'll eventually take off like he always does. He's been living out of a suitcase since he became an adult. I don't know why he seems so determined right now, but his focus will fade...and then he'll disappear." Watching him give up on me again would hurt. But it would also be a relief once he was gone.

I WAS STANDING at the counter in the shop when Finn walked inside.

Shirtless and in his running shorts.

Soldier was with him, on his navy blue leash.

Finn pulled the earbuds out of his ears as he walked inside, his chest glistening with sweat. His muscles shifted and bulged with his movements.

Abby was hanging up lingerie, and she stopped what she was doing and dropped her jaw as her eyes watched Finn walk across the room. Like a deer in the headlights, she couldn't move because she was so focused on what she was looking at.

I couldn't blame her...because he was so sexy, it was ridiculous.

I met his look and pretended to be unaffected by his perfection...but I wasn't very good at it.

He reached the counter, his eyes locked on to mine like he didn't care about the other women gawking at him at that very moment. "Hey, baby. You look beautiful today." He treated me like he owned me, like he still had me on his leash.

It was easy to melt at the words, but I stayed frozen. "I told you not to call me that."

"And you know I don't listen."

Soldier rose on his back legs and pressed his front paws against the counter so he could look at me.

One look at him and I really did melt on the spot. "Hey, sweetheart." I rubbed him on the head.

"You're a lot nicer to him than you are to me."

I gave him a glare. "Because I actually like him."

He set the leash on the counter. "You wanna borrow him for a few days?"

I eyed the leash before looking at him again. "Are you trying to manipulate me with him?"

"No. I just know Soldier misses you. And I can tell you miss him. So how about I leave him here? I'll pick him up in a few days." He didn't mention Brutus even though it was so awkward the last time we were all together.

"Brutus thinks you're using Soldier to seduce me."

A slight smile stretched his mouth. "You know I don't need a dog to seduce a woman."

Memories of our nights together came back to me, when his

hand was deep in my hair, and he claimed me like I'd be his forever. "I guess I do know that. Jane does too."

Within the snap of a finger, his smile disappeared. Pain moved into his eyes, like the insult really hit him where it hurt. "Baby..."

"Did you call her that too?" Just when I thought I was indifferent toward him, my anger would flare up. It was a bad sign because it meant that I cared...and I didn't want him to know how much it bothered me. I convinced myself he meant nothing to me, but imagining him with someone else still made me sick to my stomach.

"No. You're my only baby."

"But that wasn't enough to get you to stay, huh?" He said romantic things that made me weak, but then I twisted them around and reminded him what he'd done.

He watched me with his sad eyes. "I'm sorry that I hurt you... but I'm also relieved that you still care."

Shit. "I just want you to leave me alone, Finn."

"No, you don't. Trust me, I would know if you really did."

I didn't call his bluff. "I'll take Soldier. You can leave now."

He continued to linger at the counter. "I know this doesn't mean anything coming from me, but I don't like Brutus."

"You're right...it doesn't mean anything." I was doing bookkeeping on my laptop, but since this conversation was going nowhere, I shut my computer and looked into his blue eyes.

"I'm serious, baby. That guy...is not respectable."

"Really?" I questioned. "You think he made his billions from bank fraud or tax evasion? You think he's a cheater and a liar? It's ironic for you to throw insults when someone could say the same about you."

"I know I fucked up, but at least I'm honest about the things I fuck up on."

"What's that supposed to mean?"

He held his silence, staring me down and keeping his secrets to himself.

"Finn? What aren't you telling me?"

He backed away from the counter. "Just take my word for it." He walked out of the store and put his earbuds back in his ears. Then he ran past the windows of the store until he was out of sight.

16

COLTON

AFTER SHOOTING HOOPS IN THE DRIVEWAY, WE WENT INTO HIS living room and opened a few beers while we waited for the pizza to be delivered. The game was on the screen and Finn seemed to be into it, but since I didn't like to watch sports, I hardly paid attention. "Pepper told me you and Brutus got along well..."

"The guy is a prick." He kept his eyes on the TV, the bottle resting between his thighs.

"Everyone else likes him."

"Because he wants you to like him." Finn had a permanently dark look on his face, carrying his sadness like a billboard. Soldier wasn't there because he'd let Pepper borrow him, so he was in the house all alone.

I felt bad for him. "He seems like a good guy to me."

"Trust me, he's not."

I turned to him, wondering what kind of legitimate excuse Finn could make up. "You don't even know him, Finn."

"You don't need to know a serial killer to know if he's a murderer."

"Well...Brutus isn't a murderer."

Finn finally pulled his gaze from the TV and looked at me. "No. But he's a little bitch."

"What did he do?" I asked, not expecting a good answer.

"I'll tell you, but you have to promise you won't tell Pepper." He set his beer on the end table beside him.

Now, it was getting interesting. "You know I don't keep anything from her."

"Well, you're gonna have to promise, or I won't tell you."

"If you have dirt on him, why wouldn't you want her to know?" If Finn had something that could bury Brutus, then Brutus would be out of the way and Finn could have a better chance with Pepper.

"Because I thought he would be man enough to tell her himself...and he didn't." He shook his head. "A real man is honest about the stunts he pulls, no matter how bad they are. I told Pepper I slept with someone while in Uganda, and she hadn't even asked. That's what men do—they're honest."

"Honest like when you proposed to Pepper then ditched her?"

His eyes narrowed in hostility. "Honest like when you married her but were attracted to men?" he snapped. "It's not the same thing at all."

"Well, don't put yourself on a pedestal when you don't belong there."

"I'm just saying, this guy isn't as perfect as she thinks."

"Okay...then what did he do?"

"Are you gonna keep your promise?"

"Are you gonna explain why it has to be a secret?"

He sighed. "Because I don't want to win her that way. I don't want her to come back to me because this guy hurt her. I don't want to win her because I kicked him out of the race. And where I come from...you never snitch. It says a lot more about you than it does them. So, are we going to keep this between us?"

I never kept secrets from Pepper, but my curiosity was getting to me. "Alright, fine. Tell me."

He walked into the kitchen, got something out of a drawer, and then came back to me. He held two pieces of a ripped check. He put them together then laid them on the couch so I could see.

It was a billion-dollar check made out to Finn. A cashier's check.

I stared at it then lifted my gaze to meet his. "What does this mean? Brutus wrote you a billion-dollar check?"

He nodded. "Said this check was mine if I left Seattle that night."

I knew my brother wouldn't lie about something like that, so I believed him. And that was also a real billion-dollar check. Brutus was the only person we knew who could afford a bribe like that. "When did this happen?"

"He came to my doorstep last week?"

I pulled my eyes away from the check. "He just showed up?"

He nodded. "At like nine in the evening. He told me to leave and handed me the check."

"Why is it ripped?"

"Because I ripped it in half. I only kept it in case I needed it for proof someday..."

My brother was offered a billion-dollar guarantee, and he said no? He tore up the check and said goodbye to a life of fortune and luxury? He traded all of that in so he could keep fighting for Pepper, even though he might never get her back? I stared at him in disbelief, looking at my brother with new eyes.

Finn held my gaze, his brooding expression dark. "That was low of him. One, it was insulting. And two, he had no right to meddle in a relationship he knows nothing about. Maybe Pepper doesn't want me to leave. Maybe she wants me to stay. He's a pussy who makes his problems disappear with his wallet.

There's no respect in that. If he came here and threatened me the old-fashioned way, at least I would have respected him. But this..." He glanced down at the check. "It's low. And the fact that he thinks Pepper is worth such a small amount is insulting."

"Small?" I asked incredulously.

"For someone like Pepper, yes." He grabbed the pieces and folded them in half. "She shouldn't be with a man who pulls stunts like this. It's controlling and possessive. Not to mention, it's also creepy." He tossed the papers onto the coffee table.

It was a lot to take in, so I was still absorbing it. Brutus tried to bribe Finn to disappear, to take the money and run.

But he didn't.

He was sitting on the couch beside me, watching the game like any other night of the week. He gave up his position at Doctors Without Borders to live a normal life with Pepper. Then he turned down a fortune to stay here, to keep living a normal life. If that didn't mean he loved Pepper...I didn't know what did.

Finn could read my mind. "I really love her, Colt." Emotion escaped in his voice. "I know I fucked up, but it was a mistake. I'm here now, and I'm never going to leave. This is where I belong. Will you help me?"

"Help you how?"

"You've been rooting for Brutus. Now it's time to root for me."

"It doesn't matter who I root for. This is Pepper's decision—"

"But she listens to you. Stop whispering in her ear and saying how great Brutus is. Start telling her I'm great...that I deserve another chance. Come on, man. I need you right now. I need you on my side. Otherwise, this is going to be a million times harder."

"So you want me to influence her?"

"Yes."

"You don't think she should make her own decision?"

His eyes narrowed. "You told her to stick with Brutus and

never give me a chance. How is that not influencing? I turned down a billion dollars, when ninety-nine percent of men wouldn't. That has to count for something."

It did...it counted for a lot. "Alright..."

"Thank you."

"But just to be clear, I'm not doing this because you're my brother. I'm doing this—"

"Because it's the right thing to do."

WE GOT lunch in the middle of the day, and Soldier came with us. We sat outside at the picnic tables near the front door of the deli. I got a chicken salad sandwich while she went with a meatball sub, getting sauce all over her face.

"You've got shit all over your face."

She shrugged. "Whatever, it's just you."

"You used to be a little cleaner when we were married."

"But now we aren't sleeping together anymore, so I don't care." She kept eating, the red marinara around her lips.

Soldier whined for a scrap.

Pepper was weak, so she tossed him one of her meatballs.

"You guys are inseparable."

"He's such a sweetheart." She eyed him fondly before turning back to me. "He's like my best friend. I even talk to him like he's a real person. Just the other night, I complained to him that my Chinese food took forever to be delivered."

"Sounds like a free therapist."

"I swear, he knows exactly how I feel when I feel it. He comforted me the entire time Finn was gone for that one month. I just wish he had been there with me after Finn dumped me." She stuck her hand in her bag and snaked out a few chips.

That was my opening to say something positive. I wanted to

tell her that her boyfriend tried to buy Finn off for a billion dollars, but I'd promised not to. "I've been spending more time with Finn... He seems sincere about everything."

The chips crunched in her mouth as she ate them.

"He's miserable without you."

She ignored what I said.

It seemed like my words meant nothing to her. "I know you think Finn is just here for a short while...but I don't think he is. I think he knows he really messed up, and now he wants to make it right."

"How much did he pay you to say that?"

Interesting choice of words. "Come on, you know I wouldn't say that unless I really thought it."

"Don't let him wear you down."

Turning down a billion-dollar check was pretty powerful. I couldn't ignore it. "I know how much you were hurt by him so you keep your walls up high. I get it. But I don't think Finn would do that again."

"Doesn't matter. I'm never taking him back."

Maybe Finn should have taken the money.

"Because you think he'll hurt you again?"

"I *know* he will." She kept eating her chips. "I don't want to talk about him anymore. I'm with Brutus, and I'm staying with Brutus."

I didn't know how I felt about the guy anymore. He showed up to Finn's house late at night to make him disappear. It was a little intimidating...having Pepper date someone with that much power. What else was he capable of? "Do you love him?"

Her answer was immediate. "No. But that's not what I'm looking for."

"So what's your plan? To be with Brutus until you do love him?"

When her bag of chips was empty, she folded it then tossed

it on the tray. "When I fall in love with someone, it happens quickly. With you, within a few days, I knew I loved you. With Finn, it happened within seconds. I haven't felt that way about Brutus...so I don't think I ever will. But that's perfect. Without love, you can't get hurt."

That sounded boring. "Without love, what are you sticking around for?"

"Well, the sex is good. He's easy to talk to. He gets along with all of my friends. He wants to have a family."

"With that criteria, you could have picked any guy."

"Exactly," she said. "Which is why it's easy. If he ever pulls a stunt, it won't hurt."

I hadn't realized the extent of Finn's damage until now. Pepper openly admitted she wanted to be with a guy without any concrete reason. She wanted to be in a relationship, maybe even have a family with him, but she didn't love him. "Pepper, you need to listen to me."

She rolled her eyes. "Please don't let this be the same conversation we've already had..."

"Look, it's fine if Brutus is just some fuck-buddy rebound. But don't be in a loveless relationship. Don't give up on the institution altogether. It's out there. You will find the right guy who you love and who loves you."

"Well...I already found the man I fell head over heels for. He made me feel things I never felt before. It was beautiful, crazy, and so damn deep." She spoke with emotion, but her eyes were empty. "And he left. He took back his ring and left. So I'm not looking for another relationship based on love. I've done it twice now, and it's blown up in my face. I'm not ashamed to admit Brutus is easy. I've said the same thing right to his face. You're making a big deal out of nothing."

"I'm making a big deal because you're selling yourself short. Be with a man you love—"

"I already love a man, and I'll love him for the rest of my life." When she stared at me, she seemed both alive and dead at the same time. "But that doesn't mean I should be with him. That's not enough to be with someone who doesn't treat you right, who doesn't stick around when you need him most. I could spend the rest of my life trying to fall in love again, but I'll never love anyone the way I love Finn. It's the sad and horrific truth. So I'll find someone I don't love—but who has everything else."

I didn't say a word in response because I was speechless. The whole time I had been pushing Brutus on her, in reality, I had been encouraging this loveless relationship. She just admitted that she was in love with Finn, that he was the only man she would ever love. And I'd been pushing Brutus on her this entire time. "If you really thought Finn wouldn't fuck up again, would you take him back?"

She rested her arms on the table and considered my question with wet eyes. She shook her head slightly as she continued to think of what she might say. "I don't know. I really can't picture a reality where he won't fuck up again...so I can't even entertain the question."

WHEN I GOT HOME LATER that night, I called Finn.

"Hey," he said in a brooding voice. "What's up?"

"I had an interesting conversation with Pepper today."

After a long pause, he spoke again. "Yeah?"

"She told me she's with Brutus because she doesn't love him. If she doesn't love him, he can't hurt her."

"Well...I figured that."

"I kept pestering her about you...and she said she's still in love with you. She says she'll always be in love with you."

He took a deep breath, like those words meant the world to him.

"But she doesn't trust you not to hurt her...and she never will."

Finn was quiet for a long time, absorbing my words as he sat in silence. His breathing was barely audible, but it slowly picked up the longer time went on. "Thanks for telling me, Colt. That means a lot to me."

"You're welcome. But you still have a long road ahead of you. You burned her bad, man."

"I know," he whispered. "I'll wait as long as she needs me to wait. I'm in no rush."

17

PEPPER

Soldier sat on the floor and stared at me.

My fingers dug into my bowl of popcorn, and I popped a few kernels into my mouth.

He whined and focused those pretty brown eyes on my face.

"Alright..." I grabbed a piece and prepared to throw it.

He got into his pouncing stance.

I tossed it into the air.

He snapped at it with his powerful jaws, eating the piece with a crunch.

"Good job."

As soon as he had one piece, he wanted another.

A knock sounded on my door.

Once there was an intruder, Soldier went into defensive mode. He walked to the door and started to sniff through the crack. When he got a scent he didn't like, he growled.

"Soldier, what's gotten into you?" I chuckled as I headed to the door. I'd never heard him growl since I'd known him. He was an old police dog, but he seemed too sweet and affectionate to work with crime all day. I opened the door and saw Brutus on the other side. "Hey."

Soldier growled louder, moving between my legs like he was trying to protect me.

Brutus held a bag of Italian food that he'd picked up on the way over, and he immediately stepped back when he spotted Soldier baring his fangs.

"Soldier, come on." I kneeled down and rubbed his back to make him relax. "It's alright. Calm down." I rubbed behind his ears until he stopped growling, but he still looked at Brutus like he didn't like him. "That's weird...I've never seen him do that before."

Brutus was too scared to come in, so he stayed in the hallway with his food tucked under his arm.

"Soldier, come here." I patted the cushion on the couch until he obeyed. "Be nice, alright? Brutus is a good guy. Don't worry about him."

When the coast was clear, Brutus came inside and carried the food into the kitchen. "Still spending time with that dog, huh?" He didn't sheathe his dislike for anything that concerned Finn, even an animal.

"He's a sweetheart. I'm not sure why he's tense around you."

Soldier started to growl again.

"Soldier, come on." I scratched behind his ears again. "Be nice." I left the couch and joined Brutus in the kitchen. "Sorry about that..." I rose on my tiptoes and kissed him on the cheek. "Thanks for picking up dinner."

"No problem." He pulled out the containers and helped himself to the silverware in my drawer. "How was your day—"

Soldier snuck up on us, and now he growled at Brutus again, down in his defensive stance with his teeth bared. Then he started to bark, turning into an attack dog that seemed like he was going to bite Brutus's face off.

Brutus scooted closer to the counter. "Can you get rid of him?"

I didn't want to kick Soldier out of the apartment, but I clearly couldn't have the two of them in the same room together...which was strange. "Soldier, what is up with you?" I grabbed his leash and hooked it around his collar before I pulled him toward the door.

He kept growling, keeping his eyes locked on Brutus at all times, like he was too afraid to let him out of his sight.

I tugged on his leash and took him across the hall. I walked inside and found Colton and Tom eating dinner together at the dining table.

"I knew it," Colton said. "She smelled food."

I kicked the door shut behind me. "Actually, can I leave Soldier here until tomorrow morning?"

"Sure," Colton said. "But why?"

"He won't stop growling at Brutus."

Colton stopped eating, his interest piqued. "Really? Soldier?"

"I don't get it either." I unhooked his leash. "He can't stand Brutus. I really thought he might bite him or something." Now that we were across the hall, Soldier returned to his normal self, being a happy dog with a wagging tail. "I've never seen him act like that before."

"Dogs have phenomenal senses when it comes to smell," Tom said. "Maybe he doesn't like the smell of Brutus's clothes or cologne..."

"Maybe." He didn't seem very potent to me.

"They also have powerful instincts," Tom said. "Maybe there's just something he doesn't like about him..."

"Like what?" I asked. "Brutus is harmless."

Colton shrugged. "Too bad we can't ask Soldier what his deal is."

"Well, Brutus brought dinner so I'll get Soldier in the morning," I said. "Thanks for watching him. And just so you know, he takes up half the bed and snores...thanks." I headed to the door.

"Sorry, Tom," Colton said. "Looks like you aren't sleeping over tonight…"

I returned to my apartment and found Brutus in the kitchen. He took our food out of the containers and put it on two plates. He'd already opened a bottle of wine and had two glasses filled.

"Sorry about that." I was a little embarrassed by the interaction, but I was also concerned about Soldier. That dog had never been anything but loving, loyal, and affectionate. He got along well with strangers when we went on our walks and never barked at the customers in my store. Brutus was a fluke.

"It's okay. He's not coming back, right?"

"Not until the morning."

"Good." He handed me a fork.

"I've never seen him act that way. Maybe it's your cologne or something."

"Or maybe he's just a stupid dog."

I flinched at the insult, offended by his words just as if he'd said them about Colton or Stella. "Excuse me?" I lowered my fork and stared at him hard, feeling so much anger in just a nanosecond. I was apologetic a moment ago, but now my blood was boiling.

"He nearly attacks me, and you're mad at me?"

"Don't call him stupid. He's not stupid."

He rolled his eyes. "Fine."

I let the argument drop because it wouldn't go anywhere positive, but a sinking feeling entered my stomach. Anyone else would brush it off because Soldier was just a dog, but he wasn't just a dog to me. He was someone I loved, someone I trusted. He was just as important to me as Colton or Stella. But I had to remind myself that Brutus probably didn't like him because he was Finn's dog…and maybe that was why there was so much tension in the room.

Baby. Finn's text message popped up on my screen.

I was so used to hearing and seeing that name that I didn't need to check who it was. *How many times do I have to tell you not to call me that?*

As many times as it takes for you to give up.

If he were in the room, I would have rolled my eyes. Soldier was sitting beside me, so I said, "Your dad is an asshole."

He placed his snout on my thigh so I would pet him.

I texted back. *I don't give up easily.*

And I never give up.

I recognized the double meaning of his words. *What do you want?*

My dog. If you're ready to give him up.

I never wanted to give him up, but I knew I had to...at least for a little while. *You can come and get him.*

I hope you're hungry because I just picked up Mega Shake.

I could eat Mega Shake anywhere at any time, but I knew this was just a ploy to stay in my apartment. *You can drop off the food and leave.*

And eat it when it gets cold? No, I'm eating it on your couch.

I started to text back when there was a knock on my door.

Soldier ran to the door and started whining, like he knew Finn was on the other side. He seemed to be able to see through solid pieces of wood. Or at least he smelled through them.

I opened the door, wearing my black leggings and a loose shirt around the house. My hair was pulled back in a bun, and I'd skipped the makeup because I'd thought I would be alone tonight. Maybe my plainness would chase him off.

Like always, Finn looked at me like I was the most beautiful woman he'd ever seen. His eyes softened slightly as he took in my features, from my pale cheeks to my green eyes. Slowly, a smile entered his face, like I filled him with unexpected joy.

Soldier whined again, wanting his father's affection.

He ignored him. "Hungry?" He held up the bag with grease stains all over it.

It didn't matter how much I disliked Finn. I couldn't say no to a fresh burger and fries. "Get in here..."

He grinned in victory and stepped inside. "My baby can't say no to hot fries."

I smacked his arm. "That's insulting on so many levels."

"It's cute on so many levels."

When Finn entered the apartment, Soldier wagged his tail and jumped on the couch, excited that both of us were in the same room.

Finn moved to the couch, wearing his sweatpants and a t-shirt. He probably had been home watching the game when he hopped in his truck and came over here. Whether it was sweatpants, jeans, or a suit, he looked like a million bucks. He pulled the food out of the bag so we could eat it.

I ate my food and kept space in between us.

Soldier clearly missed Finn because he practically lay on his lap.

"How was your day?" Finn asked, pretending everything was normal between us.

"Fine. I went to the gym early in the morning with Stella then worked for a few hours. Then I took a nap on the couch and haven't moved since."

He chuckled. "Sounds like a nice day."

"Except for the gym part. Stella is a crazy bitch."

He laughed. "Maybe she should train me."

"Nah...you're good." He already had eight percent body fat. What more could she do for him?

He placed a few fries into his mouth and chewed. "I talked to one of my old military buddies today."

"Oh?"

"Yeah, he's stationed in Texas now. He'll be in the states for a while."

"That's nice. He'll have a break."

"I told him to come up for a visit if he ever has time."

"You think it'll happen?"

"Fingers crossed."

"Did you work today?"

"Yeah," he answered. "The morning shift."

"How's it been back at the hospital?"

"Good. Nothing has changed. Time stands still there."

"Have you seen Layla…?" I would always dislike that woman, even if I had no reason to. She could sleep with him, and there was nothing I could do about it.

"I've worked with her a few times." He kept eating like mentioning her was of no consequence.

"She must be happy you're single." I was playing a dangerous game. I told Finn we would never be together so he could do whatever he wanted, but I would lose my mind if he hooked up with her.

He finished chewing another handful of fries. "She doesn't think I'm single."

Relief swept through me instantly. I never wanted her to sink her claws into him. I never wanted her to have him…even if he wasn't mine at all.

"I've told everyone we're still together."

"But that's a lie."

"It won't be a lie forever."

His commitment shouldn't mean anything to me, but it softened my hardened exterior. Having Finn as the man who was completely devoted to me was still a fantasy. I remembered the first time he told the world he was taken...I felt so special. Being the only woman this man wanted was a dream come true...even now. But the feeling was fleeting and wouldn't last forever. "It wouldn't have to be a lie at all..."

He didn't stop eating his food as he brushed off the comment.

I ate everything then left the wrappers on the coffee table. It was dark in my living room because I only had a few lamps on. My TV was off because I'd been scrolling through my newsfeed when he texted me. Now it was just the two of us on the couch without any distractions.

He finished and wiped his fingers on a napkin.

"Brutus was here a few days ago, and Soldier wouldn't stop growling at him."

"No surprise there."

"Have you ever seen him do that before?"

"Nope." He leaned back against the couch and looked at me, Soldier in between us. "Never."

"I thought it was strange..."

"It's not that strange. Soldier doesn't like him. It's as simple as that."

"But Soldier doesn't know him."

"A dog doesn't need to know someone to know if they like them or not. They have instincts we can't understand. Soldier is a public service officer. His job is to protect you. Maybe he felt like you needed to be protected."

"Brutus is harmless..."

"Maybe Soldier disagrees." He kept watching me, his handsome jawline sexy because he'd just shaved. He had an old-fashioned movie star look, like he belonged on the big screen rather than in a set of scrubs. It was fortunate he had such blue eyes, soft features that made him seem less formidable. He was such a beautiful man...but there was so much underneath that pretty face.

I remembered how humble he was when he received the bronze star award. I remembered how he defended Colton when his boss was an asshole. I remembered the way he came to my rescue when the guy tried to hurt me at the bar. I remembered the first time he said he loved me...how he wasn't afraid to say it. There were so many admirable qualities about him. If only he weren't such a drifter, things could be different. But some people never changed.

He didn't blink. "What are you thinking about, baby?"

I hadn't even realized I'd been staring at him so hard. "Nothing..."

"I know that's a lie."

"I was thinking about the ways I admire you...your humility and your loyalty."

His eyes softened.

"But I was also thinking how people never change... including you."

His eyes tightened once again, becoming guarded. "Some people do change...when they find the right reason to."

He was several feet away from me, but I felt his presence like he was pressed right against me. I could feel the heat between us like a roaring fire was coming out of an invisible hearth. Just the way we used to sit together when we first knew each other, there was this unspoken chemistry. It was so heavy in the air that it was like the room was filled with smog. I never had these tense moments with anyone else, when lust and passion mixed together to form a fiery substance. It wasn't just because Finn was gorgeous. Brutus was a beautiful man too, but we never had this kind of intensity. It was more than just attraction, more than just desire. I just didn't know what that thing was.

"Baby, I've changed." He spoke quietly, his deep voice filling the space between us. His hand moved to his chest, resting over his strong heart. "I'd marry you tomorrow if you said yes."

"You made that promise before..."

"I asked you to be my wife, and then I left. What I'm saying now is, I'll marry you the second the courthouse opens in the morning. I'll be legally bound to you as long as you'll have me. I'll carry all your shit to my house and put your name on the deed. I'll put a baby in your belly tonight if you wanted to start our family. Baby, I'm not offering those things to you to get you back. I'm offering them because I want them...so much. Please give me another chance. Please."

Moisture built up in my eyes because I wanted to say yes so much. That picture he painted was an artistic masterpiece. To be deeply in love, to sleep in his arms, to have an entire future with him sounded magical. But that wasn't enough to erase the damage that been done. My heart had never been put back together because there were so many pieces I never found. "Stop this..."

"I'm never going to stop, baby. I'm your family...be my family."

The moisture bubbled into a tear and streaked down my face. "No..."

"I'll never leave you ever again—"

"You can't make a promise like that—"

"You bet your ass, I can. I've lived my life without you, and it's unbearable. If you took me back, I would spend every day of the rest of my life trying to keep you. I would worship you. I would be the best husband there ever was. I'm so committed because the only time I want to live without you is after you're dead...because I won't have any other choice. I know it's hard for you to forgive me and trust me, but I promise you I'm not going anywhere."

I wiped my tears away and turned my cheek, unable to

handle the desperation in his gaze. I didn't let myself break into sobs, but the tears kept coming.

Finn moved over Soldier and came to my side of the couch.

"Finn, no."

He cupped my cheek and pressed his forehead to mine. He didn't kiss me, but his touch was more intimate than sex. His fingers moved into my hair, and he cradled me close to him, letting our chemistry combust once we were combined. "Baby..." He closed his eyes as he held me, touching me just the way he used to when we made love. "You have to forgive me. We belong together...I know we do."

I wanted to pull away, but I didn't have the strength. His touch was so comforting, like heat after a long winter. His flames were so warm that I never wanted to leave his radiance. This felt like home, like what I'd been missing since the day he left. I wanted to close my eyes and stay there forever...feel safe forever.

But I would never be safe with this man. I would always be afraid of the moment things changed, when an offer popped up that he couldn't refuse, when modern life became too boring for him and he needed something new. "No."

"Baby—"

"I said no." I got to my feet and escaped his embrace. "You want me today, but when domestic life bores you, you'll crave something more."

He bowed his head forward and closed his eyes.

"I know how you are, Finn. You'll get tired of me eventually. And if you stay, you'll just resent me."

"That's not possible...because being with you is the only place I want to be."

"Just go." I headed for my bedroom. "I mean it, Finn. Go."

I LAY in my bed with Soldier by my side, my eyes closed once the tears finally stopped.

Curled up into a ball, he lay beside me, his eyes opening once in a while to check if I was still there.

Turning down Finn was the hardest thing I'd ever had to do —but I knew it was for the best.

My phone started to ring.

It was Brutus. I wasn't in the mood to talk, but I didn't want to ignore him either. It felt deceitful. I answered and did my best to keep my voice normal, to stop the cracking sound my throat produced. "Hey…"

"Hey. I'm surprised you're still awake."

"Yeah…I lost track of time." I usually went to bed early since I had Stella's class at the break of dawn, but I was too depressed to go tomorrow.

"Something wrong?" He must have detected my tone of voice. I was usually perkier than this, even if I was tired. We hadn't known each other very long but got quickly acquainted with each other.

I liked the honesty in our relationship, so I told him the truth. "Finn left not too long ago…"

Silence.

"He came to get Soldier, but then we started talking…told me we should get back together. Said he wanted to marry me and he would never leave me again…but I told him no." I sighed as I remembered the conversation, the tears still in my eyes.

"You want me to handle it?" He quickly turned hostile, sounding terrifying. "I can get him to leave you alone."

It was a strange thing to offer, and I wasn't sure if I liked it. "No, it's okay…he's fine."

"Why does he keep trying?"

"I don't know…"

"Do you still love him? Did you tell him that?"

The answer was sitting in my heart and I didn't want to tell a lie, so I told the truth. "I do still love him...but I didn't tell him that."

Silence once again.

"He'll give up eventually...at some point."

"I think it's pretty rude to keep trying when you're in a relationship with someone else." Seething with anger, he made it obvious this whole thing annoyed him. We were happy until Finn returned to town. Our relationship had never been the same since.

"I know. I'm sorry."

"You don't have to be sorry," he said ominously. "He should be the one who's sorry..."

"WANNA PLAY MONOPOLY?" Colton picked up the box from the counter. "It's a classic."

"That game is so long," I said. "And a bit boring. Brutus, what do you think?" With a glass of red wine in my hand, I turned to Brutus.

He was in jeans and a t-shirt, his muscular arm around my waist. "It is a classic. But I'm down for anything."

"Come on, don't be diplomatic," I argued. "What do you want to play?"

Brutus shrugged. "Doesn't matter to me."

I turned to Tom. "Veto Monopoly."

"What about Stella and Zach?" Tom asked, using them as a scapegoat. "Maybe we should wait and see what they want to play."

"And Finn," Colton added.

I should have known Finn was coming. We hadn't spoken

since our emotional conversation in my apartment a few days ago. He had the sense to give me space after breaking my heart all over again.

Colton looked up when he detected the tension in the room. "What? Do you want me to disinvite him?"

"No," I said quickly. "I just didn't know he was coming—"

"Yes," Brutus interrupted. "It would be nice if you didn't invite him to every little thing."

Colton shifted his gaze back and forth between us.

Tom was still.

I took a long drink of my wine and depleted the entire glass until it was empty.

Colton finally addressed what Brutus said. "Noted...I just thought he could play with Tatum."

"You can play games with an odd number of people." Brutus grabbed his beer and took a drink.

The situation was just getting worse. "Brutus, let it go..."

Brutus dropped his arm from my side and didn't say anything, but it was obvious he was mad. "I'm going to wash up." He excused himself to the bathroom.

Colton rounded on me the second he was gone. "What happened?"

"Finn and I had a long conversation a few nights ago about getting back together... Brutus wasn't happy about it."

"Well, I don't think Finn is gonna stop anytime soon, so Brutus'll have to get used to it. And since Finn is my brother, I can't just exclude him from game night."

"No, I understand. He's just kinda grumpy about the whole thing."

The front door opened, and Finn walked inside, wearing a dark blue shirt with a leather jacket. When he'd first returned to Seattle, the size of his body had shrunk from the lack of exercise and proper nutrition. He'd been hitting the gym religiously, and now he looked like the behemoth he used to be.

I was the first thing he looked at, as if Colton and Tom weren't in the room.

I turned my gaze and looked at Colton again, refusing to let my eyes settle on him for too long.

Finn approached the kitchen and grabbed a beer without acknowledging anyone.

"Hey, Finn," Colton finally said. "We're trying to decide what game we should play."

He twisted off the cap of his bottle. "Baby, why don't you decide?"

I stilled at the nickname because Brutus was right behind him. He'd returned from the bathroom, and he'd obviously heard what Finn said because his eyes narrowed like two bullets. He rejoined us and slid his arm around my waist, his eyes full of menace so Finn would know he'd overheard his endearment.

Soon, these two men would never be able to be in the same room together.

Or maybe soon was now.

Finn drank his beer and looked at Brutus like he didn't give a damn if he pissed him off.

Colton cleared his throat. "You're right, Monopoly is too long. Let's play Cranium."

"No," Tom said. "Finn will kick our asses."

Finn kept staring at Brutus, having a silent confrontation with just his eyes.

I felt Brutus's arm tighten around my waist, like he was restraining himself as much as possible.

"What about Sorry?" Colton asked, doing his best to dissipate the hostility in the room.

"Too boring," Tom said.

"Well, that leaves us with Monopoly," Colton said. "Unless we want to do Pictionary."

"Not a bad idea." Tom nodded.

Finn finally broke eye contact and glanced at my empty glass. "More wine, baby?" Now he said it directly to Brutus's face, staking a claim on me even though he wasn't touching me. He grabbed the bottle from the counter and refilled my glass.

Brutus was turning red in the face. "You really don't want to do that..." The threat was subtle but there nonetheless.

"Or what?" Finn corked the wine and returned it to the counter. "You're gonna write me a check to make me stop?"

It was an odd insult, but it was obviously effective because Brutus tensed beside me.

Brutus clenched his jaw. "You don't want to find out what I'll do...so I suggest you shut your mouth."

Colton eyed them back and forth then looked at me, his eyes wide with terror as the two men continued to exert hostility in the kitchen. He looked at me like he hoped I would have a solution to bring this standoff to an end.

"Maybe other men are afraid of your wallet, but I'm not." Finn took another drink of his beer. "Real men fight with fists, not cash. But you've probably never been in a fight in your entire life...or rolled up your sleeves and got your hands dirty. Pepper fell in love with me because I'm a man who puts his money where his mouth is. She's just using you to keep her bed warm. We both know you don't mean a damn thing to—"

Brutus lunged at Finn.

"Stop it." I grabbed Brutus by the arm and dragged him back. "I mean it."

Brutus obeyed me but kept his eyes on Finn.

Finn hadn't moved an inch, drinking his beer like he wasn't afraid of any kind of swing coming his way.

I was angry Brutus jumped to violence, but I couldn't blame

him because Finn had antagonized him. Finn had the upper hand, and he knew it. "Finn, you're being an asshole, and we all see it. Don't call me baby, and don't insult Brutus like that. If you can't play nice with everyone, then you should leave."

Finn didn't move an inch.

Colton bowed his head because he wanted to stay out of it.

Brutus calmed slightly when I finally addressed Finn's obnoxious behavior.

"Pissing off Brutus isn't the way to get me back," I snapped. "Instead of all of us having a good night and enjoying ourselves, you decided to ruin it. I'm not your baby, and I'll never be your baby again. So get out, and don't come back until you understand what kind of behavior is acceptable."

Finn set down his beer and stared at me, his hands still on the counter like he might not move. Brutus and everyone else didn't seem to exist. It was just the two of us. His eyes were full of disappointment, like I'd somehow crossed the line. "You are my baby. He may have his arm around your waist, but I have you forever. If you were madly in love with someone, I would back off and leave you in peace. But you don't love this guy. You're just using him to feel good about yourself. Everyone in this room knows it—including Brutus." He stepped away from the counter and walked toward the door. "But I'll go—because you asked."

———

GAME NIGHT WASN'T much fun because we kept thinking about the episode with Finn.

No one seemed to be paying attention.

At the end of the night, we started to clean up the crumbs and empty bottles. Brutus filled the trash bags with old beer bottles then carried them into the hallway to drop into the chute.

"Well, that was fun," Colton said sarcastically.

"My god, this is a nightmare..."

"And I don't think Finn is going to back off."

"It'd surprise me if he did."

Colton rinsed off the dishes and placed them on the right side of the sink to be scrubbed later. "What are you going to do?"

"What do you mean?"

"Finn seems determined, and Brutus seems fed up. You're going to have to choose at some point."

"Choose? I have chosen." I told Finn I wanted to be with Brutus. End of story.

"Until you break it off with Brutus to be with Finn, or you marry Brutus, I think this problem isn't going to go away. Maybe if Brutus weren't so proud, he would leave. No guy would deal with this otherwise."

"Yeah..."

"Unless he's in love with you."

"I doubt it."

He shrugged. "You never know. Either way, you need to put a stop to this somehow. Because kicking Finn out of your life just isn't possible, not when we are best friends who live across the hall from each other."

"Yeah...I think you're right."

18

FINN

I worked an additional two hours of overtime because the ER was swamped.

There weren't enough rooms for the patients, so beds were parked in hallways and even near the printers. Two codes came in that night, which stopped the flow of patients. Patients kept piling up, and eventually, it turned into a shitshow.

So I stayed.

I saw a couple more patients until the craziness of the ER died down. I discharged a few of my patients and admitted a few others. The remaining critical patients were handed off to Layla, whom I worked with often.

"Heading out?" Dressed in her blue scrubs and white coat, most of her tattoos were hidden from view. The stethoscope around her neck hid some of the ink that appeared out of her deep V-neck.

"Yeah." I pulled on my leather jacket. "If I don't leave now, I'll be here forever." I set the charts next to her computer, signing out my remaining patients to her care. I didn't even bother doing my dictations like usual because I was fried.

"Alright, have a good night." Ever since Pepper had

confronted her outside the airport, our relationship had been professional. She only spoke to me if it was work-related. Sometimes she asked what was being served in the cafeteria. But that was the extent of it. If she knew Pepper and I weren't together, I suspected she would be playing a different tune.

I'd be lying if I said I didn't find her attractive. I'd also be lying if I said I wasn't extremely hard up. The last time I got laid was in Kenya. I missed sex. But sex with someone else wouldn't be fulfilling. Pepper was the only woman I wanted to screw. It would be amazing, just the way it used to be.

That's what I wanted.

So I kept holding out for it.

It bothered me that she was sleeping with Brutus, but I tried not to think about it. I always felt sick to my stomach whenever I did. "Bye, Layla." I pulled my satchel over my shoulder and walked out the rear entrance. My truck was in the parking lot, so I walked into the cold evening air and moved down the line of cars until I saw my vehicle under the lamppost.

I stopped when I spotted a group of men leaning against the bed of my truck.

In the center was Brutus, dressed in his dark jeans and black blazer. His eyes locked on me, and an evil sneer spread across his face, like he'd been waiting hours out in the cold for me to emerge under the light, exhausted from my fourteen-hour shift saving people's lives.

I never turned down a fight, even when I was tired and outnumbered. There was still time to turn around and run, but that wasn't my style—especially when Brutus was my opponent. I kept walking.

Brutus righted himself then sauntered toward me, his shoulders relaxed like he'd already won the battle about the take place. Four large men were behind him, looking like bouncers doing security inside a club. "You look like shit."

"That's what happens after a long day of work...not that you would understand." I stood a few feet in front of him and pulled my satchel off my shoulder. I let it fall to the ground beside me, ready for the fight about to take place. It was cheap of him to catch me off guard after work, but at least we could settle this once and for all.

His eyes flashed with menace. "I warned you not to piss me off."

"I told you I don't want your money."

When he came closer to me, his men crowded around him. "Why didn't you tell her?"

I had no idea what Pepper saw in this guy. He didn't possess an ounce of honor. He was slimy like a snake. "Because I thought you'd be man enough to tell her yourself."

His eyes narrowed. "One more chance, Finn. Disappear or suffer. What's it going to be?" He crossed his arms over his chest.

"I'd love the chance to break that pretty-boy face." I stripped off my jacket and tossed it on the ground. "If you think you're ever gonna get rid of me, you're wasting your time. I love her and she loves me. You're only borrowing her for the time being."

"If you really loved her that much, you wouldn't have left. All I see is a pathetic guy who stalks his ex-girlfriend and makes her miserable."

My hands balled into fists.

"If you won't walk away, I'll make you walk away." He gave a slight nod, an indication to his men.

The four of them started to move forward.

"Wow, you're that much of a pussy?" I took a step back, and my fists came up automatically, prepared for a fight. "Won't even fight me like a man?"

He leaned against the bed of my truck and got comfortable. He crossed his ankles and grinned. "I'd rather watch."

The four men converged on me, all much bigger than I was. I

had more experience in combat and could stay calm and conserve my energy to survive, but I knew I couldn't outmatch this many guys, maybe two at the most.

My other option was to run.

But I'd rather break every bone in my body than cave.

Fists started to fly, and I did my best to keep moving, to evade their hits and stop my limbs from being snatched. But that only lasted a few seconds. Two of the men grabbed both of my arms then kicked my knees out from underneath me, making me fall to the concrete.

"Last chance, Finn." Brutus was enjoying his victory, grinning wider than I'd ever seen.

These men would beat my face until my features were indistinguishable. I'd probably have broken bones and a long recovery. If they hit me in the wrong place too many times, I could even die. But I refused to give him what he wanted. I refused to cave to this psychopath. I refused to let him win. "There are cameras everywhere. All I have to do is press charges and take you to court."

"Then do it," he said. "Be a rat."

My honor meant too much to me. Being a snitch was one of the worst things you could be. I could tell Pepper what happened tonight, but I wanted her to leave Brutus and be with me because she finally trusted me, not because I used this night to sabotage her relationship. All of these things were happening because I provoked them—so it was all my fault. "You'll regret this, Brutus."

He nodded to his men again. "I don't think I will."

MY EYES WERE CLOSED as I lay on the frozen asphalt. The distant sound of traffic reached to my ears, along with the sound of an ambulance. As I came into consciousness, the agonizing pain hit me so hard. Every time I tried to breathe, it hurt. Blood caked my face and stained my scrubs. When the panic set in, I tried to breathe harder—but it just hurt more.

I was in worse shape than I thought.

I could barely remember what happened after the first few punches.

My hands pressed into the concrete to lift my body—but I couldn't even do that.

Too weak.

"Finn?" Layla's hysterical voice shrieked into the night when she found me. Her shift ended a few hours after mine, so I must have been lying there for a couple of hours. "Oh my god!" Her feet echoed against the pavement as she ran toward me then kneeled over me. "What the hell happened?" She turned my face toward her so she could get a better look at me.

I opened my eyes, but everything was blurry.

"Shit. Let me get the EMTs. I'll be right back, okay? You're going to be alright."

I'd said those same words to so many people before—then I watched them die.

Was she saying the same thing to me? "Tell Pepper I love her, okay?" It hurt my chest to get those words out, but I forced them from my lungs. "Please tell her that for me..." My eyes closed again because I couldn't keep them open.

"Just rest, Finn." She turned my face back against the asphalt. "Just stay awake. I'll be right back."

I tried to stay awake but couldn't. I slipped back into the darkness...and assumed I would never emerge.

19

COLTON

I'D JUST FINISHED A LOAD OF DISHES AND LAUNDRY, SO NOW I GOT to sit on the couch and watch *Family Feud* before bedtime. My ass had just touched the cushion when my phone started to ring. It was a number I didn't recognize, so there was a good chance it was just spam.

But it was almost midnight, so that seemed unlikely.

That was the only reason I answered. "This is Colton." I twisted off the cap on my beer and took a drink.

"Colton Burke?" A hysterical woman was on the other line.

"Uh, yeah. Who's this?"

"Finn's brother, right? I remember he said your name was Colton."

This conversation was only getting weirder. "Yeah...what's this about?"

"God, I don't know how to tell you this...but Finn is in the ER right now. I walked to my car in the parking lot and found him on the ground. A group of guys jumped him and messed him up pretty badly."

I had a million questions, but they all faded away when I heard the final thing she said. "Is he okay?"

"Like I said, he's in bad condition. He'll live, but he has a lot of injuries. Blood loss, two broken ribs, lacerations everywhere... He's in a lot of pain. This is Layla, by the way. He finished his shift hours before mine, so he must have been in the parking lot for a while."

"Jesus..." I got to my feet and stared blankly at the TV, ignoring Steve Harvey as he made another joke. I gripped the side of my skull as my heart started to pound with adrenaline. "Jesus Christ, I'll be down there right away. Tell him I'm coming. I'll be there as soon as I can." I left the beer on the coffee table and grabbed my keys and wallet from the counter.

"He's not awake right now, but if he does open his eyes, I'll tell him."

"Thanks." I hung up then sprinted out of the apartment. I moved to Pepper's door and banged my fists hard against the wood because I didn't want to waste any time. There was no sound on the other side, not the sound of footsteps or her TV. "Pepper?"

No answer.

She must be with Brutus.

I didn't have time to call her, so I left and got to the hospital as soon as I could.

I BURST into the room and found my brother lying there, broken. He was the strongest man I'd ever known, but he looked so lifeless in that bed, so small. His eyes were closed, but they were so swollen and purple it didn't seem like he could open them anyway. He appeared to be asleep. An IV was in his arm, and the monitor beeped as his vitals were taken repeatedly.

Layla sat in the chair, still in her scrubs. She watched Finn with a tear-stained face, her heart on her sleeve.

I slowly crept to the bed and felt the tears start all the way in my chest. "Shit..." His face was so bloody, I wouldn't have even recognized him. He was bruised everywhere, along his shoulders and down his arms. I couldn't see the rest of him because his skin was covered by the gown and the sheets, but I imagined he didn't look much better there.

I moved to the edge of the bed and placed my hand on his. "Finn, it's Colton. I'm right here, alright?" Even if he couldn't hear me, I didn't care. I wanted him to know I was there, that I was heartbroken over this. "What happened?" I turned to Layla for an explanation.

She shook her head. "The police are looking at the footage and trying to figure out what happened. I'd assumed he was mugged...but he still has his wallet. So I don't really know what happened."

Finn was the strongest man ever, so he must have been outnumbered. Otherwise, this never would have happened. "He'll be alright?"

She nodded. "It'll take a while for his ribs to heal, along with his other injuries, but the scans show no internal bleeding. He took a serious beating, but his core is so strong that it seemed to spare him serious damage."

I guess all those hours at the gym paid off. "Fuck...I can't believe this." I knew I should call my parents and tell them what happened. And I should also call Pepper...even though it would rip her heart into a million pieces. I wanted to spare all of them of this terrible pain...but I knew I couldn't.

AN HOUR LATER, Finn woke up.

His eyes opened, and he looked straight at me. My hand was on top of his, and he moved his fingers in response.

I was glad to see him awake, but I wished he would keep resting. "Hey, how are you feeling?" Layla left once I was here, knowing he should be with just his family right now.

He cleared his throat and sighed, like he was battling the agony.

"You want me to get the nurse?"

When he spoke, his voice was raspy. "No."

I scooted closer to his bedside, wanting to feel my brother alive and well under my fingertips. "Let me know if you need anything. I can get you anything you need." I didn't know what to do in situations like this. I wanted to make it better, but I didn't know how. I'd never been confronted with something like this. It was ironic that Finn had served in the military for a decade without getting a scratch...but walking to his car after work mutilated his body.

"What's going on?" As usual, he became pragmatic. He didn't complain about the pain or try to get out of bed.

"The doctor said you have a couple of broken ribs and severe swelling all over your body. Lots of bruises and cuts. But you don't have any serious injuries that require surgery. You're going to be okay."

He closed his eyes and released a grateful sigh.

"The doctor said you can go home in the morning. They're just watching you for the right. He wrote you a prescription for a lot of serious pain medications, so you'll be comfortable while you heal. And obviously, you'll need to take at least a month off work."

He opened his eyes again, not saying a word.

"Do you remember anything that happened?" Was his attacker someone he knew? A patient who was displeased with his level of care?

He just shook his head. "No...not really." He turned his head and looked at me again. "Where's Pepper?"

I figured he would ask that. "She's on her way. I'll wait to tell Mom and Dad until the morning. They'll just freak out and be here all night... I assumed you wouldn't want that."

He shook his head. "No."

I patted his hand. "You're going to be alright, and that's all that matters."

"Thanks, Colt." He didn't seem to be in a mood to talk, so he sat there quietly.

I didn't ask any more questions.

A knock sounded on the door, and the police entered. "Finn Burke? I'm Officer Hewitt. We wanted to talk to you about the assault that took place here in the parking lot." They helped themselves into the room and approached his bedside, dressed in their deep blue uniforms with their guns on their hips.

Finn turned to me. "Can you excuse us for a moment?"

"You want me to leave?" I asked blankly.

"You don't want to hear this, Colt," he said quietly. "Just give us some privacy."

I wanted to argue, but it seemed insensitive to argue with a man in so much pain. So I nodded my head and stepped out.

20

PEPPER

I WAS CRYING BEFORE I BURST INTO THE HOSPITAL ROOM.

A man who carried himself with such strength had been reduced to a broken body in a bed. A veteran who had spent the previous twelve hours saving lives had almost had his taken away from him. Seeing someone so respectable stripped down like that was a difficult pill to swallow.

He was awake when I walked inside, his face swollen from all the injuries he'd sustained. I couldn't see the rest of his body, but it was obvious he was injured everywhere. My eyes locked on his, and I drifted to his bed, the pain in my body matching the pain he felt in his.

Colton silently excused himself from the room because he knew we needed privacy.

I took his vacated seat at the bedside and grabbed his hand. "Colton told me you're okay...but are you okay?" Tears kept falling down my cheeks even though I tried to stop myself from crying. The weight of moisture in my eyes was too heavy, and they cascaded down my cheeks.

Despite the swelling and discoloration of his face, he gave me a slight smile. "Baby, don't cry for me..." His fingers interlocked with mine, and he squeezed my hand. "I'm alright." His eyes softened as he looked at me, watching me sob over his crippled figure.

"Who did this to you...?" Who would assault a doctor walking to his car at night? Who would do such a terrible thing?

"A group of guys. I don't know who they were."

"And they just attacked you?"

He shrugged. "Maybe one of them was a former patient...I don't know. Doesn't matter."

"But it does matter."

"The doctor said I'm going to be alright. Just some broken ribs and a few bruises. No big deal."

"It is a big deal, Finn." I squeezed his hand and felt the tears begin once again. When I got the call, I had been with Brutus at his penthouse. I dropped everything I was doing and left his place. He was smart enough not to try to come with me. "You don't deserve this... You're such a good person."

"Bad things happen to good people...they usually happen to good people." He lifted his hand and wiped the tears from my cheeks, even when he winced as he did it. "I like watching you cry over me. But I don't want you to be in pain."

"How can I not be?"

"I'm pretty strong, baby. I'll get through it."

He'd called me baby again, but this time, I didn't object to it. I was so grateful he was still on this earth, I didn't care what he called me. The world was a better place with him in it. I squeezed his hand a little harder because I didn't want him ever to slip away. "I'm glad it wasn't worse..."

His fingers gently caressed my hand, like he was comforting me instead of the other way around.

"Do you get to go home?"

"In the morning."

"How long are you off work?"

"At least a month."

Finn wouldn't take any time off work if he didn't have to. That meant his injuries were pretty painful. "I'll take care of you. I'm not working as many hours at the store, so I have the time."

Instead of rejecting my offer, he smiled. "That sounds nice."

"You'd let me?"

"Definitely. Who doesn't want a sexy nurse to take care of them?" Finn always made a joke about everything, even the most serious situations.

But it was one of the things I loved about him. "Where're your Mom and Dad?"

"Colton wanted to wait until the morning. You know how my parents are. No reason to wake them up just to have a heart attack."

"Yes, your mom will definitely be upset."

He rolled his eyes. "She overreacts."

"I don't think she could overreact to this."

"Which is why I want to tell her even less," he said with a slight smile. "I know she just cares, but I hate worrying her. The entire time I was in the service, she was terrified. Now her worst nightmares came true in her own backyard. She'll think I'm never safe."

He'd been all over the world, in the most dangerous countries, but the worst thing that had ever happened to him occurred in Seattle, a fairly safe metropolitan area. "I guess we really never are safe."

"Which is why I like it when you borrow Soldier. He's a good protector. If he'd been there, he would have eaten all of those guys."

"Do you think the police will figure out who it was? There have to be cameras in the parking lot."

He shrugged. "I don't think it matters at this point. The

police will continue the investigation and make their own decisions about it."

"But they'll ask you if you want to press charges."

It was the first time he pulled his gaze away. "I have more important things to worry about than pressing charges against some thugs." His fingers continued to caress mine. "So, were you serious about taking care of me?"

"Of course I was..." He wasn't my problem, not after he'd left me, but I wanted him to make a full recovery. I wanted to help him get back on his feet and be strong again. I wanted to take care of him every day. It didn't feel like a burden at all.

He smiled through the discoloration of his face. "Good. Because Soldier is a great service dog...but not a great caretaker."

AFTER HIS MOTHER sobbed into his shoulder and his dad held his hand, his parents calmed down and appreciated the fact that Finn wasn't worse off. His stomach was wrapped in gauze to support his broken ribs, and he was discharged with enough pain medications to last him through the month.

He managed to walk on his own, but at a very slow pace. He grimaced from time to time, the pain from his ribs making it difficult for him to move fluidly. But when offered a wheelchair, he turned down the offer like he was offended. He got into the truck on his own, and we headed to his place while I picked up Soldier on the way.

Finn made it into the house in the same scrubs he'd wore the night he was attacked. The clothes were covered in dried blood, and it was everywhere. It soaked into so much of his clothing that it seemed like his scrubs had been originally red instead of blue. He also had his satchel with him, which the men had left behind.

Which was odd.

Soldier understood Finn was injured, so he stuck to his side and whined, like he wanted to help in some way.

Colton came in with the medications and instructions for Finn's care. He placed Finn's satchel on the counter. "I'm gonna make some lunch. How do tacos sound?"

"I'm not hungry." Finn took a seat at the dining table, slowly lowering himself and making a quiet grunt once his body was still.

I knew Finn had impeccable hygiene, so he wouldn't sit in his kitchen in bloody scrubs. He would normally strip off his clothing right away and jump into the shower. He was clearly struggling with the pain but didn't want to admit it out loud.

That broke my heart. "Colton, make some anyway. Finn might get his appetite back, and if he doesn't, we'll have leftovers." He'd already started his pain medication, and losing his appetite was one of the side effects.

Finn continued to sit there, breathing through the pain.

"Need some help?" I asked, trying to take the attention off Finn so he wouldn't be embarrassed.

"I don't think so," Colton said. "I already preheated the oven, and I'll sauté the meat in a second."

"You can get me a beer," Finn said.

I ignored him. "How about we get you out of those clothes and into a shower?"

He eyed the stairs like the task was daunting. "Sure. But I think I'm going to need some help, Colton..."

"Sure thing." Colton left the pan on the stove and helped him out of the chair. While holding most of his brother's weight, he got him up the stairs and into his bedroom.

I came behind.

Finn sat on the bed, rubbing his ribs where they were broken. "Thanks, man. I can take the rest from here." Finn would never ask for help unless he absolutely needed it, so the carefree attitude he gave off was just a cover-up of the agony he felt inside.

I got the shower started and set up the towels. When I returned to his bedroom, his bottoms were on the floor because he'd untied the drawstrings, but the rest of his clothes were still on.

I refused to look at the bulge in the front since that was inappropriate. "Let me help you." I grabbed his shirt and slowly lifted it up his body. When I got to the top, he finally lifted his arms above his head long enough for me to get the material off.

He lowered his arms again, grimacing from the stretch.

I saw the bruising across his abdomen as it peeked out from under the gauze wrapping. He looked mutilated.

"It's not as bad as it looks." It was a lie—an obvious one. He said it just to make me feel better.

I wanted to cry again, but I kept my emotions in check. Seeing me pity him would only make him pity himself. "Can you do your boxers?"

He rubbed his ribs. "I don't think I can bend over that way."

I looked into his eyes and realized I was about to strip him down until he was naked. I hadn't seen him in just his skin for a long time. I was seeing Brutus, so I felt like this crossed a line. "Maybe Colton should help you..."

"I'd rather do it myself than let Colton see my junk. But if you don't want to, it's fine." He grabbed the waistband of his boxers and prepared to bend over.

"No." I grabbed his hands and steadied them. "I can help you." I grabbed the top of his shorts and pulled them down, closing my eyes as I got to my knees so he could step out of the material.

"Baby, you've seen me a hundred times."

"But still...I want to respect your privacy." I got to my feet again and kept my gaze on his face.

"We both know I don't want you to respect my privacy." He started to walk into the bathroom, moving slowly because his body was too sore to move the way his mind wanted him to.

I opened the sliding door for him so he could get inside easier.

"You want to join me?" He stepped under the water inside the shower we'd shared so many times. He flashed me his charming smile as his hair became damp.

"I'm here to take care of you—not sleep with you." My motivation to be there was completely out of love, loyalty, and even friendship. To ask such a thing was slightly offensive. How could I be aroused when he was so injured? How could I hop in the shower with him when I was still with another man? Maybe he was joking, and maybe he wasn't. Either way, I didn't like it.

His smile faltered. "I'm sorry. That was a stupid thing to say."

I pointed to the towel on the rack. "I'll wait in your bedroom until you're done...just in case you need help."

AFTER HE DRIED OFF, I replaced the gauze around his chest as he instructed and got him into his pajamas so he could get into bed. I tucked him in and pulled the sheets to his chest.

Once he was lying still, he released the breath he was holding, as if he were relieved that the pain from his movements had stopped. He closed his eyes for a moment, his hands lying by his sides.

I sat beside him and ran my fingers through his hair. "Hungry? I'm sure Colton is finished with dinner."

"No thanks." He kept his eyes closed. "My doctor wrote me a

prescription for Vicodin. Could you bring a tablet up with some water?"

I didn't know anything about medications, but I knew Vicodin was a major pain killer, one of the biggest you could take. If he was asking for it, then he was suffering in a world of pain, unable to do anything but lie there and take it. "Yeah... sure." I pulled my fingers out of his hair and left his bedroom, keeping the tears back long enough to get into the hallway.

By the time I made it downstairs, tears streaked down my cheeks.

Colton didn't have tears the way I did, but his eyes were filled with the same pain. "Are you alright?"

I looked through the prescriptions until I found the right bottle. "It's just so hard to see him like this. He's trying to put on a brave face for us, but I can tell he's suffering so much..." It killed me inside that this had happened to him. He didn't deserve this kind of treatment, not when he made sacrifices for strangers all the time. "I wish I could take all of his pain for him."

"I know..." The tacos were ready to be eaten, but it seemed like no one had an appetite. "It's not right."

"What if something worse happened to him?" I leaned against the counter and crossed my arms over my chest. "What if...?" I didn't want to say the words out loud, so I refused to finish the sentence. "I couldn't live without him. I couldn't go on if we lost him... I love him so much." I cupped my mouth with my hand to stifle my tears so Finn wouldn't be able to hear them up the stairs.

Colton wrapped his arms around me and hugged me in the kitchen. "I know...but thankfully that didn't happen."

Soldier walked out of the kitchen and ran up the stairs, his collar making a gentle noise as he made it all the way to Finn's room. He was probably going to lie in a ball right at his side, to comfort him the way he comforted me.

Colton rubbed my back. "The important thing is, Finn is going to be alright. We need to focus on that and remember that this is just going to be a terrible memory someday. Finn will get through this. He's the toughest guy I know."

"I know he will…" I let my tears soak into his t-shirt. "But it still hurts so much…"

I SAT at his bedside and watched him sleep. After he took his painkillers, he finally relaxed enough to drift off. He didn't have dinner, but since he was in so much pain, I didn't force him to eat.

Soldier lay beside him, opening his eyes once in a while to check on Finn.

I considered spending the night, but I didn't want to stay on the couch. I had to open the shop in the morning and work a few hours before I came back over here in the afternoon. I left a plate of tacos for him in the fridge so all he had to do was heat it up when he woke in the morning. There were also instructions on what pills he was supposed to take.

I didn't want to wake him to say goodbye, so I left his bedside and headed to the door.

"Baby?" His deep voice was raspy, like he was half asleep.

I turned around and saw him open his eyes slightly, his body still rigid. I slowly came back to the bed. "Go back to sleep. You need to rest." My fingers moved into his hairline, and I stroked his dark strands, trying to make him doze off again.

He kept his eyes open. "Are you sleeping here?"

"Actually…I was going to go home. But I'll be here around

noon tomorrow. I just have a few things to do at the shop. There are tacos in the fridge, so all you have to do is heat them up."

"You can always stay here…"

"I don't want to sleep on the couch. It hurts my neck…"

"You can always sleep in here." He turned to see Soldier beside him. "You know, if the dog will move over."

Helping him get into the shower was already bad enough. I couldn't sleep here…even though I would love to stay by his side through the entire night. I wanted to be there if he needed anything, to make sure he didn't hurt himself. "You know I can't…"

His eyes fell in disappointment. "Yeah…I understand." He said the right words, but judging from the expression in his eyes, he didn't mean them. "I'll be alright. I've got my dog right here." He patted Soldier.

I was so tempted to stay, I almost changed my mind. That bed never looked more comfortable. I missed sleeping in between Finn and Soldier, in between the two men in my life. Now that I'd almost lost Finn for good, I didn't want to let him slip through my fingers again. I didn't want to waste another moment being apart.

But then logic took over—and it reminded me of all the reasons we weren't together in the first place. "Call me if you need anything."

"Alright. How about you take my truck? I won't be using it anyway."

"Are you sure?"

He nodded. "It'd be a lot easier for you to get dog food for Soldier, get groceries, and do whatever else you need."

"Alright…good night."

"Good night." He stared at me with those blue eyes, like seeing me leave his house was almost too painful to watch. I'd return in the morning, but that wasn't quick enough. The longing and affection were two beacons in those glorious eyes.

"Yeah...good night."

———

WHEN I GOT HOME, I called Brutus. I knew he didn't like Finn, but he probably wanted an update anyway.

"Hey," he said when he answered. "Long day?"

"Yeah...very long."

"So...is he gonna be alright?"

"Yeah. He's beaten up pretty badly and in a lot of pain, but he'll recover. It'll take some time, but he'll get there."

"Good...any idea what happened?"

"No. Finn said they were just some random thugs."

Brutus was silent for a while. "Well, at least no serious harm was done."

"Yeah...but it hurts so much to see him like that. He's such a good man. He doesn't deserve that."

"It's not retribution for what he did to you?"

The question was so ridiculous, I didn't know what to say. "Absolutely not. He may have broken my heart, but he traveled to a third world country to help complete strangers. Regardless of what he does to me, that man sacrifices everything for the good of mankind. I wish I could take his place so he doesn't have to go through this..."

Brutus sighed into the phone. "He's a strong guy. He'll get through it."

"Yeah...I just wish he didn't have to."

After a long pause, he spoke again. "Want to have dinner with me tomorrow night?"

The last thing I wanted to do was have fun. I wouldn't be able to enjoy myself because all I could think about was Finn.

"I'm going to be taking care of Finn a lot for a while... I don't think I'll have time."

"Why is it your responsibility?"

"It's not, but Colton works all day—"

"He's off by five."

"I'm sure we'll take turns. But for now, I want to be there for him. I know we have a past, but he's still important to me..." I understood why my new boyfriend didn't appreciate me spending time with my old boyfriend, but right now, I didn't care.

"Look, I'll be supportive for a few weeks. But after that...I won't be."

"What's that supposed to mean?"

He sighed into the phone. "He's been a huge thorn in this relationship since he returned to Seattle. I can only put up with so much, Pepper. If this keeps going on, you're going to have to choose—me or him."

That comment only angered me. "At game night, I told him off and asked him to leave the party. I've held my ground with him before. Do you not understand that he could have died last night? He was in the parking lot for hours before someone found him. If he had internal bleeding, he would have died."

"I get that," he said gently. "But it didn't. The guy is gonna make a full recovery—"

"But he needs help getting there. He helps so many people, and now he's the one who needs help...and I'm happy to give it."

21

FINN

Pepper went to the grocery store, and Colton stopped by the house to check on me.

"Mom made you some cookies and muffins." He carried the basket to the kitchen table. "Want one?"

I was sitting on the couch in my sweatpants with the gauze tight around my torso. "That woman knows I don't eat cookies or muffins..."

He chuckled. "She thinks we're still kids."

I felt closer to old age than adolescence at this point in my life. "How's Pepper doing?"

"What do you mean?" Colton moved to the back of the other couch and looked at me.

"With this whole thing...I can tell it's been hard for her."

"Yeah...she's pretty devastated. I think she's taking it the hardest."

That woman loved me. I saw it written all over her face. I saw the regret in her eyes every night she left. She wanted to crawl into that bed and never let me go. She wanted to love me with everything that she had—she just wasn't there yet. "I'm going to be okay, Colton."

"I know. She knows that too. But it's still hard for her…"

I could see it in her eyes every time she looked at me. She wanted to take all of my pain and feel it herself just to spare me. Her love was so obvious that it filled the area around her, like a halo of emotions.

Soldier finished eating then hopped onto the couch beside me, taking his usual spot at my side. He'd been my companion through the ordeal, caring about me more than playing with his toys or going on a walk. Normally, he grabbed his leash and brought it to me when he was restless, but he seemed to understand I was in no condition to resume our old lifestyle. "Colton, I need to ask you for a favor."

"Anything. What is it?"

That was the answer I was looking for. "I need you to do something for me—no questions asked."

Now his eyebrows furrowed.

"You can't ask me about it ever. And you can't tell Pepper about this either. Do we have a deal?"

"Uh…can you tell me what it is first?"

"Nope."

"Hmm…"

"Come on, man. I need this."

Colton had more questions written on his face, but he let his curiosity slide. "Alright…what is it?"

"I need to borrow your phone for ten minutes. Wait in the front yard until the ten minutes are up."

"Wait, why do you need to borrow my—"

"No questions asked, Colton."

He shut his mouth then dug his phone out of his pocket. He placed it on the couch beside me then headed to the entryway. "Alright…you've got ten minutes." He opened the front door then disappeared.

I waited a minute before I scrolled through the phone and

found Brutus's number. I preferred to confront him in person, but since I could barely walk and Pepper had my truck, I couldn't make that happen. This was the next best thing.

He answered. "Hey, Colton. Sorry to hear about your brother."

I almost laughed into the phone. "Wow...you're a great liar. Not a good quality for a man to have."

He turned silent, recognizing my voice right away.

"You didn't think your plan all the way through. Now Pepper is stuck to my side day and night. The thought of losing me is only making her realize how much she needs me. I guess I should be thanking you. Without you, this wouldn't be possible."

Brutus was caught off guard, so he had no idea what to say. He just got his ass handed to him, and there was no clever response he could make.

"I don't have any regrets. But I think you do."

22

PEPPER

I WAS ONLY WORKING HALF DAYS AT THE SHOP NOW, SO I STOPPED by my apartment and did a little laundry before I headed to Finn's. Soldier was still a young dog with a lot of vitality, so I took him on a long walk to keep him healthy as soon as I walked in the door of Finn's place.

Finn was sitting on the couch in his sweatpants with the gauze wrapped around his waist when we returned. "How was your day?"

I walked into the living room and removed Soldier's leash from his collar. "Good. The store was busy all day, so my employees weren't bored. And Soldier really enjoyed his walk. He was tugging me along the entire time." Walking in the door and talking about my day only reminded me of our old lives. We used to do this every day, kiss each other, then exchange stories.

"Soldier was getting restless, so I'm glad he got some fresh air."

I moved into the kitchen and examined the food in the fridge. "What are you in the mood for?"

"It doesn't matter to me. I'm not that hungry." He almost never had an appetite, probably because he was sedentary and not burning calories the way he used to. Coupled with his medication, he just didn't have an appetite.

"You need to eat more, Finn."

"I can't force myself to have an appetite, baby."

I stared at the chicken breasts and asparagus in the fridge, letting that nickname wash over me. I felt like I'd ventured back in time, living in a much happier moment. No other man ever called me that, and if they did, it wouldn't have sounded so good. I pulled out the meat and vegetables and decided to cook a plain dinner because that's what he would usually eat. "Well, I'm making dinner, and you're eating it."

"Whatever you say, baby." The TV was on, but he hadn't taken his eyes off me since I'd walked in the door.

I set everything on the counter and tried to ignore that hot stare. He could make me feel his presence right up against my side, like his lips were almost pressed to my shoulder. It was an unnatural ability he had, to touch me without actually laying a hand on me.

"I appreciate you doing so much for me, but if you want to take the night off with Brutus, I understand. I can't be the center of your universe, and I can always call Colton or my parents if I really need something."

My response was automatic. "No, I want to be here." I knew it was how I really felt because I didn't think twice before saying those words. "You're the kind of person that won't ask for help even if you need it, so long as I'm here, you never have to ask." I kept my eyes down and washed the asparagus before dropping it on the cutting board. After I rinsed the chicken, I added salt and pepper for taste and began cooking.

Finn continued to watch me, far more fascinated with me than the TV.

I kept my eyes down and tried to avoid his look, doing the best I could to keep an invisible distance between us. My heart was still locked inside a solid cage, but with every passing day, the lock came a little looser.

If I weren't careful, that door would swing wide open—and let him in.

WE WATCHED TV together on the couches. I was on one side of the room, while he was on the other.

We watched the basketball game together, both rooting for the same team. Since he couldn't drink while he was on his medications, he was limited to water...which he wasn't happy about.

Soldier was usually stuck to my side like glue, but since Finn was hurt, he chose to lay his head on his thigh.

The game ended at almost ten in the evening, so it was time for bed.

Finn rose to his feet and made his way to the stairs, moving slowly.

"You need help?"

"I'm too heavy for you, baby. I can manage." He gripped the banister and pulled himself up as he moved to the second floor of the house.

Soldier sat at the bottom of the stairs and waited until Finn was in the bedroom before he followed.

I grabbed a glass of water and some of his pills before I joined him.

Finn was in bed, his eyes closed because the journey to his bed was trying.

"You know, we could put a bed downstairs so it's easier for you."

"No. I need some exercise. Plus, if I don't use those muscles, they'll atrophy."

"Yeah, but it's only been a week. Don't push it." I sat at the edge of his bed and placed the glass of water down along with the pill.

He snatched it up the second I put it down and swallowed it dry, like he couldn't get it into his system quick enough.

That meant he was still in a lot of pain. "Is there anything I can do?"

"More than you've already done?" he asked incredulously. "No."

My fingers moved into his short strands, and I rubbed his head gently, doing my best to get him to relax. "It'll be over eventually. Just try to stay positive."

"I hope the pain ends soon. I've never broken a bone before, so this is new."

"You're young so you'll heal quicker."

"I guess I do have that on my side." He turned his head and looked at me straight on as I continued to massage his scalp. Wordlessly, he stared at me, like the connection between us was enough entertainment.

The bedroom was dark since he was about to go to bed, but there was enough light for us to see each other.

His arm moved to my thigh, where his fingers rested against my jeans. He gripped me possessively, like he wanted to touch me as I touched him.

"I wish I could take all this pain for you..." I didn't want to carry the burden just because he was a good man. I wanted to do it because it caused me so much pain to see him like this, to see him struggle to walk and breathe. A man in his prime had been cut down so easily...and it wasn't right.

"I know you do." He squeezed my thigh. "But I would never want you to. I'd rather suffer a million times than let you experience any pain... You have no idea how much I mean that."

My hand trailed down his neck until it rested against his

chest, settling on his strong heartbeat. I looked at the man I loved and felt the exact same feelings I used to feel on a daily basis. I wanted to hold him and never let go. I wanted to make love to him because he meant so much to me, not just because I was as attracted to him as I ever was. I wanted to kiss him so he could feel my love through my embrace. Brutus was everything I was looking for in a partner, but not once did I ever feel that way about him.

Not the way I felt about Finn.

I continued to feel his heartbeat thump against his chest. Slow and steady, it tapped against my hand, telling me he was still as strong as a horse. If something had gone wrong, I could have lost this heartbeat forever.

He'd hurt me so much, but losing him would have hurt even more.

Now I wondered if I should give him another chance, if I should risk getting my heart broken again. He was already a proven flight risk...but maybe he'd changed. I wanted to believe he'd changed.

As if he could read my thoughts, he addressed exactly what I was thinking. "I'd rather live the rest of my life like this than spend it without you." His hand moved to mine, and he squeezed it. "I see the way you look at me, the way you love me. You see the way I look at you. Neither one of us will ever look at someone else that way. I know this is where I belong...and I'm never going to leave. And I know you believe me..."

It was late in the evening when I asked Brutus if I could stop by.

I took the elevator directly into his living room and saw him standing there in just his sweatpants. He was a beautiful man with a beautiful body. I wasn't entirely sure how I'd managed to win the affection of two gorgeous men.

He seemed to assume I was there for sex, that this was a booty-call situation. He walked up to me and slid his hand into my hair as he leaned in to kiss me.

I turned my cheek away instinctively. "Actually, I wanted to talk..."

He pulled away, his hand coming down slowly. His eyes narrowed with hostility as he studied the trepidation on my face. It only took a few heartbeats for him to figure out exactly why I'd come that night. "Don't be stupid, Pepper."

"I think I have to be..."

"He's not gonna change. People don't change."

For some reason, I believed that he had.

"Don't let him get inside your head. Don't let his injuries twist your mind. You were fine before all of this happened—"

"That's exactly why I feel this way. Because if I'd lost him...I wouldn't have survived. Seeing him like that made me realize how much I still love him, how much my heart beats for him. I'm sorry, Brutus. You're a great guy. I wouldn't change anything about you. But...I just don't feel that way about you. With Finn... I feel things I can't even explain."

"That's not necessarily a good thing. Relationships based on emotion always burn out like rockets into space."

"I know...but I think we're different."

He bowed his head and rubbed the back of his neck.

"I think he's changed. And even if he hasn't, I'm willing to take that risk. Because the idea of losing him someday terrifies me. I want to spend every day with him as long as I can...before something really serious happens. You just never know when your time is up. What if his time was up last week? I would have regretted so much..."

"Fuck, this is a nightmare." He dragged his hand across his jaw, his eyes steaming like boiling water.

I excused his outburst because I knew he was hurt. "I'm sorry, Brutus. I am."

He wouldn't look at me. "I think this could go somewhere, Pepper. I'm looking for an easy relationship like this. I'm looking for a good woman to give me a family, someone who doesn't care about my money."

"And you will. But you should also fall in love. I know you're scared... I was too. But relationships are meant to have love... otherwise, they just don't work. You deserve to keep looking until you find the right woman, the woman who will love you the way you want. Don't give up on that."

"I'm sorry, Pepper. I just don't think that exists."

"I think it does. And I think you'll find her."

He sighed as he looked at the ground.

"I'm sorry...I wish I could make this easier."

He raised his head to look at me. "I think you're making a mistake."

"Maybe...but I have to make it anyway." I didn't know what it was about Finn that kept making me come back, that made me believe. But we had something special I couldn't replicate with another man. "Good luck." I wanted to move into his chest and hug him, but he seemed too upset for that.

He refused to look at me.

"I know you'll find someone you deserve...someday."

23

COLTON

I WAS DEAD ASLEEP WHEN MY PHONE RANG ON MY NIGHTSTAND.

"Ugh..." I squinted my eyes and stared at the clock on my nightstand, barely making out the time. It looked like it was midnight—and I had a big meeting in the morning. But since it might be Finn asking for help, I answered. "Everything alright?"

"I'm at your front door. Can you let me in?" It was Pepper.

"Can we talk in the morning?"

"We could...but I want to talk now."

"Ugh...alright." I hung up the phone and walked to the front door. I opened the door, my eyes still half closed, and then walked back to bed. I dove back into my sheets and got comfortable.

Pepper joined me, dressed in her pajama shorts and a tank top without a bra. She stuck to her side of the queen mattress.

"So, what's up?" I faced her with my head on the pillow, seeing her clean face without makeup. It was late in the evening and she was usually in bed hours before now, but she seemed wide awake. "Finn alright?"

"Yeah, he's fine," she said quickly. "It's not about him."

"Something happen with Brutus?"

"Yeah...I broke up with him."

I was so tired just seconds ago, but now I was wide awake. "Why?"

She was quiet as she tried to find the right words to express herself. "So many reasons...but I guess Finn is the only reason I care about."

My brother's dream had just come true. "You're going to take him back?"

"No...I just couldn't keep seeing Brutus. Every time I'm around Finn, I just feel so much...and it makes me realize I'll never feel that way about Brutus. It makes me realize I want to feel that way...that I want to believe Finn is here to stay this time."

"I think he is."

"It's just getting harder and harder to be around him, to not tell him I love him whenever it pops into my head. And almost losing him made me realize how much I love him...and how much I would regret not being together."

"He's gonna be so happy, Pepper. The guy has been so miserable without you."

"I know...but he can't know."

I stared at her blankly. "What do you mean?"

"I don't want him to know just yet. I want to be by myself for a little while. If he knows, he's gonna be all over me, and I don't want to rush anything. I'd rather him think I'm still with Brutus so he'll respect my space."

I didn't know if I could keep such a big secret to myself, especially when my brother needed good news right now.

"You'll keep it to yourself?"

I didn't know how I would look my brother in the eye and not tell him. "You're putting me in a tough spot."

"Colton."

"How long are you going to keep this a secret?"

"I don't know...for a while."

I was loyal to Pepper, so I would do as she asked...but I wouldn't be happy about it. "Alright..."

"Thank you." She pulled the sheets to her shoulder and closed her eyes. "I'm too tired to go back to my apartment. Can I sleep here?"

"I figured you would—and then raid my fridge in the morning."

She gave a guilty smile. "You caught me."

ONE OF THE girls called in sick, and Pepper had to manage the store.

So I took Finn to his doctor's appointment. Over the last two weeks, he'd made significant improvement. He could move up and down the stairs without cringing, and he was able to lift heavier objects again. He cut back on the Vicodin and now only used it sparingly.

We sat in the waiting room for a while before he was taken back for his X-rays. Twenty minutes later, we ended up in the doctor's office to review them.

It was hard to be in the same room with him when I knew Pepper had been single for the last two weeks—and he had no idea. But I didn't feel too guilty about it because I knew she would take him back when she was ready. It wasn't like she was going to run off and date someone else.

Soon, everything would be back to the way it was.

Everyone would be happy.

The doctor came in and reviewed the X-rays with us. The ribs had healed nicely, so now he would do physical therapy a few times a week until he was back to normal. He had some scars that would be on his body forever, but the cuts and bruises on his face had nearly disappeared.

He was in great shape.

I drove his truck back to the house. "I'm glad I finally got a driver's license. This is a nice ride."

"You're lucky I'm letting you drive it." He sat in the passenger seat.

"Hey, you're lucky I got the day off to take you to the doctor."

He looked out the window and grinned. "Yeah...you're a pretty good brother." He patted me on the arm. "I appreciate everything you've done for me these last three weeks. I know it wasn't easy, but you didn't complain."

"I didn't mind, Finn. One day if something happens to me, I know you'll be there."

"Yes. And I'll let you borrow Soldier."

We arrived at the house then walked inside.

"So...how's everything with Pepper and Brutus?" His tone dropped the second he mentioned their relationship.

He'd never asked about Brutus so I never had to lie about the relationship, but now I was put on the spot. "Uh...I don't know."

"What do you mean, you don't know?" Finn pulled out a protein shake and drank it at the counter. "She tells you everything."

I shrugged. "Lately, she's only been talking about you."

"Good things?"

"Uh...I guess."

Finn was observant and intuitive, so he noticed the discrepancy between my usual demeanor and my current tone and body language. "Why are you being weird?"

"I'm not being weird."

"There's obviously something you aren't telling me."

"And you're obviously being paranoid."

"Fine." Finn backed off. "Keep your secrets...but I thought you were on my side."

"I am on your side."

"Then why won't you tell me?"

"Because it's none of your business, alright? You told me not to tell Pepper about Brutus writing you that check. Would you want me to blab that to her?"

Finn drank from his container.

"Then leave it alone." I grabbed a beer out of the fridge and took a drink.

Finn didn't press it any further.

"Wanna watch the game?" I wasn't ever off this early on a weekday, so I had time to kill before Tom got off work.

Finn was always in a bad mood when he didn't get his way, but he tried to cover it up as much as possible. "Alright."

24

PEPPER

After I took Soldier to the vet for a checkup, I ordered dinner and headed to Finn's house. There was this Mediterranean place he liked near my apartment, so I picked up some kebabs and hummus before I pulled into his driveway.

Soldier and I walked into the house and found Finn on the couch.

Soldier barked and ran up to him like he hadn't seen him in days rather than hours.

Finn gave him a good rubdown before he stood up. "How'd it go at the vet? Everything good?"

"Yes, he's perfectly healthy. I picked up some treats for him to celebrate." I pulled the food out of the plastic bags and set everything on plates.

"If you keep feeding him that stuff, he won't be healthy for long." He walked into the kitchen, his posture straight and his core strong. He still had the gauze around his waist, but he wasn't wincing with his movements anymore. He was the strong man I remembered, making a full recovery in a relatively short amount of time.

I stared at him and felt my eyes water.

He stopped when he noticed my emotion that sprung out of nowhere. "Baby, what's wrong?"

"I'm just happy to see that you're feeling better." I released a heavy gasp of air from my lungs, feeling the relief flood through my veins. I didn't have to watch him swallow painkillers anymore. Now he would return to the life he had before, one where he was happy.

His hand moved to the middle of my back, and he came close to me. His head tilted toward mine, like he was about to kiss me.

Good thing he still thought Brutus was in the picture—otherwise, he would kiss me.

His eyes locked on to mine. "Because of you." His hand snaked up my neck and moved into my hair. "You're the one who took care of me. You're the one who put me back together. You did this." He pressed his forehead to mine and held it there for a moment before he pulled away.

Once his possession was gone, I felt lonely. I missed those embraces. It was like being swallowed up by warm honey, getting lost in a good bath. It was the most comfortable I'd ever been in my life. I didn't want him to pull away. I wanted him to lift me onto the counter and make love to me for the first time in almost a year.

"This looks good." He eyed the food. "Thanks."

My mind was nowhere near food. "Yeah..."

He took our plates to the dining table and sat down.

I took the seat across from him, my mind still thinking about a passionate night with this man on top of me. He probably wasn't well enough for sex, but I could always be on top. I cut into my food and tried not to let the dirty thoughts explode into fantasies.

Finn took a few bites before he looked at me. "When Colton was here a few days ago, I asked about you and Brutus. He was a little weird about it. When I pressed him on it, he wouldn't answer."

Good thing Colton was loyal to me over his brother.

"Something going on?" He still held his fork, but his eyes were focused on me, like he didn't want to miss even a slight reaction.

I didn't know what to say. He'd confronted me, and I could spit out a lie, but I didn't see much point in that. I'd had two weeks to think about my feelings, to think about what I wanted. I was still afraid that Finn would hurt me...hurt me worse than he did last time. Unfortunately, there was nothing he could do or say to persuade me that nothing would ever happen again... because there wasn't that kind of proof in existence. "Uh...yeah."

He watched me closer.

I didn't want to meet his gaze because it was too hard. But I forced myself to look up and be unafraid. "I broke up with him a few weeks ago."

Finn didn't have an overt reaction, but there was a tiny explosion in his eyes. His entire body tightened with the information, his fingers curling around his fork like it was a weapon. He'd clearly been anticipating different news because he definitely hadn't expected that answer.

"I didn't tell you because I knew exactly what would happen...and I wanted some time to think."

He was still rigid as a statue, as if he didn't know how to process this information. "Think about what?"

"You know..." I hadn't expected to have this conversation now over dinner, but it was happening...and we had to roll with the punches.

"I want you to tell me, baby. I want to know exactly what you're thinking, exactly what you want. If you don't tell me, I'm gonna knock all this shit on the floor and take you on this table."

He dropped his fork and pushed his plate aside as if he wanted to make good on his threat.

A part of me wanted that, to be devoured by him once again. But I had to focus on the reality of our situation, of what I really wanted from him. "I...I guess I'm still thinking about what I want. After what happened to you, it made me realize I could lose you at any moment, and if I did, I would regret all this time we've lost. I know I want to be with you. I know I want us to be what we were."

He closed his eyes like those words were too good to hear.

"But I'm still scared. So, I'm stuck at a crossroads. I want to be with you, but I don't..."

"Then why did you break it off with Brutus?"

"It just didn't feel right anymore. It didn't feel like we were in a relationship...because I'm in a relationship with you."

He folded his hands together and rested them against his mouth, like he was withholding his excitement. "When did you end it?"

"About two weeks ago."

He laughed to himself, as if he couldn't believe I had been available that entire time and he'd done nothing about it.

"I'm taking it slow...trying to figure out if I can really do this." My heart wanted to be with Finn. My body wanted to be tangled around his all night long. "I'm so scared...it's hard to trust you again."

He lowered his hands back to the table. "How about this?" Our food was abandoned now that the conversation had begun. "I'm yours whenever you want me. Keep taking your time until you're ready. And when you are...we'll be together. I'll wait as long as it takes for you to figure that out."

So basically what we were already doing—but now he knew about it.

He rose from the table. "I'll be right back." He left the room and ventured up the stairs.

I stayed at the table and considered the conversation we just had, the way my heart beat so frantically in my chest. I thought Finn would rush me and force me to be his, but he continued to be patient, to give me whatever I wanted to make this relationship work.

He returned to the table with something clenched in his hand. He stood beside me and placed an item on the surface, a white gold ring with a single diamond in the band. It wobbled for a moment, and the diamond flashed with a brilliant prism.

The second I looked at it, I recognized it. "You didn't sell it..."

"No." He dropped into his chair again. "I couldn't. I guess I thought I might need it someday. I guess I knew I was making the wrong decision as I made it. I guess...I knew I wanted you to have it whether you married me or not."

I stared at the ring without touching it, remembering how happy I had been when he'd originally given it to me. It had slid onto my finger so effortlessly, like it was made just for me. It brought me so much joy...but so much heartache when I had to take it off.

"I meant it when I said I would marry you if you would have me."

I pulled my gaze away from the ring and looked at him.

"So, when you're ready to have me, ready to forgive me, ready to trust me...put that on. Keep in mind, when I see that ring on your finger, I'm not going to hold back. I'm going to assume that means you're mine, so I'm going to take you like you're mine, move all your shit over here like you're mine, and marry you like you're mine."

Colton sat across from me in the café, splitting a turkey sandwich with me. He was dressed in his slacks and collared shirt because he had to look like a million bucks every day at work.

Since I worked fewer hours, I kinda dressed however I wanted. Today, I was in jeans and a t-shirt, my hair in a slick ponytail because I didn't feel like styling it.

"How was work?" he asked, phrasing the question in a bored voice like he was already bored with my answer.

"It was fine. I just do bookkeeping now, which is nice. But I do still book appointments with my major clients because they like working with me. That's always fine."

"Dressing up women in lingerie is fine?"

"You know, if you were straight, you would understand how sexy that is."

He chuckled. "Touché. How are things with Finn? Still keeping him in the dark?"

"Actually...I told him the truth a few days ago. I'm surprised he didn't tell you."

He sipped his coffee and almost spat it out when a cough overtook him. "I'm surprised too. What did he say?"

"Well, he didn't pounce on me like I thought he would. He actually said something pretty sweet."

"What?"

"He still has my engagement ring..."

"Really?" Colton clearly had no idea because his surprise was genuine.

"Yeah. He gave it to me and told me to put it on whenever I decide I'm ready...and until then, he'll continue to back off."

"Wow...I didn't think Finn was capable of backing off."

"Me neither."

"But that is sweet. I really think he loves you, Pepper. I'm not just saying that because he's my brother. I had my reservations about him in the beginning, but I think he's really changed. I don't justify his earlier behavior...what he did was fucked up. But I don't think he'd ever do something like that again."

"Yeah...I'm starting to believe that. I guess I'm just taking my time."

"Take all the time you need. I'm sure he'll wait."

"Yeah..." I thought he would too.

"I'm excited for you guys to get back together. We can all be happy again...and live out our lives together. We can have our families and just enjoy life. No more drama. No more secrets. It'll be nice."

"What secrets?"

"Um...you know...about you breaking up with Brutus and not telling him."

"Oh yeah," I said. "I guess. I'm eager for a happily ever after too. I guess I still have some reservations...but in time they'll fade. Honestly, I love him so much that I'm willing to get hurt again. I just hope he doesn't make the same mistake twice."

He gave me a confident look. "I don't think you have to worry about that, babe."

WE WENT to the bar that night, Colton, me, and Stella and Zach.

It seemed like all we'd been talking about lately was Finn, so I avoided that subject—and tried not to think about him either.

"Have you heard from Brutus?" Stella asked.

I didn't realize I hadn't thought about him once until Stella mentioned him. "No, he hasn't tried to contact me."

"I'm surprised he didn't try to get you back," Stella said. "And I'm still surprised you broke it off with a billionaire."

"Money isn't everything." In fact, it meant nothing in the grand scheme of things. Finn could be homeless, and I would still love him until my dying breath.

"Yeah," Zach said. "You love me, and I'm just an average guy."

"Obviously," Stella said. "But I might love you a little more if you won the lotto..." She brought her glass to her lips and took a big drink.

"Ignore her," I said to Zach. "She's just drunk right now."

"Isn't she always drunk?" Colton asked.

Like she was living in her own universe, she blurted out, "Where's Tom?"

"He's spending the evening with his parents," Colton said. "Family night."

"You guys have been together for a while." Zach kept his arm around Stella's waist, so when she started to sway, he could straighten her again. "Think about making it more serious?"

"Actually...I was thinking about asking him to move in."

"You should." I smacked his arm playfully. "That would be amazing. You guys would be so happy. And we all really like Tom."

"I like him too," Colton said. "Well, I love him...but you know what I mean. I was always afraid that maybe I shouldn't since he's my first and we met in a bar...but I don't feel like I need to find someone else just to validate my feelings."

"You don't," I said. "If he's the one, he's the one." I rubbed his shoulder. "And he's so handsome."

"But not rich," Stella said. "That's the one drawback."

"Good thing Brutus isn't around anymore," Zach said. "Otherwise, I would have competition, apparently..."

"Nah," Stella said. "Friends don't date each other's exes. That's weird."

Just when I finished off my glass, a full one appeared right before my eyes. Another vodka cranberry with extra ice. I smiled because I knew exactly who'd slipped this drink under my nose.

"Hey, baby." Finn emerged at my side, flashing me his handsome smile as he leaned against the table. He'd made a lot of progress with physical therapy, and now he was strong once again. He would have dull aches and pains for a few more months, but he was back at the hospital, working part time. "I like that dress."

It was black and simple, but it showed a great deal of cleavage. "Thanks."

He stood close to my side, like he wanted the world to know I was taken without actually touching me. Instead of drinking scotch, he stuck to beer. It seemed like he'd sworn off hard liquor for good. As always, he glanced at my left ring finger, hoping to see my engagement ring. When it wasn't there, he looked away. "What did I miss?"

"Colton is gonna ask Tom to move in with him," I said. "Isn't that great?"

Finn's eyes lit up like he was genuinely happy. "That's awesome, man. Congratulations." He moved around me and hugged his brother. "I never wanted to influence you, but I've always liked Tom. He's a good and classy guy. Perfect partner for you."

When Colton's eyes filled with affection, it was obvious his brother's approval meant a lot to him. "Thanks...I appreciate that."

"When are you going to ask?" Finn stood beside him with his beer still in his hand.

"I don't know...maybe over dinner?" Colton asked. "I don't want to make it a formal thing just in case he's not into it."

"He'll be into it," I said. "Come on, he loves you."

"Yeah, but we haven't been together for two years yet," Colton said. "I just don't want to ruin things by moving too fast."

"You won't," Finn said. "Love doesn't need to move at a certain speed. It's different for everyone...and when you know, you know. So ask him and be happy." He patted Colton on the shoulder.

"Yeah," Colton said. "Maybe you're right."

"STELLA HAS HAD ENOUGH. I'm taking her home." Zach wrapped his jacket around her shoulders then lifted her into his arms.

Once her head was against his shoulder, she closed her eyes, ready to go to sleep the second she was weightless.

"I like it when she drinks because she's feisty." Zach looked into her dead-tired face. "But when she's like this, I don't get any action at all. It's hard to find that balance. Well...good night." He carried her out of the bar and to his car in the parking lot.

Colton had already taken off to see Tom, so it was just Finn and me.

Alone.

We'd been alone many times, but now it was more intense than before. We were both thinking the same thing at the same time, wondering when I would put that ring back on my finger so we could pick up where we'd left off.

A part of me wanted to make out with him in the middle of the bar until he took me home and ravished me the way he used to. But I knew I hadn't committed to this completely just yet. There was still lingering doubt, like I might be making the worst decision of my life—twice.

Finn stood beside me with his fingers wrapped around his beer bottle. "Ready to call it a night?" Ever since I'd told him Brutus was gone, he'd kept his distance and didn't try to rush me into a physical relationship. He couldn't stop staring at me, but he didn't try to get me into bed. Knowing we were together without actually being together was enough for him. He was willing to be patient since he was so close to finally having me.

It gave me plenty of time to think. "Yeah." I finished the rest of my drink and left the empty glass on the table.

"Can I give you a ride home?"

"I assumed you would."

We left the bar and took his truck to my apartment. As always, he parked at the curb and walked with me all the way inside the building and to my floor. His footsteps echoed against the hardwood floor as he accompanied me to my front door.

I fished my keys out of my clutch and sighed as I prepared to face my empty bed alone. I didn't just miss sex since Brutus and I broke up. I missed sex with Finn. I missed that passion, the way our sweaty bodies slid past each other as we fucked ourselves into ecstasy. But I didn't give in to my desires, not when I wasn't sure what I wanted yet. "Thanks for the ride..."

"Of course." He stood in front of me, his hands in his pockets.

"Well...good night." I turned away.

"You know what? I can't take this anymore." He grabbed me by the arm and turned me back to him. His powerful arms wrapped around my body, and he pulled me into his chest, hugging me as his lips pressed against my hairline.

The second I felt his hard body against mine, I closed my eyes and treasured the reunion between our bodies. My arms rested on his, and I kept my forehead against his chest, his scent exploding in my nose. It was just as good as I remembered, just as magical. His affection was just as good as sex.

His hand cupped the back of my head, and he kissed my forehead. "I love you so much..." He kept his lips in place as he breathed with me, as he enjoyed this unbridled love. His fingers moved in my hair as he relaxed.

I could stay there all night.

After a few minutes, he pulled away and looked into my face, his eyes full of longing.

"I love you too..." I'd missed telling him that, missed feeling him like this.

His hand cupped my cheek, and he pressed my back into the door before he kissed me. His fingers tugged my hair lightly as his lips massaged mine, trembling slightly once they came into contact with my mouth. He released a gentle breath as the desire struck him so hard.

It was just as good as I remembered, just as wonderful as I remembered. My hands gripped his arms, and I felt the love and passion I'd been afraid of. I felt myself fall headfirst into this terrifying bliss. I'd never felt this way for anyone else, including Brutus. Kissing Finn was the closest to heaven I would ever get, at least on Earth.

His mouth opened and closed as he took mine, sucking in breath then returning it at the same pace. The kiss was so delicate, so soft. It was the kiss a man gave when he was in love, not when he was looking for a weekend fling. He pressed me against the door as he made love to my mouth with his, stole my breath away, and gently touched my hair like I was a fragile doll.

A single kiss with him was better than months of sex with Brutus.

He ended the embrace abruptly, as if a little voice inside his head was telling him not to push this too far. "I'm sorry... I just miss you." With his body pressed against mine, I could feel his dick was hard in his jeans, pressing against me like he wanted to break through his clothing to get to me.

"I know...I miss you too."

He rested his forehead against mine for a moment before he pulled away. "I'll let you go..." He stepped back, pulling back his warmth and tenderness with his movements.

I didn't want this to end. I wanted to be weak, just for the night. "Unless you want to stay..." The words tumbled out of my mouth all on their own.

He turned back to me, his eagerness obvious. "I'd love to stay...if that's what you really want."

"Well, it would just be to sleep..."

He barked out his answer. "That's fine with me."

I got the door unlocked, and we entered my apartment. Shoes were kicked off by the door before we made our way to my bedroom. I peeled off my dress and let him see me since he'd already seen me naked so many times. I stood in just my thong because I couldn't wear a bra with this dress.

His jeans were on the floor, and his eyes were locked to my figure. The bulge in the front of his boxers moved noticeably with a jerk.

I turned around and pulled a t-shirt over my head, hiding my naked torso from view. When I came to bed, he was already under the sheets, bare-chested.

He snatched me right away and pulled me close to his chest, wrapping our limbs together as we became one person. He hiked my leg over his hip and rested his large hand on my ass as he held me close. His hard dick was impossible to ignore because it poked me like a very large and hot stick.

His beautiful eyes stared into mine, not blinking as he took in my features like it was our first night together. It was steamy and intimate, the way we looked at each other with nothing in between us.

He moved his head closer to mine on the pillow, until his face was just inches away. He could kiss me if he wanted to, but somehow, he kept himself under control.

I had to do the same.

"I can't wait to do this with you every night for the rest of our lives..." With emotion deep in his voice, he said the most beautiful words I'd ever heard him say. Sincerity with a touch of remorse filled the air between us.

When he left, he'd hurt me so much. But when I saw this

look on his face, it was hard to believe he would ever hurt me again. His devotion was concrete. His apology was deep. It seemed like the only place in the world he ever wanted to be was by my side...forever.

FINN WOKE me up at the break of dawn. "I'm sorry, baby. I have the morning shift today."

"Ugh..." I kept my eyes closed, so comfortable in his arms that I didn't want him to leave.

He kissed me on the forehead then the lips. "I'll let myself out." He moved his face into my neck and sprinkled a few kisses there, his warmth pressing against my delicate skin.

I moaned as I felt him kiss me, missing those sessions of morning sex we used to have. He would give me a load before bed and then another first thing in the morning. I tilted my head back so he could kiss me more as his hand slid up my leg. "Don't go..."

"I wish I could stay... You have no idea." He gave me a final kiss on the mouth before he got out of bed and got dressed.

I stayed under the covers and watched him, seeing that chiseled physique disappear under the clothing that blocked his sexy abs from view. Now that I was awake, I didn't know if I would get back to sleep, so I got to my feet and walked him to the door.

He stopped in the doorway and gave me a tight hug. "Come over tonight."

"Alright."

"Pack a bag if you want." He kissed my hairline before he stepped into the hallway, like he didn't want an answer to my request.

I watched him go before I shut the door and returned to bed.

The sheets weren't nearly as comfortable without him there. They were already cold the second he was gone. I lay there wide awake and wondered if I should sleep over at his place. Even without sex, last night was the best night of sleep I'd ever gotten.

I opened my nightstand and searched through the random crap that turned the drawer into a junk haven. I pushed aside old necklaces and earrings until I found the necklace he'd given me the night he left.

His dog tags.

It had taken me three months to take them off, and I hadn't thought I'd ever wear them again.

But now it felt wrong leaving them buried with other meaningless crap.

I put them around my neck and felt the tags sit against my chest in the exact same spot as before. Like they'd been there all along, they felt weightless. The metal was cold around my neck, but the sensation slowly faded away as the heat brought it back to a comfortable temperature. My fingers played with one of the tags, his name engraved in the metal. I wasn't quite ready to give myself to him once again...but it was obvious he already had me.

25

COLTON

AT MIDDAY, I WENT AROUND THE CORNER TO THE COFFEE SHOP TO get a refuel of caffeine. I ordered my coffee then lingered in the back, waiting for the barista to call my name once he finished making my nonfat soy latte.

I was going to scroll through my phone when I noticed a tattooed beauty walk inside. In her blue scrubs with her hair pulled into a slick ponytail was the woman who'd called me on that unforgettable night. She must have been picking up a coffee before her shift, or maybe she needed a pick-me-up after a long day.

Since she was the one who had found Finn, it felt weird to ignore her. "Hey, Layla." I would address her by her full professional name, but I couldn't remember what it was. "Going to work or just got off?"

"On my way, actually." She smiled like she was happy to see me, but there was also a hint of discomfort since I was Pepper's best friend...and she'd tried to steal Finn away. "Finn is working the morning shift, and I'm so happy he's back on his feet. That was such a horrific night...he didn't deserve that at all."

"Yeah. I'm glad he made a full recovery. He was in a lot of pain there for a while..."

"And those painkillers are terrible for the body," she said. "Hopefully, this is just a bad memory for him now. I can't believe he didn't press charges against the asshole who did that to him. I understand the guy is rich and powerful, but that's no excuse not to fight back."

Finn told me it was a pack of nobodies that had ganged up on him, but that never had made any sense to me. The words that just tumbled out of her mouth made even less sense. "Rich asshole? What are you talking about?"

"They released the security footage to all personnel of the hospital for safety issues. It didn't take long for people to recognize him. But no one's doing anything about it...which is ridiculous. I told Finn to press charges and make him pay all of his hospital bills and medications, but he refused."

"Recognize who?" My entire body tightened and turned hot at the same time, as if I already knew the answer without hearing it from her lips. The truth filled me with so much dread, so much uncontrollable rage.

"Brutus Hemmingway... He didn't tell you?"

I stared at her blankly, imagining Brutus jumping him in the parking lot.

Layla got her answer. "Maybe he was trying to protect you... I shouldn't have said anything. I'm sorry."

Brutus went behind our backs and attacked Finn like a coward. He beat him up in the parking lot and could have killed him. For what reason? Because he wouldn't leave Pepper alone? Was this guy a psychopath? "Can you send me the video?"

"Sure...but are you sure—"

"Yes. Send it to me."

She pulled out her phone and sent it as a text message.

I opened up the footage and saw Finn being cornered by

four large men and Brutus. The men wrestled Finn to the ground, pinned his arms behind his back, and after a short conversation, beat him violently. Their fists slammed into his face and abdomen, striking him even when he was clearly unconscious. It wasn't just a simple fight. It was an execution. I almost couldn't watch it.

Layla's eyes shone with sympathy.

I forced myself to watch until the end, until Brutus and his cronies drove away.

And left Finn there to die.

I TOLD the office I had an emergency and headed over to the lingerie store.

Pepper was standing at the counter, a large binder in front of her where she kept notes on all her expenses and her payroll. She looked up when she noticed me. "Hey, Colton. Why the long face?"

"I need to talk to you—in private." She had girls on the floor and behind the counter. When she saw that video, she wouldn't want to be around anyone else but me.

"Uh...okay." She led me into the office and shut the door behind her. "You're scaring me. Everything alright?"

"No, everything is not alright." I pulled out my phone and opened the video. "I just ran into Layla, and she told me who jumped Finn that night. You aren't going to believe it."

"Who?" she demanded. "No one we know, right?"

I felt so stupid for rooting for Brutus, now that I knew he was a fucking psychopath. When he didn't get his way, he tried to terrify his opponents until they disappeared. He must have been pissed when Finn didn't take the check, and then when Finn kept calling Pepper baby, he wanted retribution. "Brutus."

Her mouth immediately dropped open, and her eyes narrowed like she didn't believe it. "Brutus? Brutus would never—"

"This is the security footage they pulled from that night. It's definitely him." I held up the phone to her gaze and watched in horror as she covered her mouth with her hands and started to cry once she saw the damage Brutus had caused.

When I pulled the phone away, tears were soaking her cheeks.

I didn't want to show it to her, but she had to know.

She covered her face with her hands. "Oh my god...why didn't he tell us?"

I couldn't think of a justifiable reason. Finn should have pressed charges. "I don't know...but there's something else that happened. Finn told me to keep it a secret, but I don't think I can anymore."

She dropped her hands and looked at me, her eyes still soaking wet. "What?"

"A few months ago, Brutus showed up on Finn's doorstep with a billion-dollar check. Told him the money was his if he disappeared and never showed his face again."

"Jesus, are you kidding me?" She gripped her hair and practically yanked it out of her head. "Who the fuck does he think he is?"

"And Finn didn't take the money...as you probably figured out."

She was too upset to soften, too upset to care about how devoted Finn was.

"He showed me the check. It was a cashier's check, and he ripped it in half. So if you're still worried that Finn isn't a hundred percent committed...you're worried over nothing."

"Why did he make you promise not to tell me?"

"Said he wasn't a rat. And he wanted you to choose him, not go to him just because Brutus was out of the race."

"But what about this?" she demanded. "This is assault. How could he not say anything?"

"I don't know... I came straight here when I heard the news. Knowing Finn, it's probably some macho thing, proving that he's tough and can take anything, that he won't run to the police. Why he didn't tell you...it's probably for the same reason."

She dragged her hands down her face again. "I'm giving that motherfucker a piece of my mind." She stormed out of the office, her eyes filled with blood lust like a general about to embark on war. "I'm gonna kill him...fucking kill him."

I chased after her. "What are you going to do?"

"I just said it." She got to the street and waved down a cab.

"Pepper, I'm pissed too, but I don't know if confronting him is the best—"

The taxi pulled up to the curb, but before hopping inside, she turned to me. "Oh, I'm confronting him. I'm gonna make that son of a bitch pay for doing that to Finn. Classy bitch is gone. Psycho bitch is here to stay."

I DIDN'T KNOW what was going to happen once we came face-to-face with Brutus, but I wasn't skipping out. I had to protect Pepper if he raised a hand to her—and I needed to get a few punches in myself.

She stepped inside his elevator and entered the code to rise to his penthouse.

The elevator started to move.

"He didn't change his passcode...idiot."

We rose to the very top of the building then the elevator doors opened to a beautiful living room. Luxury was obvious in every inch of the place, from the cashmere rug to the grand piano that didn't have a speck of dust.

Pepper marched inside. "Brutus!"

I came in behind her, surveying the living room for weapons.

Footsteps sounded a moment later, and his legs emerged as he descended the spiral staircase that led to an additional floor. In just his sweatpants, he was streaked with sweat because he must have just used his personal gym.

He walked toward us, rigid as he looked at Pepper. "What are you doing here?"

Fearless, Pepper made her move. "It was you! You're the one who almost killed him!"

He glanced at me then looked at her again, not denying the charges.

"You fucking asshole! What the hell is wrong with you?"

"He wouldn't back off." Brutus spoke with calmness, as if beating a guy in the parking lot was no big deal. "I warned him and gave him a chance to get out of it, but he refused."

"So you jump him?" she asked incredulously. "You think you're the mob or something? How dare you?" She launched her momentum forward at alarming speed and slapped her hand across his face so hard he actually staggered back.

I couldn't help but be proud—because I'd taught her that.

"You piece of shit." She slapped him again then shoved him as hard as she could.

He landed on the floor. "Pepper—"

"How does it feel?" She kicked him in the knee. "Huh? You like that?"

She didn't even need me to jump in.

"Stop." He grabbed one of her legs to steady her.

"Oh, you want me to stop?" She tilted her head, looking crazy. "Did Finn ask you to stop?" She dropped to her knees and slammed her fist hard into his dick.

Brutus screamed and crawled into a ball, cupping his dick like he'd been shot. "Fuck!" He writhed on the floor because the pain was so excruciating, he couldn't do anything else but breathe through the hurt.

Pepper turned around and marched off. "Go fuck yourself, Brutus." She walked past me and headed to the elevator.

I wanted to get a few punches in, but seeing him practically weep on the hardwood floor was enough revenge for me. With a punch like that, it would hurt every time he peed. And getting hard was probably so painful it wasn't worth it.

"Let's go, Colton." She held the door open.

I turned around and joined her and watched the doors close.

"I hope I broke his dick," she said as the elevator descended to the ground floor.

"Even if you did, I don't think that's punishment enough."

"I agree. I wish I could mutilate his face with a baseball bat..."

I wanted to take it a step further... I wanted to bury him six feet under.

26

PEPPER

My mind had been in a daze since I'd heard the horrific news.

Brutus was responsible for the worst day of my life.

The man had no right to do what he did, to cross the line in such an egregious way. He didn't even do it to protect me. He did it for himself.

And he could have killed the man I loved.

I sat on the couch with Soldier and struggled to slow the adrenaline pumping through my heart. Attacking Brutus in his penthouse and punching his dick didn't give me the satisfaction I wanted. Even if I broke his heart and ripped out his ribs, I still wouldn't be satisfied. Nothing could ever avenge the pain he'd caused.

My temple throbbed with my pulse, and my fingers kept tightening until my knuckles were hard. Brutus was responsible for this, but I felt like the one to blame. If I'd never dated him at all, this wouldn't have happened.

Finn wouldn't have ended up in the hospital with broken ribs.

Soldier knew something was wrong, so he kept looking at me with those sad puppy eyes.

I was too furious to be sad.

Minutes later, the sound of the motor opening the garage fell on my ears. The truck entered the space, the engine loud. Then it died, and the door slammed shut. Seconds later, Finn entered the house, his satchel over one shoulder while he wore his scrubs.

I stared at him, both happy and pissed.

He didn't notice me until he set his satchel on the dining table. "Hey, baby. I didn't see you there..." He tensed when he saw the livid look on my face. He must have seen the rage in my eyes, a billowing inferno that was about to engulf the entire house.

I rose to my feet and walked up to him, my stature so intimidating, he actually stepped back. "Why didn't you tell me?"

He held his stance, clearly bewildered.

"Finn."

"You're going to have to be more specific."

"Why? You have a lot of secrets?" I stepped toward him again. "Colton showed me the security footage from that night... He showed me the video where Brutus ganged up on you with four men and nearly killed you in the middle of the parking lot in the freezing cold. And you said nothing?"

When his secret was out in the open, his eyes filled with despair.

"Why didn't you tell me?"

He bowed his head.

"How could you not tell me? How could you not tell me that he paid you a billion dollars to leave me?"

He still had nothing to say.

"Finn." I stomped my foot to get his attention. "Answer me."

He lifted his gaze again. "I didn't tell you about the money because I didn't want to give him the satisfaction. I didn't want to be a rat. I didn't want to win you back because I kicked him out of the race. That's not how I wanted this relationship to form."

"You don't think turning down a billion dollars for me would get us back together?"

His eyebrows fell as he considered it. "I still wanted you to choose me on your own."

"And the hospital? How could you not tell us that he's a psychopath?"

His answer didn't come easily. "Again, I didn't want to give him that satisfaction. He wasn't going to get me to cave."

I would never understand his machoness or his code of ethics. "What he did was so wrong... You should have told me."

"I had the chance to get out of it, but I didn't."

"What did he say to you?"

"He told me to disappear and he wouldn't hurt me...so I told him to do his worst."

I closed my eyes as I remembered that image from the film, seeing blood fly out of his mouth from being hit so hard.

"I didn't tell you because I wanted to use it against him."

"Against him how?"

"Because when I was hurt, all you wanted to do was take care of me...and that's how I got you back. I made him regret his decision, made him suffer knowing he was the reason we came back together. Everything he did only pushed us closer together. He offered me that money thinking he could get rid of me...but he only forced me to prove how much you meant to me. He gave me everything I needed to get you back. All I had to do was be patient."

All the doubts I'd had about Finn seemed ridiculous now that all this information was on the table. I was so scared he would hurt me again, that I preferred to be with an asshole with no morals. "I'm so sorry..." Tears bubbled in my eyes. "This is all my fault."

"No," he said quietly. "It's not your fault at all."

"But if I hadn't dated him—"

"I was the one who provoked him—and I have no regrets."

I wiped away my tears with my fingertips even though my eyes continued to water. "When Colton told me the truth, I couldn't think straight. I marched to his penthouse and gave him a piece of my mind..."

"He didn't hurt you, right?"

"No...but I hurt him."

His eyes narrowed.

"I slapped him a few times then punched him in the dick."

A slight smile appeared on his mouth. "That's my girl."

"I can't believe he did that to you. You should press charges. You could get a lot of money for damages—"

"I've never wanted his money. Couldn't care less about it. The only thing of his I wanted is now mine. So let's forget about him for good. I already have." He pulled the stethoscope off his neck and tossed it onto the table before he walked up to me. The distance separating us diminished until there was no space in between us. His arms wrapped around me and pulled me close. "Marry me tomorrow." He grabbed my left hand and placed it on his chest, letting my engagement ring catch the light. Without looking at my hand, he seemed to have noticed it was there, must have noticed the ethereal glow from its endless prisms.

"Tomorrow?" I whispered.

His hand moved into my hair as he tilted my chin up. "I don't want to waste another day like this, not when we should be so much more. I want to wake up in the morning and see my wife next to me. I want to come home to her every day, eat her medi-ocre cooking but pretend to like it to spare her feelings. I want to start a family with you, make lots of babies and have them climb all over the furniture like monkeys. I want us to be a family...to live to a ripe old age then be buried side by side in the graveyard for eternity, until the sun explodes in five billion years and brings us into permanent darkness. Say yes."

"I can't..."

His eyes filled with sadness, like I'd ripped his heart out of his chest so I could watch him die.

"I want Colton there. I want your parents there. I want our friends to be there. How about Saturday instead?"

The darkness quickly disappeared as the affection returned to his eyes. His fingers gripped my chin, and he looked into my gaze like I was the most beautiful woman he'd ever seen. Love shone in his eyes brighter than the sun. His fingers gripped me possessively, like he never wanted to let me go. "I guess I can wait until Saturday..."

FINN SHUT THE BEDROOM DOOR, closing it right in Soldier's face.

Soldier whined through the wood.

"Sorry, boy. Not tonight." He pulled his V-neck over his head, revealing the strong physique that had survived the cruel punishment he'd endured just a month ago. The bruising had faded away, and the scars were almost impossible to see because his tattoos commanded all the attention.

He untied the drawstrings, so his pants fell to his ankles. His muscular legs stepped out of the material before he pulled his boxers down, letting his enormous cock pop out and steal the show. With a thick vein along the shaft and an impressive crown, he had the kind of dick an artist would love to paint.

I'd missed it.

Proud of his junk, he crossed the bedroom and came to me,

lifting me into the air and pulling me against his chest. His large hands supported my ass as he cradled me against him and kissed me.

My arms moved around his neck, and I squeezed his hips as I used my strength to keep myself up. My fingers ran through his hair, and my nipples dragged against his soft skin. My mouth ached for his lips, ached for the reunion of our bodies.

I was about to fall headfirst into the greatest love I'd ever known—and I wasn't scared at all. This man wouldn't hurt me. He wouldn't break my heart again. He would be everything he promised. That ring would stay on my left hand forever because he would never ask for it back.

When our kisses became so heated we could barely breathe, he rolled me onto my back and maneuvered between my legs, like his dick couldn't wait to get inside me. One arm hooked behind my knee while the other dug into my hair. Like he remembered every angle of my body, he tilted his hips and slipped inside me, inching deeper and deeper until he was balls deep.

"Oh Jesus…" My nails clawed down his chest as I moaned in ecstasy. His dick felt exactly the way it used to, hard as steel, warm, and so fucking big. This was the dick I fantasized about when I was alone, the dick I wished were inside me when it was just me and my vibrator. I couldn't wait to have this monster inside me every night for the rest of my life.

"Fuck." He breathed against my mouth as he enjoyed the slickness he'd just slid into. "Baby, I'm not gonna last long…" He remained idle as he enjoyed my tightness, as his dick got reacquainted with my pussy once again. He tilted his hips and throbbed in between my legs, practically coming apart the second his cock got wet.

At least I knew he'd really been celibate these last two months. "Me neither." I guided his lips to mine and kissed him, starting off slow as our bodies got used to each another. I moved the fingers on one hand into his short strands of hair, while my other hand gripped his muscular bicep. I was stuffed full with his cock, and he didn't need to move for me to enjoy it.

Sometimes he couldn't focus on kissing me because he lost his breath, so absorbed by the tightness between my legs. He hadn't even started to move yet, but he was like a virgin who could barely hold his load because sex was too good to handle.

That kind of reaction from a man like Finn was hot, seeing him enjoy me so much, remain celibate just for me.

He kissed me again then started to move, thrusting his hips as he pushed deep inside me. It was nothing but slickness the entire way through, so much wetness that it dripped down my crack to the sheets underneath us.

No wonder why he enjoyed it so much.

He stopped kissing me and looked into my eyes, his jaw clenched as he kept moving. He glanced at his old necklace between my tits, taking in the sight of metal with affection, then slid his gaze back to me. "Fuck, I'm gonna have a sexy wife." He pressed his forehead to mine as he kept rocking, doing his best to hold himself together so he wouldn't ruin the moment by coming so soon.

But watching him struggle the entire time was sexy. When he had sex on a regular basis, he could last forever, could fuck me a million ways without losing his control. But during a dry spell, he turned into a teenager all over again.

With our gazes both heated and combustive, we stared at each other as we moved, our bodies gradually moving quicker because we wanted more of each other. My body started to squeeze because I could already feel the arousal hitting me hard. I was burning all over, white-hot and scorching. I wanted to explode before he finished, but I could tell he was barely holding on. And then it happened...the best orgasm of my life.

"Finn...Finn." I'd missed whispering that name in bed, missed coming around his perfect dick.

"Baby..." He came too, filling me with his enormous load of come.

I could feel it sit inside me, feel the hot heaviness. It made my climax last longer, made it more potent. I squeezed his arm as I finished, feeling his dick throb inside me. "Yes..." My left foot cramped because I'd tightened so much, but I didn't care at all. The euphoria was just too incredible.

He was so hard up that he didn't even soften inside me. His dick was just as aroused as before, ready to keep fucking me like nothing happened. He rocked his hips again and moved farther on top of me, possessing me the way he used to. He fisted my hair so he could have a good grip on me as he pressed me hard into the mattress. "I love you..."

It was worth the risk. It was worth everything...having this. "I love you too."

COLTON OPENED the door without knocking.

I'd just gotten home from the gym, so I was in my leggings and sports bra. "You're gonna have to start knocking. Finn and I could be doing it on the couch, and I don't want you to be scarred by the sight." My ring felt perfect on my finger, especially when I talked with my hands and felt the weight of the diamond. I wore it everywhere I went, even the gym. It was such a part of me now that I never wanted to not wear it.

"Well, I knew you weren't doing it on the couch."

"And how did you know that?"

Finn walked in behind him, wearing his gym clothes like he was about to work out. "Because we're packing your things and moving them to my place."

"Right now?" I asked blankly.

"Yep." Finn stood beside his brother, his hands on his hips. "Our life together starts now, not later. I'm not going to bed on Saturday night knowing you still have your shit here. This apartment is gonna be empty by this evening."

"I still have the place for a couple more months, so there's no rush—"

He stared me down like he was a general and I was a petty officer. "Yes, there is a rush." He nodded to Colton. "Throw her clothes in a bag and toss it in the back seat of the truck. Then we'll get her couches and put them in the bed."

"Whoa, hold on." I waved both of my arms in front of them. "I appreciate what you're trying to do, but do we even want this furniture at your place? Where is it going to go?"

"Good point," Finn said. "Let's donate it. I already have dishes, kitchen appliances, towels, a bed...all you need are your clothes. So let's take everything down to Salvation Army."

"Well, I didn't mean let's donate all of it." This was happening so fast. He'd burst through my door the second I got home and started making all of these decisions. "How about we take a step back, alright? I'm sleeping with you tonight, regardless of what we do with this stuff—"

"No." Finn stepped toward me, taking the reins and stealing my voice. "I warned you what would happen when you put that ring on. You're mine until we're both dead. So we need to take care of this shit now. What do you want to keep, and what do you want to donate? I have a big storage facility if you want to keep stuff there until you figure it out. But we aren't keeping this apartment."

Colton tried to sneak into the corner and disappear from this conversation.

"Is this how it's going to be for the rest of our lives?" I asked incredulously. "You bossing me around—"

"Yes. At least when it comes to stuff like this. So, you better make your decisions fast. Otherwise, I'll make them for you." He turned to Colton. "Start packing her clothes. I'll do the kitchen."

Both men broke off in separate directions, and Colton was happy to go into the other room.

I stared at Finn's back as he walked into the kitchen. "You're crazy, you know that?"

He grabbed a box and started piling everything inside, keeping his back to me. "Yes."

"I'm serious."

He turned around and looked at me, his expression practically cold. "Losing you has made me a little crazy."

"More like big crazy..."

He leaned against the counter and crossed his arms over his chest. "You can keep anything you want. I'm not making you get rid of it. Bring anything you want to the house. All I ask is you leave this apartment behind and live with me. Maybe you think that's crazy...but that's your fault for loving a crazy man."

27

COLTON

"I DON'T THINK THIS IS HOW THIS IS SUPPOSED TO WORK." I SAT beside Finn as he sat in the leather chair.

The artist kept the needle directed on his left hand and carved the ink into his skin. It looked and sounded painful, but Finn stared out the window like he didn't feel an ounce of discomfort. "Meaning?"

"You're supposed to get the ring after you get married."

"I have to wear a bandage for a few days, so I need to do it now." He pulled his wrist to his chest and looked at the time.

"But can you work with an open wound?"

"As long as it's covered." He turned to me. "So, you picked up the last boxes from her apartment?"

"Yeah, I put everything in the storage shed." Finn, Zach, and I had cleaned out her apartment yesterday. We dropped off stuff for donations, moved her clothes to Finn's place, and put the rest of her stuff in storage because she didn't know what to do with it right on the spot. "She's gonna drop off the keys to the landlord tomorrow, but she might have to keep paying rent for a while."

"She's not paying rent with me, so it shouldn't be a big deal. Are you okay not living across the hall from her anymore?"

It would be weird since we'd been doing it for nearly two years now, but we were both moving on with our lives. "Actually...I talked to Tom about moving in together."

"Yeah? What did he say?"

"He said he wanted to do it." I had been so nervous at the time, so when he said yes, I showed every single tooth in my mouth when I smiled. It would be nice to wake up to him every single day, to have dinner with him every night. "But he suggested we move in to his place since it's a lot bigger...and I agreed."

"So you're both leaving your apartments?"

"Guess so."

"Wow...talk about a lot of change."

"Yeah." Pepper and I had come so far. Just a few years ago, we were married, and now we were with different people. "She'll be married to you on Saturday, and Tom and I will probably get married someday... A lot of good things have happened."

"I think everything is exactly as it should be."

"You're going to have to work on not keeping secrets."

He looked at me, his eyebrow raised. "What are you talking about?"

"You didn't tell her about the check or the fact that Brutus assaulted you. That's pretty important information..."

He shook his head slightly. "My secrets are behind me. I'm an open book."

"And you're certain you want to do this?" I knew what his answer would be, but I wanted to test him anyway.

He looked me square in the eye, like I was the one who needed to be convinced—not him. "Not a doubt in my mind, man. All that time in Uganda was a fucking mistake... I wish I could take it back."

"But you can't run off again. You can't travel the world. You're gonna be in one spot for the rest of your life...and be a dad someday. You do understand that, right?"

He actually rolled his eyes at me. "I want to be with her every day for the rest of my life. I want to sleep in the same bed, live in the same house, and die in the same city. I'm not scared, Colton. A few years ago, I would have felt differently, but when you meet the right woman, nothing else seems important. There's no exotic place that's more enticing than our bed. There's no lost opportunity that I'll regret. Being with her is a whole different kind of adventure...and I'm looking forward to it. You done grilling me now?"

"Yeah, it's my job. I'm the closest thing she has to a family."

His eyes looked off into the distance, as if he were thinking of an old memory or something someone had said a long time ago. "I'm her family now, Colt. It's my job to take care of her."

———

I SAT on the couch with Tom as we watched the game at Finn's house. Finn was sitting on the other, Soldier sitting close beside him.

Then Pepper's voice rang from the top of the stairs. "Colt, come here. I want to show you something."

I sighed as I eyed the stairs, the entire floor I'd have to ascend to see what she wanted. "How about you just come here?"

"No," she snapped. "Get your ass up here."

I sighed as I put down my beer. "Sometimes I feel like we're still married."

Tom chuckled.

"Colt," Pepper shouted again.

Finn kept his eyes on the TV. "I think she wants to show you her wedding dress."

"Oh, I didn't know she was wearing one." They were doing this wedding on such short notice that I hadn't thought she was getting anything.

"She needs gay approval," Tom said. "Now don't keep the bride waiting."

I moved up the stairs then entered the bedroom she shared with Finn. She wasn't wearing a traditional wedding dress like I'd imagined. Instead, it was a simple halter top dress that produced a noticeable line of cleavage right in the center of the neckline. It flared out, reaching slightly past her thighs. In her white heels, her legs were a foot longer, and with her slightly tanned skin color, the dress was perfect on her. "Wow, that looks nice."

"You really think so? Not too slutty?"

"That's exactly why it looks nice."

She swatted my arm playfully. "Come on, I'm being serious. What do you really think?"

"I really think you look stunning. It's better than a traditional wedding dress. Even if you planned a wedding a year in advance, Finn would still want you to wear that."

"You don't think your parents will think it's a little...inappropriate?"

I shrugged. "Who cares what they think? It's your day, not theirs. Besides, you already wore a traditional dress for them once. Now you should wear whatever you want. And I can tell you right now, Finn is gonna rip that thing off you the second you get home." A year ago, I would have had to stop myself from gagging after saying something like that. But now...I didn't see her as mine anymore. Now, she was Finn's...and she was just my friend.

She caught the sadness in my eyes. "I know it's a little weird... I'll be your brother's wife."

"But you're still my best friend. And we'll be siblings-in-law, so that's pretty cool. We'll always be together...no matter what. And truth be told, you couldn't have picked a better guy. I had a talk with him the other day, and his commitment didn't shake at all."

"I don't think we need to worry about that again, Colt. I think we should leave the past where it belongs..."

"Yeah. I think it's time." I hugged her and rested my chin on her forehead. "You guys will have a long and happy life together."

"I know we will."

I kissed her forehead. "Can I give you away tomorrow?"

"I was hoping you would."

I squeezed her tighter. "You want to stay at my place the night before the wedding?"

"Yeah, right," she said with a laugh. "Like Finn would ever go for that."

"I always thought you'd be wearing the pants in this relationship."

"Not possible. Being with Finn is like being in a relationship with a very stubborn dragon."

I chuckled at her analogy. "Let me know if you change your mind. There's plenty of room for both of us in that bed."

"And what about Tom?"

"He could squeeze in there too." I pulled away and dropped my hands from her limbs, knowing it was one of the last times it would just be the two of us. Now Pepper would be my family because she would be married to my brother. Our marriage would be a distant memory, a time that would fade away as we moved on with our lives. It hurt a little bit, but it was also exhilarating at the same time. We were finally where we were meant to be...it just took a while to get there.

28

PEPPER

THE NIGHT BEFORE THE BIG EVENT, WE LAY TOGETHER UNDER THE sheets, our faces close together on the same pillow. Our naked skin came into contact as we touched each other, as we scooted closer or felt each other intimately.

I'd suggested that I stay with Colton for the night, but as I'd expected, he shut down the idea immediately. In his eyes, we were already married. We'd already committed ourselves to each other for all eternity. Tomorrow was simply a celebration. "I've been meaning to ask you about your hand..." Gauze was wrapped around his left ring finger, like he'd cut himself at work.

"It can come off tomorrow. I got some ink done, and it should be healed by the morning."

"You got a tattoo?"

"Yeah. My wedding ring."

"Really?" The man was covered in ink, but I thought he might choose a traditional ring. Something that would contrast against the black tattoos on his body. But the ink would be permanent...something he could never take off.

"I'm not a fan of jewelry. And I like knowing everyone can

see my commitment regardless of what I'm wearing. At the hospital, I only wear a watch because it's easier than trying to find the time somewhere else. But I couldn't imagine wearing a ring on my hand. It would get in the way or get dirty...this is better."

"And it saves me money."

He reached for the gauze and removed it.

"Shouldn't you wait?"

"No, it's fine." He set the wrapping on the nightstand then rested his hand on the sheet between us. In black ink was a thick line around his left ring finger. Solid and full, the line was unmistakable. It contrasted against his hands because he didn't have any ink past his wrists. "What do you think?"

"I think it's sexy..." My fingers brushed over the area.

He smiled. "I thought you might like it."

"I guess I like how permanent it is."

"That's why I like it too. It's you and me forever, baby."

"Forever is a long time..."

"Not to me." He hooked his arm around the curve of my back and tugged me a little closer so our foreheads were touching. My tits pressed against his chest, and my nipples hardened the second I came into contact with his heat. "I was thinking we could take a little trip after the ceremony."

"Yeah? Where did you have in mind?"

"I rented a cabin out in the woods. It's got a nice fireplace, a great view of the lake, and it's in the middle of nowhere... It'll be a little honeymoon."

Being away from everyone so we could enjoy our nuptial bless sounded perfect. "What about Soldier?"

"He's coming too. I knew you wouldn't want to leave him behind."

"You know me so well."

"Yes, I do." He rolled me over onto my back and moved his hips between my thighs. "And I know you want me again."

"Shouldn't we save some for tomorrow?"

He slid inside me, getting balls deep instantly. "I could make love to you all night, and I'd still want you even more tomorrow."

I WENT to Colton's apartment to get ready.

Stella curled my hair while Tatum did my makeup.

"That dress is so sexy on you," Stella said. "He's gonna eye-fuck you like crazy the second he sees you."

"I hope his parents don't notice," I said with a chuckle.

"Knowing him," Tatum said, "I don't think he'd care."

Stella pulled the curling iron away then sealed the curl in place with hairspray. She ran her fingers through it until it was perfect.

Tatum finished my mascara then applied a new shade of lipstick to my mouth. "Ta-da."

"You look perfect." Stella stepped back and studied her handiwork.

I stood up and balanced on my heels, admiring my appearance in the mirror. My dress was a little slutty because it was short like a summer sundress, but Finn would definitely like it—so I would like it.

Besides, this was my second wedding. It didn't matter what anyone else thought.

Colton came into the bedroom and looked me up and down. "Sometimes I wonder if I'm still straight..."

"Oh, shut up." I walked past him, practicing in my heels.

"I'm serious. You look great."

"You really do," Stella said. "The man is gonna eat his heart out."

"Then eat you out later," Tatum added.

"Wow...is this my wedding day or a bachelorette party?" I said with a laugh.

"Maybe both?" Colton was in slacks and a collared shirt with a tie, looking dressed up but not overly formal.

"What's Finn wearing?" He and I had never talked about it.

Colton shrugged. "You'll have to wait and see."

"If he could, he would be naked," I said. "That's the kind of man he is."

"And I don't think anyone would mind if he showed up naked..." Stella smiled at Tatum.

I would have to live with women checking out my husband all the time, so I might as well get used to it.

Husband.

It was the first time I'd called him that...and I really liked it.

Colton looked at his watch. "We should get going. Are you ready?"

I didn't need to give it a second thought. I was going to marry the love of my life, the man who would move mountains to make me happy. We would be family in just a few hours... We would be soulmates.

29

FINN

I waited at the courthouse with my parents.

The courthouse wasn't the most exciting place in the world, but it was still the most exciting day of my life. Any moment now, my future bride would walk up the stairs and enter the building, looking gorgeous in whatever she decided to wear. If she showed up in a paper bag, I would still marry her because she would rock it.

That was how hot my baby was.

"You look so handsome, sweetheart." Mom kept smoothing out my jacket and keeping every little wrinkle out of my clothing. She'd even pinned a flower to the front of my suit to make it official.

Since she was so excited about today, I let her do whatever she wanted. "Thanks, Mom."

Dad clapped me on the shoulder. "You got yourself a good one. Don't fuck it up again."

"Trust me, I won't." I'd lived a terrible existence without her, so I wouldn't make the same mistake twice. The second I returned to Seattle, I was committed to her. I was her husband even though she wouldn't take me.

Soldier sat beside me and whined when he wanted attention.

"She'll be here soon." I patted him on the head. He had a black collar around his neck and a matching flower pinned to it.

"I was always afraid you would end up with someone who wasn't good enough for you," Mom said. "But she's really lovely. Honest, classy, and she loves you so much..."

"I know, Mom." I would have loved her the same even if my parents didn't like her, but it meant a lot to me that they did, that she would be part of our family forever.

Finally, Colton opened the door and escorted her inside, his arm extended so she could hold on to it. He got her in the door first, and the girls followed behind.

It was a special moment because she didn't notice me right away. Her eyes were on the ground because she was getting used to her heels with the change of foundation. She wore a short dress that flared out around her waist—and her tits looked amazing. A sea of hair fell around her shoulders, the curls loose and easy to fist. The second I looked at her, I pictured myself between her legs, consummating our marriage before I could even get that dress off her. We would make love by the roaring fire as I made my wife come over and over again, starting off our lives in the best way possible.

Sex was the first thing that popped into my head anytime I looked at Pepper.

Come on, how could it not be?

But as she came closer to me, I thought of the other reasons why I was marrying her. But only one reason actually mattered.

I loved her.

It was real. It was true. My heart beat for hers in a way I couldn't explain. I wanted to spend my life by her side every single day, protecting her, loving her, and giving her a reason to stay with me.

My time overseas and in the rural places in foreign countries taught me how to be alone, how to thrive in solitude. I became so good at it that I preferred it over companionship. Women were good for one thing—sex. When I first met Pepper, it wasn't like that. The more I got to know her, the more I wanted from her. I didn't just want to fuck her—I actually wanted to kiss her.

I wanted to be with her.

Now the idea of returning to that solitude terrified me.

Because it would mean she wasn't there.

I couldn't be without her ever again. I learned how much better my life was with her. I realized my bachelor days were over the second I stepped inside that apartment that one afternoon.

Even then, I knew she was the one.

Even when I left, I knew she was the one.

And now, I knew it even more.

When she looked up, her eyes focused on my face, taking in my appearance like she thought I was the hottest man she'd ever seen. She eyed my shoulders in my suit, noticed the way I'd done my hair just for her, and when her gaze settled on my face, there was a special twinkle in her eyes.

I hoped she looked at me like that every day for the rest of our lives.

When she reached me, Colton let her go.

"You look... Jesus Christ."

Everyone laughed at my crass remark, even my parents.

I meant the words when I said them, but they didn't complement all the thoughts I'd just been thinking. It didn't match all the true feelings I harbored for her, the unstoppable force that existed inside my chest. Maybe she fell in love with me because of my qualities.

But I fell in love with her because she was my soulmate. "You still want to marry me?" Maybe that was a stupid idea, to let her think she had the option. If she changed her mind, I would just make her change it back.

"Yes." She slid her hand into mine and looked up into my face. "I do."

COURTHOUSE WEDDINGS WERE QUICK. They ran through the lines, told us what to say, and then they moved on to the next couple.

But when I locked my eyes on to hers and listened to her say I do, time seemed to stand still. It seemed like it was just the two of us, two people so madly in love that no one else existed. She was so beautiful, so happy, that I didn't even focus on what the guy marrying us was saying.

"Finn," he repeated. "Do you take this woman to be your lawfully wedded wife?"

I kept my eyes on her. "Sorry...all I can think about is kissing you."

My parents and everyone else laughed.

She smiled, tears in her eyes. "You can kiss me after you marry me."

"Then I do."

"By the powers vested in me, I now pronounce you husband and wife. Kiss your girl."

I grinned as I pulled her close, my hands shaking because she was finally mine. All of the torment was officially over because she was my wife—my other half. She promised to love me for the rest of our lives, to stand by my side through thick and thin.

How did I get so lucky?

I bent my neck down and kissed her, pulling her tight into my chest so I could remember this moment as long as I lived.

Her mouth crushed against mine, and I felt so good inside, like all my suffering had disappeared.

It was all a bad dream.

Everyone clapped as they witnessed our first kiss as husband and wife.

Pepper was officially my wife.

Mrs. Finn Burke.

When I ended the kiss, I scooped her up into my arms and held her against my chest. "Bye." I walked through our friends and family and carried her away, stealing my bride so we could run off to the cabin and start our new lives together.

They all laughed and cheered as I took her away, to make love to my wife for the first time. Soldier barked then caught up with us, knowing he was coming along for the ride too.

With her arms wrapped around my neck, she looked happier than I'd ever seen her, the love shining in her eyes and the emotion in the slight trembling of her lips. "We're family now...all three of us."

"Yes...and we'll always be family."

IT STARTED to rain after we arrived.

I got a fire going in the large hearth to keep the place warm. The heater hadn't been on in so long that it was chilly.

Pepper sat on the edge of the bed, still in her little white dress.

I stripped off my tie and then my jacket, dropping everything onto the floor because I had no intention of ever wearing it again.

She watched the pile of clothes grow bigger. "I've never seen you wear a suit before."

"And you won't see me wear one again until our kids get married."

Her eyes glowed as she watched me strip down to my bare skin. She stared at my hard cock when it was visible, licking her lips because she knew she owned my junk forever.

Watching her want me only made this night more incredible.

I kneeled in front of her, naked and on my knees. My fingers slipped off her white heels, and then I laid her back as I reached under her dress and I pulled down the sexy white thong. I took my time as I peeled it away, as I pulled it down her sexy legs until she was bare. I'd just had her the night before, but when she looked so perfect like this, with the glow of the fire bringing a rosiness to her cheeks, it felt like the first time.

I lifted her up the bed then raised her dress to her waist.

"You don't want me to take it off?"

My thighs separated hers as I positioned myself between her legs, my cock so anxious to be inside her that it could find her entrance all on his own. "No." I fantasized about the way I wanted to take her the moment I looked at her in that dress. I wanted to enjoy the sight of her in that dress a little longer—and really take my time getting it off.

I held myself on top of her and slowly sank inside, slowly slid through the moisture that had been building on the hour ride here. My dick landed like a plane on a runway, and I sank into her so perfectly, making her gasp as she felt me stretch her apart.

She widened her legs and gave me ample room to take her, to make her my wife all night long. "Finn..." Her hands moved up my chest, and her mouth gaped open as she moaned, so turned on that she was already writhing for me.

"Mrs. Finn Burke." I thrust inside her, seeing the light of the flames highlight her face as I made love to her in the middle of nowhere, the sound of the fire accompanying the light rain falling outside. It was a beautiful setting to fall deeper in love, to strengthen our relationship until it was unbreakable.

She rocked with me, gasping and scratching.

"You look so fucking beautiful." It was an image I could beat off to for the rest of my life. The way her eyes filled with emotion, the way her lips parted so she could breathe. Her perfect tits shook with my thrusts. The best part of all was that diamond ring on her finger, the ring she'd agreed to wear for the rest of her life.

Because she wanted me for the rest of her life.

I pressed my forehead to hers as I kept moving, kept making love to my wife for the first time. "Thank you for marrying me." I hated to think of what would have happened if I hadn't gotten her back. I would have ended up in the bar alone every night, drinking away all my regrets while someone else got to be exactly where I was now.

She cupped my face and breathed with me. "Thank you for not giving up on me."

"I'll never give up on my baby...not ever."

EPILOGUE

FINN

We'd been married five years.

Five beautiful fucking years.

They went by so fast.

First, it was just the two of us and Soldier.

Then Neil arrived.

With the same dark hair and blue eyes I possessed, he was a miniature version of me. But he had Pepper's fierce attitude, so he was the perfect little boy I wanted. He was sweet to his mother and disciplined when it came to me.

I loved having a little boy. But I knew he wouldn't be little forever...and I wanted him to be a man I was proud of.

I took my eyes off him for one second, and he knocked his apple juice onto the floor and spilled his milk and cereal everywhere. In just an instant, he made a huge mess—after I'd just cleaned everything.

I could lose my temper and scream.

But I didn't want to be like that.

With apology on his face, he looked up at me, embarrassment in his eyes. "Sorry, Daddy..."

Sometimes it was impossible to get mad at something so

precious. He could do anything, and I would still love him so damn much. He had Pepper's innocence and emotional intelligence. Yelling at him was like yelling at her, which was impossible to do. "It's okay, champ. Accidents happen sometimes. But let me show you how to clean it up." I grabbed a few paper towels and then a soapy dishrag, and together, we cleaned up the little explosion he'd made in the kitchen. "Everyone has accidents sometimes, but we've got to be aware of what we're doing and try to prevent them. How did this happen?"

"I knocked over my juice..." He pushed the soaked paper towel across the floor.

"Alright. Be aware of your juice next time."

We threw away everything, and in minutes, the kitchen was clean again.

I taught him a lesson without yelling at him—seemed effective to me.

Pepper came down the stairs a moment later, her hand on her large stomach. "Why do I smell apple juice?"

Neil bowed his head. "Because I spilled..."

"And he also cleaned it up." I raised my hand and gave him a high five.

Pepper walked toward me, having that sexy pregnant glow. I loved it when she was pregnant. Sex was somehow better, knowing I was the reason she was so uncomfortable that she had to waddle everywhere. She looked down at our son and smiled. "Just pay attention, alright?"

"Okay, Mommy..." He moved to her leg and hugged her.

She chuckled as she ran her fingers through his hair dark hair. "So, you think your parents will watch him tonight so we can celebrate our anniversary? I can't drink and I'm tired all the time, but we should do something."

"Well, I had a better idea."

Soldier came into the kitchen and started sniffing, probably smelling the apple juice that had been spilled moments ago.

"Yeah?" Pepper asked. "Your mom will watch him, and we'll just stay home..." She gave me a meaningful look in her eyes, telling me she was happy to stay home and just have sex for a couple of hours.

"Actually, I invited Colton and Tom over. They're bringing the boys."

"Yeah?" she asked, immediately perking up.

"I thought we could have a barbecue and the kids could play together. Maybe we can play Monopoly, Colton's favorite game."

"That doesn't sound so bad. I feel like we haven't seen them in weeks."

I nearly rolled my eyes. "We saw them last Saturday."

"Yeah...but that seems like a lifetime ago." Even though she was married to me, she still needed Colton in her life as her best friend. They had lunch together and gossiped like any other pair of friends. I didn't mind in the least. It only made our family closer.

"So, that sounds good? I'll make some chicken."

"Ugh, no poultry." She rubbed her stomach. "I can tell she doesn't like it."

"I can make something else. What do you want?"

She smiled. "Maybe some mac and cheese...?"

When she was pregnant, she had the appetite of a child. I wanted to roll my eyes or make a joke, but since she'd already pushed out one baby, I couldn't complain about making her whatever she wanted. "Whatever my baby wants."

"Thank you." She took Neil by the hand. "I'm gonna change his shirt. He'll reek of apple juice if I wait too long." With their hands held together, they left the kitchen and went upstairs, mother and son.

I watched them go, unable to believe my own life. I never

thought I would be here. I was a father to a great boy. Now I would be a father to a beautiful little girl. And my wife was fucking amazing.

I looked down at Soldier. "I'm the luckiest man alive, huh?"

He barked.

I chuckled. "I'll take that as a yes."

SIGNED PAPERBACKS?

Would you love a signed copy of your favorite book? Now you can purchase autographed copies and get them sent right to your door! Get your copy here:

http://www.eltoddbooks.com/

CPSIA information can be obtained
at www.ICGtesting.com
Printed in the USA
LVHW110019170621
690286LV00005BA/925

9 781095 597064